Justin H. McCarthy

A London Legend

Volume 2

Justin H. McCarthy

A London Legend
Volume 2

ISBN/EAN: 9783337391522

Printed in Europe, USA, Canada, Australia, Japan

Cover: Foto ©Andreas Hilbeck / pixelio.de

More available books at **www.hansebooks.com**

BY

JUSTIN HUNTLY McCARTHY

AUTHOR OF 'DOOM,' 'DOLLY,' 'LILY LASS,' ETC.

'Coincidence, coincidence, divine coincidence! Let us
at least cling to it in legend if we lack it plentifully in life.
Let us remember that if romance is a mirror it is sometimes
a magic mirror, and the sights that we see therein are
governed, not by the weary laws of a workaday world, but
by the wonders of an Arabian tale.'

THE LETTERS OF PERTINAX.

IN THREE VOLUMES

VOL. II.

London

CHATTO & WINDUS, PICCADILLY

1895

CONTENTS OF VOL. II.

CHAPTER   PAGE

   XI. THE PLEASURES OF FRIENDSHIP -   -   1

  XII. SOLEMN LEAGUE AND COVENANT -   - 20

 XIII. THE HOUSE WHIMSICAL   -   -   - 34

  XIV. TO BE OR NOT TO BE   -   -   - 47

   XV. THE DAWNING OF THE YEAR   -   - 67

  XVI. IN RICHMOND PARK   -   -   - 80

 XVII. THE HOLLOW PLACE   -   -   - 105

XVIII. THE TURN OF HASSAN DRASS   -   - 123

  XIX. LONELY   -   -   -   - 154

   XX. MR. HEMPLETT   -   -   - 164

  XXI. THE COMING MAN -   -   - 186

 XXII. VOX POPULI   -   -   - 202

CHAPTER XI.

THE PLEASURES OF FRIENDSHIP.

They swore to be friends for ever,
  Eternally hand and glove :
They thought themselves mightily clever—
  And then they fell in love.

A Pastoral in Pink.

THOSE who have read the 'Letters of Pertinax' will remember how that philosopher and cynic defines friendship between man and woman as the first chapter of a folly or the last chapter of a lament.   But cynics are not always in the right of it, and Swift, who was no cynic, had always cherished some

VOL. II.   16

very fine ideas about friendship, which he
had plumped with many other ideas into his
' Cry for Liberty.'   He had even gone so far
as to cite with approval the theory of the
young St. Just, who was one of his heroes,
and whose portrait adorned the walls of the
Cordeliers' Club, that it would be well for
the State to formally abolish love and set up
friendship in its stead.   He had enlarged
upon the advantages of friendship between
men and women with the more impartiality
that he had never made the experiment.   He
had known loves, or what passed for loves,
and of course he counted some women—and
chiefly Lucilla—among his few friends, but
that was not exactly what he had meant
when he propounded his theory.   Now it
seemed as if Fate was according to him
what it does not always accord to philosophers, the opportunity of putting his
theory into practice.

Some friendships grow little, if at all—
remain at the last in the same cool atmo-

sphere as at first; such friendship is scarcely friendship, it is but a formalized indifference. Some friendships grow very slowly, if very surely, marking a steady if almost imperceptible progress with the course of the seasons, yet so gradually that it is only when near the end of the journey that the look-back shows the extent of the ground that has been gone over. But some friendships, and these are the best and the sweetest, ripen swiftly; the blossom succeeds to the bud, and the fruit to the blossom, with a tropical rapidity that is full of delight to people of high passions and warm pulses. To-day such destined spirits meet, salute, exchange some subtle glances, that are half-conscious pledges; to-morrow they are full of self-confessions to each other and well on the highway to sworn comradeship; the day after they are old friends and friends for life. There have been cases in which a man and a woman, swung together by the whirligig of Time, have found themselves at the end of an

exquisite week bound together by an intimacy
that seems to have lasted for years, an intimacy that makes each wonder, in the words
of the gracious poet, 'what you and I did ere
we met.'

Even such a friendship, so warm, so quick,
so glad, was the friendship between Swift
and Candida. If the week that had passed
between his first meeting with her and his
second had seemed intolerably long, the week
that passed after the second meeting, if it
seemed to fly with the swiftness of the
Arabian Bird, seemed also, like the dream of
the Arabian king, to hold the course of long
years shut up within a little space.

'With some folk,' says Pertinax, 'friendship is a river that widens slowly and surely
from its source to the sea. With others it is
a village brook that answers to every ex-
ternal influence, to the breath of every
breeze, the passing of every cloud, that
glitters in the sunshine and shivers in the
rain, and is the first to freeze in winter.

With others, again, 'tis like a mountain tarn,
darkly deep, silent, unconscious. Yet again,
with others 'tis like some mighty flood that
sweeps over every obstacle and covers a
ruined country with a great sheet of water
like a sea, but which in time subsides and
leaves desolation as the only trace of its
passage. With others, again, and these
perhaps the happiest, it is like to some
volcanic lake : yesterday it was not, to-day
it is ; it comes in one mighty moment, swift
and irresistible as the flood, but, unlike the
flood, it comes to stay.'

If Swift had read the 'Letters of Pertinax,'
he would have accepted the latter parable as
symbolic of his state. His friendship for Candida—in the core of his heart he called it his
love for Candida—had altered the world for
him, and had altered it for good. If he got to
know Candida better in the days that drifted
by, the days that made their friendship
dearer to him did not seem to make it older.
He felt that they were old friends on the day

when she kept her tryst with him by the pillar of the Ephesian Eros, the day when he first learned what her name was and learned where she lived.

'Do not think me presuming,' Swift had pleaded on that fair first day, 'if I ask to be allowed to walk with you as far as your home.'

'It is not much to grant,' said Candida, ' for I live quite close at hand. Come, by all means.'

They walked again through the long galleries and out of the Museum into the bright April sunshine. Such talk as they had on the way had turned again upon the objects around them ; they even talked as if they feared a reaction of silence after so much confidence. Candida was right when she said that she had not far to go. After they left the gates they crossed Great Russell Street and entered Bury Street. Here, at the doorway of one of the sets of flats in that street, Candida stopped.

'These are my diggings,' she said. 'Here
independent poverty has found her nest.'

'We are almost neighbours,' Swift said,
'for I live over yonder in Queen Square.'

'A dear old place!' said the girl. 'I know
it well. Till to-morrow, good-bye, neighbour.'

She held out her hand; Swift took it for
a moment. In another moment she had
entered the doorway and disappeared from
his sight, but he heard the quick sound of
her feet as they ran up the stone steps. He
stood still for a moment, then he turned and
walked away with a head humming with
delicious exaltation. He felt as if he were
the king of all the world because he had
found a friend in a beautiful, audacious
woman.

Under the spell of this sweet unreason he
could not rest, could not settle down to the
solemnities of study, could not surrender
himself to stupefaction in the dust of
Homeric commentary. So he walked over

to the Windovers, and found Lucilla and Anthony peacefully at luncheon, and they made him welcome and gave him food and drink, and he ate and drank joyously enough, for his honest appetite did not strike its flag even to a high passion.

Windover had not yet made up his mind about the Pine Hill election. In fact, it seemed that there was no need for an immediate decision. The sitting member had not yet sent in his application for the Chiltern Hundreds, had not yet, it seemed, definitely decided to do so. It depended a good deal upon some consultation of doctors who should definitely pronounce upon the state of his health. So much Windover had learned in a letter from Rockielaw, and he seemed rather pleased than pained at a delay which postponed the necessity for a momentous decision. He had also received a letter from Gabriel Oldacre, from Constantinople, full of interesting news of that marvellous city and of the doings of Amber Pasha. Anthony

read the letter aloud to Swift, and as it
attracted him, Anthony told him of the
romance of Gabriel's life, of his love for
Dorothy Perceval, who had given her love to
Harry Chandos, and how in his despair he
had consented to accompany Amber Pasha to
Constantinople, where he had stayed ever
since.

'But I do not think that he has found consolation,' Anthony said. 'I do not think that
he will ever get over it; he is the sort of man
who takes that kind of thing badly to heart.
Of course he never says a word to me of his
sorrow, but I know that his very soul is sick
with it. Poor devil!'

And Swift, listening, and flushed with the
favour of his new fortune, felt a pity for the
man he did not know, and echoed Anthony's
'Poor devil!' sympathetically.

Then the talk drifted backward from Constantinople to Pine Hill, and from Pine Hill
to London, and from London in general to
that particular portion of London which was

known by the name of St. Ethelfreda's
Without.

'Erastus Albany came to see me yesterday,' Windover said, 'at the office of *The
Arbiter*. He has been writing an article for
me on Jerome of Jerusalem, his favourite
saint, and he carried his own copy. I think
he was unwilling to trust the post with so
precious a manuscript, but he pretended that
he came because he was getting up some entertainment at Brisbane Hall, and hoped
that Lucilla would sing at it. He wants his
list to be as varied as possible. I offered
to read some pages from my Elizabethan
essays, but he declined ungratefully—said
he did not think it would quite suit the
occasion. I believe he wishes to make a
kind of variety show of it, like a music-hall.
You don't sing any comic songs, do you,
Brander?'

Swift shook his head.

'I don't do anything so diverting, and I
am afraid a harangue upon the latest

Teutonic theory of the distribution of Homer
would scarcely serve the turn. But I dare
say I could find somebody or other who
might be willing to take a hand.'

The thought of his friend the snake-
charmer had just come into Swift's mind.
He might possibly be induced to exhibit his
wizardries for the entertainment of St.
Ethelfreda's Without. Swift had a regard
for Erastus Albany, whose Christian socialism was not wholly unacceptable to the
Cordeliers, and he would always be glad to
do him a service. Perhaps a certain curiosity
to see Mr. Drass again entered into Swift's
motive; at all events, he resolved to make
the experiment.

When the meal was ended, they all three
went into the garden for a time. There was
a fountain in the garden, a queer old stone
fountain that had been set up there by
Harry Chandos. He had brought it from
Italy; it was by no means unsightly; it
could be made to play on occasion with

considerable expenditure of water. Now,
tempted by the early warmth of the year,
they turned on the little fountain and sat for
awhile to watch it splashing and sparkling,
while Windover smoked cigarettes and
Lucilla knitted. Swift was not a smoker,
though he sometimes smoked a pipe with
Budget. In his boyhood he thought that it
was un-Hellenic; the Greeks were unaware
of tobacco; the pleasures that pleased Mim-
nermus might suffice for Brander Swift. In
his later days he seemed to fancy that it did
not accord with the principles of Eighty-nine
and the politics of St. Just. The real fact
was that he did not care about smoking.

After awhile, when Swift guessed that
Windover would wish to get to his desk, he
got up and said good-bye to the garden and
the fountain, and the boy and the girl who
were his host and hostess. He left the house
as he always left it, with a not ungenerous
envy of its calm and its content. At former
times he had asked himself whether, after

all, there might not be other things in life
besides translating German scholars and
haranguing the Cordeliers. And after
asking, he had generally dismissed the question and gone back to his Cordeliers and
gone back to his German scholars. But now
he put to himself the same question and gave
himself a very different answer than ac-
quiescence. There were other things in life
than German scholarship and Cordeliers' con-
troversies; there were better things—there
were beauty and love, and a girl called
Candida. And he repeated the name Candida over and over again as he went his way,
and seemed to find it sweeter with every
repetition.

He had left the Windovers with the
determination to try and find Mr. Drass's
house, and if possible Mr. Drass. He had no
great difficulty in tracking his way to the
dingy unlovely crescent in which the dingy
unlovely house stood. When he had quitted
it on that eventful evening he had taken

note of its bearings as he steered his way through the darkness to the Windovers, and now he found that his memory served him well and carried him without much fault through the dreary streets. There is a grisly monotony about Camden Town which throws its especial difficulty in the way of the explorer, but Swift had a fair sense of locality, and in time he reached the dingy crescent and faced the dingy house. It looked strangely dead in the daylight, for every window was shuttered from basement to garret, and the playfulness of the nomad youth of the neighbourhood had asserted itself by breaking all the panes of glass that stone, propelled by hand or sling, could reach. The forlorn area, a receptacle, as it would seem, for the general rubbish of the region, was fringed with a frise of rusty railings whose rusty gateway was securely locked. Hardly a trace of paint remained on the dismal door. If it ever had a knocker, the knocker had been wrenched away long

before, and time and weather had effaced
even the marks that showed where it had
been affixed. There was a hole at the side
for a bell-pull, a hole like a wound, but there
was no bell-handle, and though there was a
bell-handle rocking on the area railing, it
rocked aimlessly, for it had no chain. The
keyhole in the door seemed to be stopped, as
if to deny wandering curiosity even so slight,
so peccant a glimpse of the silence, of the
secrecy beyond. The dirty pillars of the
absurd porch, those pillars of that porch
which had sheltered Swift a week earlier, had
flaked their stucco away in ragged seams
through which the fallacious brickwork
grinned ghastly at the exposure of its cheat.
It seemed to Swift that he had seldom seen
so wretched a sight, and he likened it to the
Abomination of Desolation spoken of by
Daniel the prophet. Was it possible that
such a sordid, abandoned exterior was the
shell for such fantastic splendour and such
strange inmates?

He ascended the crumbling steps, stood in the porch and surveyed the door, wondering in what way to effect communication with the occupant if the occupant were within. Without a knocker and without a bell the thing was a problem. He listened half fearfully, expecting to hear soft creeping sounds behind the partition, sounds of the sinuous movements of great snakes. But he heard nothing. All was still, all was silent. The outer air of deadness which the house wore seemed to be balanced by an inner deadness no less repellent. There was an ugly sense of something like enchantment about the place which forced upon Swift an odd boyish temptation to take to his heels and run away as children run from things uncanny. But he had come to see Mr. Drass, and he meant to see him if he could, so after a few moments of hesitation he drummed sharply on the panels of the door with the knob of his stick. The sounds seemed to reverberate drearily through empty echoing spaces and die away into silence. They brought no response, so he tapped again and again, yet with no greater success. But the peculiar method of his knocking arrested the attention of idle passers-by, and collected a little crowd of staring children from adjacent gutters, who eyed him curiously, taking him for a madman or a baffled tax-collector. Some of them, regarding the whole thing as an unwonted and welcome entertainment, adjured Swift to try again, and seemed vastly delighted when Swift repeated his blows and gained nothing but noise by so doing. Then a slatternly woman came out into the neighbouring area and looked up sourly at Swift, and told him that it wasn't a bit of good his standing knock-ing there all day, as there was nobody in the house, and hadn't been for days and days. Swift asked her civilly if she could tell him when Mr. Drass would be back ; to which the woman answered that she knew nothing about him, and had no cause to, thank heaven ! and that it was none of her business

to poke her nose into her neighbours' affairs.
So Swift, finding that there was nothing to
learn or gain by waiting any longer, came
down the steps again and pushed his way
through the little crowd that seemed re-
luctant to let him depart so soon, and
resentful of the curtailment of their amusement. A little farther on in the crescent
Swift came upon a policeman lounging along
with that air of languid indifference which
comes over the custodians of law and order in
such sleepy neighbourhoods. He, questioned,
was willing enough to talk, but he could tell
Swift little. The house belonged to an old
gentleman who lived mostly abroad ; it was
occupied from time to time by different kinds
of people who always seemed to be foreigners,
but who never did anything suspicious.
Often it was unoccupied for months and
months at a stretch. That was all the
policeman knew, and he told it to Swift
while the little knot of loiterers at the door
of the deserted dwelling watched the colloquy

from afar and decided in favour of the theory
of the tax-gatherer or other exasperated
creditor of some kind.   Swift slipped a
shilling into the hand of his informant and
went his way.   He had done his best to find
Mr. Drass, and it was not his fault if the
entertainment given by the Rev. Erastus
Albany to the people of St. Ethelfreda's
Without lacked the attraction of a snake-
charmer from the Indies.

CHAPTER XII.

SOLEMN LEAGUE AND COVENANT.

The world appears a gallant place
To him that loves a lovely face;
The sunlight seems to him more fair,
Touching the tresses of her hair;
And in the candour of her eyes
He finds the earthly Paradise.

A Pastoral in Pink.

THE days danced by, a delirium, a rapture. The British Museum became to Brander Swift as the very Temple of Gnidus. In his imagination it took to itself all the attributes of beauty and sanctity from its association with Candida. While they wandered together side by side through its long galleries he was indeed in outward form actively engaged in telling his companion all that she

wanted to know—and she wanted to know
much—about the antique world, about that
Athens which he knew so much better than
he knew London, and yet which, with a
curious irony, he seemed to care for now
chiefly because it had the good fortune to
interest Candida Knox. He had devoted his
life to the service of the Greeks in order that
he might answer a few questions asked by a
beautiful girl, and it did not occur to him for
a moment that there was anything dispro-
portionate between the cause and the effect.

Goethe has written in his 'Sorrows of
Werther' that when the young man who is
in love begins to consider his position, and
the disposition of his time, and says to
himself, 'I will apportion my hours between
business and pleasure, I will spend so much
of my time with my sweetheart, and so much
of my time with my occupations in life,' then
the State may have gained a good citizen, but
the world has lost a good lover. Swift was
no such man as the lover whom Goethe

scorned. Candida seemed, Candida was, all
the world to him. He had been for long
enough the willing slave of his books ; now
he pitched them all to the devil, and thought
only of a girl's bright eyes. The dust grew
thick on the top of his German dictionaries ;
the wisdom of Bonn, of Leipzig, of Leyden,
lay unheeded on his table; Cripple and
Co. must needs wait for their translations.
Cripple and Co. were in no particular hurry,
as it happened; the booksellers and the
book-buyers of England were not actually
clamouring for the wisdom of Bonn, of
Leipzig and of Leyden ; but if they had
been, Swift would have let them clamour,
for his part. He was a kind of unconscious
fatalist. Destiny had placed this unexpected
delight in his way ; it was his duty to take
that delight and be thankful. The world
was choking with books and wisdom, but
there was only one Candida.

It was lucky for Swift, while this romantic
mood was upon him, that he was in a great

degree his own master. If he chóse to let
his work drift while he danced attendance
upon a pretty girl, that was, in the main, his
own affair. He was responsible to no one;
his work was bound by no fixed times or
conditions; his scholarship, like skilled
artisanship, could always command employ-
ment. In his recent years of simplicity and
severe work he had saved much more money
than he spent, and he had in his bank a
modest sum to his name, which made him
now feel as independent as if he were a
millionaire. Swift did not deliberately
reason out his position in this way; he
simply felt that he was free, that the most
beautiful woman in the world was willing to
call him friend, and that to be with her was
the best thing in the world, and to think of
her when he was not with her the next best
thing. 'Who knows but the world may end
to-night?' he might have said, with Browning's
lover, in explanation of his mood. Candida
had come very suddenly into his life; she

might vanish from his life again as suddenly.
He did not care to dwell upon that possibility.
In the meantime she was here, and she seemed
to like him, and nothing else was worth a
thought. His friends the Windovers, Budget,
his books, his business, his adventure on
Primrose Hill, his adventure with the snake-
charmer, all these seemed to belong to an in-
definable, shadowy past, that had nothing to
do with the splendid sunlit present.

Through all an enchanted week he had
seen her every day ; but only at the Museum,
where they wandered together for hours,
looking at the treasures, and talking about
them or about themselves. But afterwards
they met elsewhere. For on the sixth day
of their strange fantastic friendship Swift
asked her if he might ever come and see
her.

They were standing at the time in the
long Egyptian Room, where Swift had been
pretending to instruct his companion in the
influence of Egypt upon Greece. It had

been a poor pretence. Their talk had drifted
away from Egypt, had drifted, as talk will
do in the dawn of delightful friendships,
to themselves and their thoughts, and experiences, and hopes, and fancies. And it
was while they were both opposite to a wall-
painting of Egyptian dancing girls that Swift
had asked her if he might ever be allowed to
come and see her.

If it was a bold request, he did not feel
bold as he made it. It had become so
natural, even in those few days, to see
Candida daily, to walk with her, talk with
her, that their friendship seemed already to
have endured through the ages. And it was
very much with the same feeling in which he
would have asked some man whom he had
met and liked if he might come and see him,
that Swift asked· this favour of Candida
Knox. For though he was more devoted to
her and her beauty with every passing day,
he had kept his devotion to himself; at least,
so far as saying nothing about it went. A

man often thinks that because he is silent he has not betrayed himself. Besides, Candida's divine frankness did not seem to invite utterances of devotion.

Now, when he asked her, she looked up at him for a moment. Then, as her eyes travelled back to the picture of the dancing-girls, she said 'Yes' very quietly, and was silent afterwards for a few seconds, during which Swift seemed to think that his heart-beats must sound like the booming of a bell. Then she spoke again.

'If I let you come and see me,' she said, 'it must be on one well-understood, well-observed condition. I am not conventional, and I do not see why you should not come and see me as you would come to see some man—why I should not welcome you as I should welcome some woman.'

She paused again. Swift hastened to agree with her theory—her theory, that had always been his theory.

'Of course not. We are true comrades.

We are none the less comrades because I am
a man, because you are a beautiful woman.'

She turned round quickly and faced him.
Perhaps the praise had called the colour into
her cheeks a little, for he had not yet spoken
to her of her beauty.

'That is just it,' she said.   'Let me admit,
for the sake of the argument, that I really
am what you are good enough to call me, a
beautiful woman.   Now, don't interrupt me'
—for Swift was about to speak—'I know I
am not ill-favoured.   You will remember
that I told you the other day that there was
one thing I did not wish you ever to talk to
me about.'

'Yes,' said Swift, 'I remember.'

'Don't think,' Candida went on, 'that I
mind your letting me know that you think
me beautiful, now and then, if you really do
think so, and if it gives you any pleasure to
let me know that you think so.   I am a
woman, if an unconventional woman, and
I like flattery sometimes and from some

people. But it is perfectly possible that if you are pleased with my face you might fall in love with me, or think that you had fallen in love with me. At least the thing is not impossible.'

'No,' said Swift, 'the thing is not impossible.'

Even now her frankness seemed perfectly natural, perfectly right, perfectly womanly. She seemed to assume that she had the right to speak as she pleased, and she acted on the assumption with a convincing grace.

'Well,' she said, 'I want you to understand at once that I do not wish you to make love to me. We are friends, not lovers; let us remain friends. If you were to fall in love with me it would be neither my fault nor your fault; but if it should happen, don't tell me about it. If I make you my friend, it is because I prize your friendship, because I believe that friendship is possible between a man and a woman, because you believe so too.'

'Of course,' Swift assented, somewhat sadly. He could not deny his own theory— the theory that he exposed at length in several of the most eloquent pages of the 'Cry for Liberty.' But he did not feel quite as confident now in its universal application.

'You must not think me vain if I talk like this,' she said. 'I do not say that you will fall in love with me. But it is possible that you might fall in love with me, as it is possible that I might fall in love with you.'

Though she spoke these words as composedly as if she were discussing some abstract question of no immediate concern to anyone, a flame seemed to pass over Swift as she spoke, and to burn out his strength, so that he trembled and felt faint. He turned to her.

'Is that possible?' he stammered, gazing with eager eyes upon her beautiful composed face.

'Why not?' she answered calmly. 'The one thing is as possible as the other, But I don't want either to happen—at least, for the present. Perhaps I prize your friendship too highly to put it in peril. Anyhow, I am a woman, and a woman is privileged to offer her friendship under conditions, and these are my conditions. I will be your friend with all my heart, and there's my hand upon it ; but we must be friends, not fools. Give me your promise that you will not make love to me, either spoken or unspoken, and we shall be the best friends in the world.'

She held out her hand, but he hesitated for a moment to take it. He was in love with her, though she did not seem to know it. Should he tell her so at once, or hold his peace ? She saw his hesitation.

'I read somewhere once,' she said with a smile, 'that between a man and a woman friendship is better than love—better, nobler, braver.'

Swift knew very well where she might
have seen such a theory, for he had formulated it himself in that terrible 'Cry for
Liberty,' and had been very proud of it at
the time. He did not feel quite so proud
of it now, which is sometimes the way of
philosophers when their theories come home
to roost.

'Don't you think that you are rather hard
upon me,' he asked, somewhat piteously, 'in
binding me down by such a hard and fast
promise as that is?'

'No,' she said slowly, 'we have only been
friends for a few hours, and it ought not to
be difficult for you to make such a promise
now. It is quite possible that you think
yourself to be in love with me at this
moment. Without vanity, I should not be
surprised if you thought so.'

'I don't think so,' Swift said beneath his
breath, with a stress upon the verb which
was to show his certainty of his state.

Candida took no notice of the interruption,

made as if she had not heard it, and went on with her homily :

'My face pleases you, my frankness interests you—there is something unexpected about this sudden friendship which charms while it amazes you. But neither charm nor amazement makes up love, though the one is love's herald and the other love's pursuivant. But I may soften my condition thus far. Promise not to make love to me until—until I give you permission. There, it is either your hand on that or your hand in farewell.'

He looked at her for a moment with a kind of wonder and a kind of hope. But there was no trace of sentiment in her voice and no look of sentiment in her eyes.

'Very well,' he said, 'I promise.'

He held out his hand, and the girl took it gladly.

'That is good,' she said. 'We shall be the best friends in the world now. And now I want you to tell me some more about the

influence of Egypt upon Greece. What was
the story you promised me yesterday, the
story from Herodotus ?'

Swift resumed the professor with a silent
sigh, plunged into Herodotus, and told the
promised story. But he had his reward, for
when they left the Museum Candida asked
him if he would like to come in and have tea
with her.

CHAPTER XIII.

THE HOUSE WHIMSICAL.

This little room is my demesne,
I am an empress here, a queen ;
Below the great world goes its way,
From daybreak to the end of day ;
The sky above my head, you see,
Spreads me a royal canopy.

Songs of Sentiment.

CANDIDA lived in a little flat at the very top of the block of buildings in which she had pitched her tent. She liked, as she explained to Swift while they climbed up the stone stairs together, to live at a height.

'I am a child of the mountains,' she said, 'not a child of the valley, and I would rather dwell in an eyrie than in a cave.'

Swift agreed with her; he would have

agreed with anything she said just then, even if she had expressed disapproval of the opinions of Karl Marx. No stairs seemed too steep that were trod in her company, no height too hopeless to which she played the guide. It was really not so very high after all, and if Swift felt giddy, it was from delight at his good fortune, not from the narrowness or the steepness of the stairs up which he followed Candida with a beating heart.

Candida's flat was very small, but very dainty. It was just big enough for her and for the single servant she kept, and for her cat, the big blue-gray Persian whom she called Omar. She opened the door with a latch-key, and led Swift across a little hall into the little room which did duty for a drawing-room. It was separated by curtains from another smaller room which served as a dining-room.

'This is my den,' said Candida, making him free of the place with a friendly wave of the hand. 'If you will excuse me for a moment I will go and see about tea. I am not sure that my girl is in.'

She vanished, and Swift was left alone in the little room, rapturously delighted to be there, but almost afraid to realize his fair fortune. He was her guest, he was under her roof; this was the very temple, the very shrine of divinity, and he, the passionate pilgrim, had been permitted to pass within the precincts.

He looked around him almost timidly: everything he saw added to his charm. The rooms were very simply furnished, for Candida had told him that she was poor; but their simplicity had all the grace that comes of distinction in taste, distinction in choice. Everything seemed to be in harmonious relationship to everything else. Form was related to form, colour combined with, or seemed to come from, colour. All seemed to be governed by that antique law of the fair and fit, from the curtains by the door

to the flowers in the Chinese jar by the
window.

A deep niche by the window was fitted
with shelves and filled with books. Swift
always looked at books at any time ; naturally, now, he looked at these with a livelier
curiosity. It was not a very large library ; it
might not have served the turn of a scholar,
but for a girl living alone it was a collection
of oddly-allied companions. Swift smiled
approval upon Goethe and Schiller, upon
Richter and Heine. He had learned already
that Candida knew German, and knew it
better than he, for all his practice in the
translation of dreary scholars. The smile
faded a little as his glance fell upon a set of
volumes of Schopenhauer's writings, but re-
asserted itself as he caught sight of Fitzgerald's translation of Omar Khayyam.
As his gaze travelled from shelf to shelf, the
expression of his face varied a good deal—
varied in shades of surprise, for the collection
was mixed, bewilderingly mixed. ' Grimm's

Fairy Tales' came next to 'La Cousine
Bette'; a row of Ibsen's plays in German
flanked several volumes of the Elizabethan
dramatists ; Carlyle's 'French Revolution'
followed the 'Saga of Grettir the Strong';
'The Origin of Species' ranged with 'Virgini-
bus Puerisque' and 'Memories and Portraits';
Hans Andersen's stories shouldered a row
of Labiche's plays; Pater's 'Renaissance'
stood next to Lane's 'Arabian Nights';
and Symonds' two volumes on 'The Greek
Poets' shouldered 'La Reine Margot,' 'La
Dame de Montsoreau,' and 'Les Quarante-
Cinq.'

It certainly was a curious collection. He
had been prepared to find, as he did find,
Tennyson and Shakespeare, Mathew Arnold
and Molière, Dante, and even Petrarch ; Don
Quixote—though the fact that this was in
Shelton's translation did a little astonish him
—and Scott, Wordsworth and Shelley, Keats
and Byron. He was less prepared to find, as
he did find, Ronsard and Clement Marot,

Charles D'Orleans and Villon, Rossetti and
Chaucer, Walther von der Vogelweide and
the Romanceiro, 'The Song of the Sword'
and 'Letters to Dead Authors,' 'Poems and
Ballads' and 'The Subjection of Women,'
some volumes of Herbert Spencer and some
volumes of Paul Verlaine, the 'Morte
d'Arthur' and 'Les Fleurs du Mal.'

'What an amazing collection!' he said to
himself. He wondered vaguely if it were not
rather muddling to a young woman's mind to
read such a queer variety of books : he was
conscious that, if he approved of some of
the volumes, he disapproved of others ; he
applauded Shelton's 'Don Quixote,' but
he frowned at 'Les Fleurs du Mal.' He
addressed himself again to the investigation
of the shelves, but he had no further time
then for his inspection, for the door opened
and Candida came into the room again. She
laughed as she saw that he was studying the
bookcase.

'You are looking at my books,' she said.

' They are rather a mixed lot, I fear—the harvests of a variety of moods. Of course I have not room for many books here, even if I could afford to buy them, which, of course, I cannot, and so I am glad that my poor little library may offer me as wide a choice of amusement and inspiration as is possible under the conditions.'

' I hope you don't read too much,' said Swift. ' Many of us nowadays are too much bound by the bondage of books. All wisdom is not shut within the two covers of a book. It is better to live life than to read about it.'

He felt that he was sententious, but he was shy, and shyness always drove him into dogmatism. He wished to be at his ease, wished, above all things, to be brisk if not brilliant, and yet the best he could do was to stammer out sentences that might very well have been portion and parcel of the ' Cry for Liberty.'

Candida looked at him thoughtfully. If

the ghost of a smile haunted her lips, her dark blue eyes seemed rather sad than amused.

'Perhaps you are right,' she said slowly. ' Books are not everything, though I believe there are one or two people nowadays who think and talk and write as if books were not merely the best, but the only business and blessing in the world. But it is all very well to talk of living life—all very well for you with your many interests, your ambitions, your translations from the German, your socialism. Yours, if you like, is a crowded, animated, living life.'

She spoke so seriously that Swift declined to believe that she spoke satirically. And yet her words, in their apparent eulogy, somehow seemed to make his life seem small and mean, and he who lived it a somewhat foolish lounger.

' It is better to live one's own life than to dream dreams,' he said with a sententiousness that was this time self-defensive.

' Perhaps,' said Candida. ' But what is a poor girl to do, placed as I am placed ? The life she can live is somewhat limited, if she is not ' — she paused for a moment, and then completed her sentence—' if she is not an adventuress.'

' Don't you like your life ?' Swift asked. ' To live alone, to be free ? I suppose you need not live alone if you did not choose.'

' I certainly have got some relatives,' said Candida with a slight smile ; ' but for the present I prefer living alone to living with them. I need not starve ; I have enough to keep us going, me and my maid and my cat, and perhaps when I get tired of idleness, or feel that mistress, maid and cat need more money, I shall turn companion or governess, or take to type-writing. But in the meantime I let things drift, and I drift with them. I like to feel almost as free as if I were a man, and I think I shall be sensible enough not to get into scrapes.'

' You will want a purpose in life,' said

Swift. 'You will want something to do. At least, you would if you were a man.'

'I believe,' she said, ' that I have heard of men who get on with their lives without doing anything.'

'Drones, not men,' Swift answered. 'No man has a right to live an idle life.'

'Nor woman neither, I know you would add,' said Candida. 'Well, you shall not blush for me, my friend. I will find something to do, be sure of that. But remember that this life, this kind of liberty, is so new to me, and if I lounge away some hours or days or weeks, or even months, you must needs forgive me.'

Swift would have forgiven her almost anything just then, as she leaned slightly forward with her eyes fixed upon his face, and her beauty heightened by the eagerness of her manner. If she had confessed to the sins of Semiramis, or avowed an affection for poisoning in the Borgia manner, it would have seemed to him natural and almost

commendable while he was under her spell.
And for a girl to plead guilty to a desire for
a man's freedom was to prove her an unconscious disciple of the ' Cry for Liberty.'
The desire for a man's idleness was heterodox,
but no great matter.

'Indeed,' he said, ' I hope you will let me
share some of your lounging hours.'

' Your time is too precious to trifle with,'
she answered.

He protested eagerly.

' Not at all, not at all. Besides, the
British Museum is my hunting-ground. We
do but follow the chase together. If I am
lucky enough to teach you anything, remember that I learn in teaching. We are all
students, even the most experienced.'

' Even the wisest of us may be wiser,' said
Candida. ' Perhaps; it is very likely. Well
I am content for the present to lounge and
learn Greek things. By-and-by, perhaps,
when I am tired of my idleness, I shall take
your advice as to work and the purpose of

life, and all the rest of it.   In the meantime,
will you have some tea ?'

The door opened, and the maid brought in
tea—a little pink and yellow maid, pink-
cheeked, yellow-haired, who looked as if she
carried a storage of country health that
could defy Bloomsbury.   At her heels,
making her look like a modern representation of the Goddess Freya, came the big blue-
gray Persian cat that played the third part
in Candida's household.   The cat came
purring to Candida, who introduced it to
Swift.

'This is Omar,' she said—'the most
beautiful cat in the world. He is named
after old Khayyam, of course.'

Omar graciously permitted Swift to stroke
his soft coat.   The maid withdrew, darting a
little shy glance of surprise at the stranger
in the yellow suit.   Candida gave him some
tea, which seemed to him the most enchanting elixir in the world, and they talked for a
little while longer—a light talk, that Candida

kept from drifting again into a serious channel.

When Swift went away a little later with Candida's promise to meet him again at the Museum on the next day, he seemed to tread on air, and he could have danced in the street if he had not remembered in time that the sight of a student in yellow skipping for joy might afford too much entertainment to the unpoetic.

CHAPTER XIV.

TO BE OR NOT TO BE.

Now Fortune, like the phantom in the tale,
Stands and allures me with a laurel wreath,
The which she bids me bind upon my brows
And wear in honour.   Shall I for this crown
Forsake my vineyards and my fruitful fields,
Woods, lawns, and waters, and my perfect peace ?
The Duke of Attica.

THE days that immediately succeeded the
letter of Colonel Rockielaw were days of
much mental searching on the part of the
two Windovers.   To enter Parliament or
not to enter Parliament, that was the
question. Miss Carteret's ambassador had
left so little doubt upon Windover's mind
that the seat was a certainty, that neither
he nor Lucilla wasted any time in con-

sidering the possibility of defeat as a
factor in the problem. It really seemed
that if Windover chose he had only to
ask and have. The question was whether
he should ask and have or no. They
discussed the subject at breakfast. They
went for a walk in Regent's Park, and
discussed it as they wandered beneath its
trees and by its waters. They discussed it
again at luncheon, and after luncheon, as they
sat by the fire; they allowed their favourite
books to lie unheeded on their laps while
they again exercised their minds over the
familiar course. It was characteristic of the
youthfulness with which Lucilla and her
husband persisted in regarding the world
and its phenomena that they found a childish
enjoyment in their game of speculation, and
that ever and anon, when their doubts were
keenest and their faces gravest, they would
be both seized by a sense of the humours
of the situation, and begin to laugh like
children. And yet, as Windover profoundly

observed, it was no laughing matter. Upon their decision—for Windover had no idea of deciding either way without the full concurrence of his wife—much must and more might depend.

To begin with, they were very well as they were. Windover liked his work and liked his quiet life. Lucilla admired Windover's work and liked her quiet life. They were well enough off for all their modest wants ; they were very happy in each other's society and in the society of their familiar friends ; they liked the ordered independence of their existence—in fact, they were exceedingly happy, and knew that they were happy. It was this happiness, this content—a content unusual among those who live the civic life and take any share in the direction of public affairs—that they were now both mortally afraid to jeopardize. Windover, who was very conscientious in his views as to the duties of any citizen to his State, could not make up his mind whether he really should be of greater service to his cause inside the walls of Westminster Palace than outside those walls. He could not make up his mind whether the very natural temptation to accept a gratifying offer was a response to the call of duty or the mere prompting of a personal ambition which lurks somewhere in the hearts of most men.

Lucilla, for her part, was distracted between a secret pride in seeing her husband take his place among the representatives of the nation and a secret fear that it would lessen their companionship. She had no doubt of her husband's success in Parliament; even Budget's suggestions about a possible Premiership had not seemed to her to be at all too fantastic. But ambition for her husband was fettered by tender alarms, lest the gratification of that ambition would mean also the mortification of becoming of less importance in his life.

Many days went by in these agitations and perplexities—agitations that followed

Windover to his desk and danced impish dances between him and the paper that waited to receive his opinions on passing events; perplexities that pursued Lucilla in all her housewifely occupations, buzzing in her ears like a swarm of summer flies. At the end of several days neither husband nor wife had advanced at all nearer towards a definite decision.

'If this uncertainty goes on much longer,' Anthony would exclaim in simulated despair, 'I shall grow gray.'

And Lucilla, imitating his mood, would assert that unless they settled the problem one way or the other she would grow wrinkled and old before her time. Whereupon Windover would immediately kiss her, and they would both start laughing, only to grow serious again and pucker their brows over the problem.

A new day dawned and found them still undecided. Windover racked himself between duty and inclination, argued with duty and

inclination. Duty to his cause and the inclination for practical politics which is so
often the passion of the theoretical politician
urged him to accept. Duty towards Lucilla
and inclination for his quiet life urged him
to decline. Lucilla, who was as fretted as
he, would probably have come to a decision
sooner if it had been left to her, though as it
was not left to her she really had no definite
idea what the decision would be. The one
thing she feared was forcing her husband
to either action against his secret wishes,
and so she watched him as a sailor watches
the sky for decisive weather signals. And
Windover could not make up his mind.

'If this goes on much longer,' said Lucilla,
half laughing and half crying, on one of these
mornings of doubt and of deliberation, 'I
shall become quite pettish, quite peevish,
quite fractious, run all the gamut that
leads from nervousness at the one end of
the scale to downright bad temper on the
other.'

Windover looked at her in some alarm. He knew that she was joking, but there seemed to be a note of seriousness behind the jest.

'It is very trying,' he confessed; 'I begin to feel rather irritable myself. Confound that fellow! I wish he had never come here to bother us. I have a great mind to——'

'To what?' asked Lucilla.

'To make up my mind one way or the other,' Windover answered, and pretended to immerse himself in the *Times*.

'Yes, but which way?' said Lucilla, and Windover, with a comic groan, answered:

'There thou hast me.'

They spoke no more of the engrossing problem that morning. Windover wrote a stalwart article for his paper on the dangers of indecision in politics. 'We want men of action, not men of speculation,' he wrote decisively, and then smiled and sighed at his own indecision. Lucilla went into the garden, for the day was fine. Lucilla sat on the edge of the basin of the fountain and looked over a little armful of books which she had hastily gathered from her husband's library in the hope of finding inspiration in their pages. They included Herbert Spencer's ' Sociology,' Sir Henry Taylor's ' The Statesman,' Bagehot's ' Physics and Politics,' De Lolme on the Constitution and Machiavelli's ' Il Principe.' She turned over their pages gallantly in the hope of finding out the perfect way for the possible politician, but they made her head ache after a while, so she quietly dropped them and read Hans Andersen instead, and thought of nothing but princesses and fairies and enchantments until it was time to go and look after luncheon.

During luncheon Windover and Lucilla were ostentatiously scrupulous in avoiding any reference to the subject which was harassing them. They talked of new books they wanted to read, of new plays they wanted to see, of places they wanted to visit. No one who overheard them would have imagined that there was such a place as Westminster in the world, or, at least, that its geographical existence was a matter of the faintest moment to either the man or the woman.

When luncheon was over they both went into the garden, and Anthony smoked cigarettes, and propounded theories of art, and looked at the vines that were trailed upon the high walls, and prophesied that if this fine weather held they would soon begin to burgeon. Lucilla walked beside him, apparently absorbed in viticulture, and her three cats and her dog gambolled in the sunshine and chased each other round the fountain. It was very Arcadian and quiet, for the garden was a large one and little overlooked, and the big chestnut-trees and plane-trees served as an effective screen against the neighbours.

Suddenly the quiet was disturbed. The

dog began to bark, the cats scattered for cover in all directions, as the maid appeared through the open window-doors closely followed by a man whose tall form and soldierly bearing had been familiar in the thoughts of both Windover and Lucilla for many days. The maid disappeared, Lucilla called to the dog to be quiet, and husband and wife advanced across the garden to meet and greet the advancing Colonel Rockielaw.

Colonel Rockielaw seemed brisker, more vivacious, more like the leader of a storming party than ever. He occupied the garden in a moment, and proceeded to carry the Windovers by a bold stroke.

'Well,' he said, after he had taken the hands of husband and wife victoriously— 'well, I hope you have decided, and decided in the right way.'

The Windovers were silent, and their silence seemed to perturb their questioner, for he glanced from one to the other with an expression of unconcealed chagrin.

'Come,' he said sadly, with a touch of sternness in the sadness, the sternness of a man who is about to declare an armistice at an end, ' you don't mean to tell me——'

He paused ; his disappointment seemed to be too much for him. Windover felt that he must say something.

' Well, you see,' he began almost apologetically, ' the fact is——'

But what the fact was Colonel Rockielaw did not give him time to say. He charged tempestuously into the middle of Windover's attempted explanation and scattered it.

'Sorry to interrupt you,' he said. 'But before you go any further let me ask you one simple question. Do you know anything of a man of the name—the absurd name—of Budget ?'

Anthony and Lucilla involuntarily glanced at each other.

'You do,' said the Colonel; 'I perceive that you do.'

' Yes,' said Windover ; 'we certainly have

a friend of the name of Budget—Mr.
Stephen Budget. But I do not quite
see——'

'What he has to do with this matter,' said
the Colonel. 'Well, there I agree with you ;
neither do I. But Mr. Budget—yes, his
name was Stephen—seems to think differently from both of us.'

'How do you mean ?' asked Lucilla.

They had heard or seen nothing of Stephen
Budget since the night when he had dined
with them and been told of the proposal to
Windover, but she still resented the kind of
advice he had given to Windover and the
way he tendered it. So she felt much
curiosity to know how Colonel Rockielaw
had come to hear of him.

'Mean, my dear madam ?' said the Colonel.
'Why, simply this : did you give this fellow
Budget—excuse me, if he is a friend of
yours, for calling him "this fellow"; but that
is how he presents himself to my mind—did
you give this person Budget any authority

to act in any way on your behalf in this
matter ?'

'Certainly not,' said both Anthony and
Lucilla, speaking together with the precision
and decision of a chorus.

'I thought not,' said Colonel Rockielaw, 'I
felt sure not. He didn't seem to be the kind
of person—excuse me again ; if he is a friend
of yours he is a friend of yours, and no
more words about it—but he did not really
seem to me to be the kind of person whom
you would authorize to act in any kind of
delicate negotiations.'

'I most certainly should not,' said Windover. 'And I should be glad to know how
he comes into this matter at all.'

'Certainly,' said Colonel Rockielaw. 'This
fellow—I beg pardon, this Mr. Stephen
Budget—came to me the other day, called
upon me at the club. He sent up a note
to me in which he asked for the favour of
a few minutes' interview. He said in his
note that it concerned the election, and he

mentioned your name as a great friend of his.'

Windover frowned slightly. Lucilla frowned strongly. They both began to feel annoyed. The Colonel went on with his narrative.

'Of course the mention of your name would have been enough for me at any time, but the mention of your name coupled with the election convinced me that it must be something of the utmost importance, that the writer was probably some emissary of yours sent either to give me your answer or to ask some further questions before deciding. So I saw your friend in the Strangers' Room of the club.'

The Colonel paused for a moment as if to observe the effect of his story upon his hearers. Windover said nothing, but he looked a little pale. Lucilla leaned forward eagerly, and spurred the Colonel's speech with an interrogative, ' Well ?'

' I do not wish to say anything uncomplimentary about anyone whom you have honoured with your friendship,' said Colonel Rockielaw hesitatingly, 'but I must say, frankly, that I was not much impressed by the man, or, rather, I should say that I was, but that my impressions were not very favourable.'

'I am not surprised,' said Lucilla rather sharply. Her latent distrust of Stephen was deepening.

The Colonel bowed gallantly to Lucilla.

'I am glad to find that we are in agreement,' he said. 'My unfavourable impressions were not removed when he proceeded to explain himself, which, to do him justice, he did without the slightest embarrassment. Indeed, he acted as if he were conferring a favour upon me by invading my club and my quiet.'

'That is very like Stephen,' said Windover with a smile, as he pictured to himself the appearance of the two men at the interview.

'He began by explaining,' the Colonel went on, 'that he was a very intimate friend of yours, Mr. Windover. I notice, by the way, that you speak of him by his Christian name—Stephen.'

'We have been friends for some time, friends of a friendship formed in journalism. Budget has a way of considering a much slighter acquaintance than ours an intimate friendship.'

'So I should suppose,' said the Colonel—'so I should suppose. Well, to make a long story short, he gave me to understand, after many circumlocutions, that it was in the highest degree improbable that you could be prevailed upon to stand for Parliament.'

'He certainly did his best to persuade me not to stand,' said Windover; 'but that gave him no right to act as the interpreter of my opinions to anyone.'

'Of course not,' Rockielaw assented. 'However, he even went so far as to urge me, all in your interests, of course, not to

press the proposal upon you. He painted
quite a moving picture, I assure you, of the
injury to your literary work, of the injury to
your domestic peace, that public life would
cause you.'

'How very impertinent of him!' said
Lucilla. Her pretty cheeks were red with
anger, and her eyes shone.

'I cannot understand,' said Windover,
'why Stephen took it upon himself to
arrange my public and private affairs for me
in this extraordinary manner.'

'Can't you?' said the Colonel. 'You will
in a minute, for the best, or the worst, of the
business is still to come. I suggested to Mr.
Budget that, if you thought public life would
be injurious to your interests, you would no
doubt be able to speak for yourself. That
was my hint for him to go, but instead of
taking it, he took me still further into his
confidence. He was good enough to suggest
that in the event, the very likely event, of
your absolutely declining the offer that had

been made to you, he himself, Stephen
Budget, would be quite prepared to accept
the candidature and come forward as the
champion of our interests.'

Lucilla gave a little gasp, half of amazement and half of triumph. She had expected
some such revelation before the Colonel had
made it. Windover was frankly astonished.

' Budget said this ?' he asked.

' As I tell you,' said Rockielaw. ' He
assured me that as the representative of our
constituency he would undoubtedly be the
right man in the right place.'

' But this is quite astonishing !'—a remark
upon which Lucilla commented with an
indignant ' Not at all !' beneath her breath.
' Stephen Budget is one of the extremest of
extreme Radicals.'

' Is he ?' said Colonel Rockielaw. ' Then,
he is also one of the coolest of cool hands, to
come to me as he did. If I had known that,
I should have asked him to step outside the
club and have laid my rattan across his

shoulders in the open street. Perhaps it's
not too late now. Do you know the rascal's
address ?'

And the Colonel jumped up in a passion,
clutching his cane and with his face very red.

Lucilla half closed her eyes as she shaped
to herself with a certain amusement a
picture of the scuffle between the big, hard,
well-knit soldier and the big, loose, flabby
Budget. But Windover hastened to calm
the Colonel. Windover was not a man who
liked scenes of any kind, or the suggestion
of scenes.

'I don't think anything would be gained
by that, my dear Colonel Rockielaw. It is
true that I have always taken Budget to
be a very extreme politician. But I may
have been mistaken ; I may have misin-
terpreted his views. Also he may have
changed his mind. We have all heard of
rapid conversions in politics. So far, at
least, the age of miracles is not past. And
Budget is a very clever man.'

'He is a very great rogue, sir!' responded the indignant Colonel. But he so far suffered himself to be mollified that he sat down again, and, placing his rattan between his knees, folded his hands over its gold head, and gazed fixedly at the Windovers. 'The question for us to consider now,' he said, 'is not what this fellow Budget is, or what this fellow Budget is not. The question is, Are you disposed to accept our offer?'

And though Windover had not exchanged a word or a glance with Lucilla, he knew as well as if they had exchanged the inmost ideas of their minds that he was only saying what she would wish him to say when he returned the Colonel's fixed gaze and answered firmly:

'I am.'

CHAPTER XV.

THE DAWNING OF THE YEAR.

Spring is in the air, my darling,
  Spring is everywhere ;
In the chatter of the starling,
  In the golden air.
Spring is in the grove whose greenness
Thinly veils the branches' leanness—
  Branches lately bare.

Spring has come at last, my sweeting,
  Earth is mad with spring ;
Listen to the cuckoo's greeting
  Hear the swallow's wing.
Fireless hearths confound the cricket,
Nightingales in yonder thicket
  Have begun to sing.

Songs of Sentiment.

POETS have raved about spring ever since
poets began to rave about anything. But
the rhapsodies of English poets are too often

a mockery.   Yet there are some seasons, rare
and precious, when our English spring, that
is too often churlish, wears a genial face—
when March carries upon its rugged shoulders
the golden mantle of a poet's May, and
April laughs like June.   So it was with this
year—this year of Swift's life when all the
elements seemed to be allied in the purpose
of making existence an enchantment.   The
dear days of that April were such days as
he had never remembered in April before—
days of golden sunlight, of soft air, days as
warm as June, days that made all the world
wear holiday aspect, days of blue skies, of
bursting buds, of an atmosphere vibrating
with heat.

London seemed gay and gallant in the
unfamiliar sunlight which gilded its dingy
streets and gave a glory to its dingy
houses.   The parks blazed with early
flowers ; people who had window-boxes rejoiced in hyacinth and narcissus ; the flower
shops revelled in a riot of colour with prim-

roses and violets and daffodils. In the green open spaces which are London's playgrounds, the oases in her desert of bricks and flags, butterflies were now and then to be seen, yellow butterflies like animated flowers wheeling in the warm ether, unexpected harbingers of all good things, like Hesperus, and luring screaming children in pursuit, an allegory of human vanity that must for ever grasp at a fluttering happiness. It was all part of a masquerade, no doubt. London had no right to be so brave, an English April no business to be so bright. There was no precedent for it ; it was almost unconstitutional, but it was very beautiful, and it made a great many people very happy —especially Swift.

The weather that the poets have called the weather of the kingfisher stayed and stayed, giving its glory to everything, and calling with voice upon voice to all lovers of the country life to shake the dust of cities from their feet and face the highways that lead through meadows to woods and lanes and waters and the hollows of the hills.

Swift began to long with a longing that was like a sickness to obey those voices, to feel upon his cheek the air of the fields, to breathe the odour of flowers, to drink from the Fountain of Youth, as he always drank when he escaped from the town into the country. Of old he would have answered the summons instantly—have thrust a book into his pocket, flung on his hat, and set out for a day-long wander, that brought him back at evening footsore, but heart-light, full of memories that enchanted, with cheeks that the sun had tanned, with clothes that the dust of many highways, the grass of many lanes, had stained. For then he was content to be alone, to walk where he pleased and how he pleased, his own master, with no need of other companion than his thoughts or the volume in his pocket. But now the voices of the spring called upon a changed worshipper. For Swift was no

longer alone in the world, no longer the
austere master of his own caprice; he
hungered and thirsted for the country as
much as ever, but he did not wish to taste
its joys in solitude. He wanted the country,
but he also wanted Candida for his companion in the country.

Hitherto his friendship for her, her friendship for him, had been bounded by a few
streets, environed by a few houses. To walk
with Candida through the echoing halls of
the British Museum, to talk to her of the
old Gods who long ago reigned on Olympus,
of the old shepherds who long ago sang in
Arcadia, this was indeed delightful. But it
would be even more delightful to walk with
her as in a living green Arcadia, to woo, in
her company, the last and greatest of the
Grecian Gods, even Pan himself, whose
shaggy coat still hides wherever a hedgerow
runs, whose goat-feet still caper wherever
woods abound and fields spread to the sun,
whose bearded face still mirrors itself in

unpolluted streams. The sound of his pipes along the hills and down the valleys is still ever the sweetest music in the world, to those happy few upon whom in their helpless cradle the rustic Pan has breathed. Great Pan is not dead to any child of the open air, for all the cry of the wind round Cape Misenum.

Swift was in a great degree a child of the open air. The necessity for making a living had compelled him to live in cities and to write in rooms, to haunt great libraries and be within touch of the printer's devil. But his heart was always with the country; he was happiest when striding across a windy common, or climbing a kindly hill, or treading the needled carpet of a pine wood. It was, Oh to walk across a common with Candida, to sit with Candida beneath the shade of some gracious tree, to hear with Candida the first call of the cuckoo—the call that wakens at once all that is sylvan in the heart of the man whose inmost spirit still remembers the green woods!

After all, why should it not come to pass? The days as they drifted by in the splendour of their sunlight, in the illumination of their gold and colour, only seemed to make the friendship between Swift and Candida more intimate, more exquisite, more ideal. Candida accepted the friendship as if it had always been portion and parcel of her life; she treated Swift with something of the frankness that would have been natural if he had been another woman or she another man. He, on his part, drunk with delight at the kindliness of her comradeship, rejoiced and amazed at the rapture of his happiness, forgot, or tried to forget, that there was a time when this friendship had never been, and exorcised, or tried to exorcise, the thought that it could cease. She was willing to see him every day, and for a large part of every day. He had been allowed to come again and again to the dainty little room in Bury Street.

April had lingered out its life in ineffable

sweetness, and now May sat upon her throne, no less royal in the attributes of summer. If London could seem so fair in the golden atmosphere of those glorious days, how would not the world show in the clear, clean country? If Candida would only come! And why should she not come, she who seemed so disdainful of conventions, she who seemed so content with the conditions of their friendship? At least he decided it could do no harm to ask her. Even if she refused she was not likely to be angered by the proposition.

He suggested to her, diffidently, one afternoon early in May, that the weather was too fine to be wasted within the walls of even the British Museum.

'You are fond of walking,' he said. 'Will you come for a walk? I have a vagrant mood upon me.'

She looked thoughtfully at him, and then glanced at a casemate in the room in which they were standing. The casemate was

open, and through its wired aperture came a
glow of sunlight.   There was a glimpse of
green trees from the neighbouring gardens,
and the chatter of birds came pleasantly
upon the ear.   Swift followed the direction
of her glance.

'Does not that tempt you?' he asked.
'If that square of sunlight and that little
glimpse of leaves seem so alluring in this
old place, how delightful the country would
be !   Let us assume that the spirits of the
woods and the waters are calling to us, and
let us obey the summons.'

'It would be pleasant,' she said softly
—'very pleasant.'

'I often take walks by myself,' said Swift,
'but it would be delightful to have you for
my companion.   I hope you do not think I
ought not to ask you?'

'Oh no,' said Candida ; 'we are friends
and comrades.   But where could we go?'

'Do you know Richmond Park?' Swift
asked.

A smile came and went on Candida's face too quickly for Swift to notice it.

'Not very well,' she said.

'I am awfully fond of it,' said Swift. 'For a place so near to town it is full of pastoral possibilities. I go there very often, and I tell you what I often do—and what we might do, if you didn't mind—I take my luncheon with me and eat it in the open air. One is as much alone as if one were in the backwoods.'

'It sounds very pastoral and primitive and pleasant,' said Candida. There was mirth in her eyes and mirth in her voice, but the proposal seemed to please her.

Swift was delighted.

'It need not tire you much,' he said. 'We can take a train to Putney, walk from there to the Park, have our picnic at the foot of some tree, and then walk across the Park and come back by train from Richmond. Do come. It would be delightful!'

'I will come with pleasure,' Candida said. 'Do not fear fatigue for me. I am not easily tired.'

'This is excellent,' he said. 'I will bring some sandwiches and a bottle of claret.'

'No,' said Candida; 'let us divide the burthen like brothers. You shall bring the claret, and I will bring the sandwiches. Besides, I am sure that my girl will cut them better than your landlady would.'

Swift, conscious of that worthy woman's heavy hand in cookery, admitted that this was extremely probable. So it was all arranged, and Swift prayed for fine weather.

Fine weather was vouchsafed. Fine weather was the appanage of that unwonted time, when the trees wore the green livery of the spring well-nigh a month before their custom, when the fervid air seemed to belong to the June of the poets, when the laburnum blazed in yellow, and the lilac blazed in mauve, and the chestnuts showed their great

white candles like green altars to nature,
and the crimson stars of the may burned
everywhere, and burning filled the air with
the incense of their strange, sweet scent.

Pessimists shook their heads over this
untimely splendour; they saw in it only the
prodigality of the spendthrift who squanders
his inheritance with headlong haste, and they
prophesied a dismal summer as the penalty
for a divine spring. But the optimists hoped
that this early glory was but the herald of
happier, hotter days; and the opportunists,
of whom Swift was one, did not trouble
their heads about either fortune, but accepted
with delight the fact of fine weather in
season or out of season, and were prepared
to make the most of it and the best of it
while it lasted.

Thank heaven the sun shines to-day—this
day that is like Hesperus, and that bringeth
all good things: clear skies and Candida,
green grass and green trees, and the colours
of flowers, and the sounds of birds, and

escape from streets and houses—that brings sweet companionship, open friendship, hidden love.

Such was the wise mood in which Swift welcomed a wonderful day.

CHAPTER XVI.

IN RICHMOND PARK.

Only I lonely long
For the woodland life, for the strong
Cry of the cuckoo's song.

The Romany Road.

THE gleams of the morning sunlight, glad-
dening Swift with the fulfilment of his hope,
seemed to shine ironically upon Swift's workroom, with its unused books and its neglected
desk. Swift, even while he joyously ate his
breakfast, joyously drank his tea, noted how
the rays fell upon the backs of volumes
which under other conditions would have
been lying wide open upon his table and
incessantly consulted. And instead of open-
ing them now, he was going off as careless as
a gipsy to wander in green places with the

most beautiful woman in the world. How much better it was to wander in green places with the most beautiful woman in the world than to bother about books! But the neglected books reminded him that he had neglected other things; that he had not been near the Windovers since the day when he sought, and sought in vain, for Mr. Drass; that he had forgotten all about the Pine Hill election; that he had seen nothing of Budget, and had not been near the Cordeliers for ages.

He felt penitent about the Windovers, but not very penitent, for he knew that Lucilla, if she knew, would readily forgive him. As for the Cordeliers, he only smiled a smile of satisfaction as he left his house to think that he was going for a walk with Candida instead of going to a committee meeting in St. Ethelfreda's Without. And yet there was a committee meeting that day, specially summoned by Budget, but Swift did not give it a thought.

At half-past eleven Swift stood at Candida's door, and rang the bell joyously. A small bottle of claret, artfully enveloped in brown paper, so as to resemble anything save its convivial self, occupied one of the roomy pockets of his yellow coat ; a volume of verse occupied the other. In honour of the expedition Swift had mounted his straw hat, sunburnt with the suns of more than one summer, and bound with a plain black ribbon, for Swift did not belong to any aquatic or athletic club, and could fly no colours.

Candida opened the door to him herself, and Swift thought she looked more enchanting than ever as she stood there, framed in the square of the doorway, in her very neat, very simple, very dainty dress of blue serge, and the cool white blouse beneath the little open jacket.

If Swift had been a man experienced in the wear of women, he would have admired the perfection with which the plain attire

was made, and the modishness of the small
straw hat that crowned Candida's dark hair.
But he was not, and he only thought that
she looked very nice, which, indeed, he would
probably have thought if she had come to
greet him garbed in an old flour-sack.   Candida held a small square brown paper packet
dangling by a string-loop from her finger.

'I was resolved not to keep you waiting
for a second,' Candida said, 'and so I came
to the door to be ready for you.   The virtue
of punctuality should not be the privilege of
man.   Here are the sacred sandwiches.'

Swift laughed and took the packet from
her, and she drew the door to behind her.

'We have plenty of time,' he said as they
went down the stone stairs.   'But it is very
good of you to be punctual, none the less.'

When they got into Oxford Street, Swift
was for calling a cab to drive them to Charing
Cross, but Candida would not hear of this
piece of extravagance.

'We have plenty of time to walk,' she

said; 'therefore let us walk. Poor people like us cannot afford to spend money in that reckless way.'

'But won't you be tired?' Swift asked dubiously. 'Remember that there is plenty of walking to do at the other end of our train journey.'

'So much the better,' said Candida. 'We are going a-walking; let us get all the walking we can. It will do us both good, and I think you will find that I am not easily fatigued. Remember that I am a country girl.'

So it was settled, and they walked along briskly towards Charing Cross in the best of spirits. The sun was bright, and made even the sordid streets look cheerful, for your sun is the best beautifier in the world and of the world, and the man and woman were as merry as a boy and girl. More than one of those whom they passed on their way looked with admiration at the beautiful girl in her simple, admirable attire, and looked with amazement

at her companion in his yellow suit and his
old sunburnt straw hat. But if Candida
noticed the admiration or the amazement,
she showed no sign of notice; and as for
Swift, he noticed nothing but his companion, thought of nothing but the fair
fortune of the fair day.

At Charing Cross they caught a Metro-
politan train to Putney. Here Swift insisted
upon extravagance, and took first-class tickets,
though Candida suggested that third-class
would do very well, and that they certainly
ought not to think of travelling higher than
second. But Swift, who was very careless
of his own comfort, and whose democratic
theories always carried him to a third-class
carriage, wanted to give Candida the best
that it was in his power to offer her. There
were not many people going out by that
train, which left Charing Cross at a minute
before noon, so they had a carriage all to
themselves, and were very merry during their
twenty minutes' transit.

Candida seemed to take the liveliest interest in everything that was to be seen from the windows of the carriage — the changing types of houses, the steady, merciless advance of brick and mortar upon what once had been smiling fields, the growing sense of a cleaner, more countrified air, as the train crossed the river. She pretended that Swift in his extravagance had secured a reserved carriage for her ; nay, more, had chartered a special train. He had never seen her so merry, in such high spirits, in all their infinite, intimate friendship, which was now some sweet weeks old. Her child-like mirthfulness made her young beauty seem yet younger, and its influence was deliciously contagious, bringing out in Swift all that was most brightly boyish in his unsophisticated nature. He felt quite sorry when the train came to East Putney, and was only able to console himself by remembering that the delight of the day was now to come, the delight of the walk with Candida.

And it was a pleasant walk. First through the Putney Street and the wide way of Putney Hill. Then across Putney Common, with its first fair breath of wildness after the servility of the abandoned, well-nigh forgotten city. Then the coming on the Portsmouth Road, with all the rich suggestions and imaginings that the union of those two simple words afforded—suggestions and imaginings of an earlier day when the history of Europe seemed to start from Portsmouth Hard, and when the demigod adventurers travelled post-chaise from the great city to the great sea-port to fight the French and find eternal glory. Then to come on Wimbledon Common, with its illustrious windmill holding its gaunt vanes to the soft sky, and the grayness of the common's tone dotted with the scarlet points of the golfers' coats. And so on, on by the gallant winding road past modern villas hideous in their modernity, and past old houses that seemed as if they must in their

day have been honest coaching inns, their
bar-parlours not unfamiliar to highwaymen ;
by trim gardens and spreading fields, until
they came to the funny little row of modest
suburban houses which, as Swift knew,
announced the immediate nearness of the
Park. The little houses were all very neat,
and their tiny front gardens won the admiration of Candida, because of the brave show
they made in flowers of the simpler favour.
But they did not linger long over these
modest houses. A few paces more and Swift
turned his companion to the right, and they
were face to face with the Robin Hood Gate
of Richmond Park.

Once inside the gates of the Park, the
wanderers seemed to pass, as if by enchantment, from town to country, from the pave-
ment to the woodland.

'Now are we in Arden!' cried Swift
joyously, waving his hand towards the tall
elms as if to congratulate them upon the
advent of divinity.

Divinity looked up at him and laughed.

'Please do not finish the quotation,' she said, 'unless you be indeed of the Touch-stone humour. "Marry, the greater fool I! When I was at home I was in a better place."'

Swift reddened slightly, and laughed too.

'That was the folly of a motley fool!' he said. 'Your coxcomb is no shepherd. Withered brain and wry wit are not made for the country life. I suppose Touchstone took Audrey back to Court with him. I wonder how she liked it?'

'Oh, famously,' Candida answered. 'She was made for the buttery hatch and chaffer with pages and men at arms. I doubt if she ever sent back a sigh towards Arden.'

'Perhaps not,' said Swift. 'Perhaps nobody ever loves the country so well as those who were born to cities. To me this place seems like the Earthly Paradise after Queen Square.'

They were walking under the great trees

skirting the wall that divides the Park from
Kingston Vale. The withered bracken of
the dead year crackled beneath their feet.
Here and there, through the dry earth and
the dead leaves, the pale green fronds of
new ferns began to peep, called into life by
the lovely spring. In front of them the
ground was a network of burrows, in and out
of which the quick, darting rabbits played or
stood still with long ears lifted, watching the
visitors' approach, and disappearing like
bubbles as the human steps drew nearer.
Above their heads a colony of rooks cawed
vociferously in the swaying tree-tops. In
the distance Swift pointed out to Candida a
herd of dappled deer moving slowly across a
green lawn, the antlers of the stags rising
and falling like the lances of a marching
army. The woods and the open were quick
with animal sights and sounds, but there
were no human beings to be seen. They
seemed to be as much alone in the beautiful
place as Adam and Eve in Eden. If it were

not for the low line of the wall, and the sight
of an occasional red roof gleaming through
the trees beyond it, they might have fancied
themselves to be in the very heart of the
country.

' Is it not a delightful spot ?' Swift asked.

His exhilaration knew no bounds. Never
before had he felt so conscious of the joy of
being alive as now in that green and golden
place, walking by the side of that beautiful
girl. Between the trees he could see the
warm air vibrating with the heat, and every
vibration seemed to arouse and to respond to
some pulse of pleasure in his own being.
The April sky flew the brave blue banner of
July, and Swift, looking up, saluted the
standard with a grateful heart.

' It is indeed !' Candida answered.

She smiled up at him in sympathy with
his enthusiasm, the enthusiasm which in him
was always so simple and so boyish. She
was silent for a minute as they moved
slowly along between the trees, going in a

direction of which Swift had constituted himself the guide. Then she said again :

'You seem very earnest in your likings. Are you always in earnest about everything ?'

Swift looked down quickly, with a vague fear that she might be laughing at him—a fear that for the second made him feel quite sick at heart, and that flung a shadow over the bright sky and the brave world. But Candida's face was perfectly grave, and her eyes were fixed upon a distant slope. He breathed again, and the shadow vanished and the sky was as gay, the world as gallant, as before.

'Of course I am in earnest. What is the good of life if one isn't in earnest about living ? Where I believe, I believe with all my heart and with all my soul ; where I like, I like ; where I love, I love——'

He stopped, with the quick colour in his cheeks, and she finished his sentence for him hurriedly :

'And where you hate, you hate, I suppose? Was that what you were going to say?'

He looked thoughtfully at a clearing across the ribbon of road some yards away, a clearing bright with sun, where the rabbits were racing about in sheer enjoyment of the game of life.

'I suppose so,' he said slowly. 'I don't know—I don't think—that I am much of a hater; at least, as far as I myself am concerned. I have never had occasion to hate anyone. I dare say I have disliked people, but hate is a great term, and it is a pity to degrade it to a substitute for spite.'

'Hasn't somebody said somewhere,' Candida asked, 'that those only love well who hate well?'

'It was Dr. Johnson, I think,' Swift answered. 'He said a great many things that he didn't exactly mean, I fancy. I don't think it is true. I hope it isn't true.'

'If anyone wronged you very much, do

you think you could hate them?' Candida asked with a gravity that defied grammar.

'I don't know,' Swift answered. 'Hate is such a hopeless kind of thing nowadays. We don't fight duels, we don't even hire bravos—and I don't write paragraphs for the papers.'

'I don't think I was thinking of a man,' said Candida; 'I think I was thinking of women. If women wronged—if a woman wronged you, could you hate her, do you think?'

'The problem hardly comes within the range of practical politics,' Swift said with a laugh; 'but I think not—I hope not. A man must be such a poor sort of a blackguard to hate a woman, it seems to me. What do you say to this tree?'

'Good-morning, tree,' said Candida, with an air of pretty pertness that made Swift shout with boyish laughter.

He had brought their walk to a halt in front of a mighty elm whose roots swelled out above the surface of the earth and sloped away in graceful curves. It was quite a lonely place—a place that seemed especially to invite wayfarers to repose.

'I am sure the Hamadryad should be grateful for your gracious salutation,' said Swift. 'But that is not exactly what I meant. I wanted to know if you thought this tree would be a pleasant kind of camping-ground for us?'

'Oh yes!' said Candida—'quite delightful. These gnarled roots will make excellent chairs.' She sat down on the biggest roots, and, leaning back against the tree, smiled up at him. 'I feel like a very gipsy. Do I look like a gipsy?'

As she glanced up at him, with her dark-blue eyes rendered darker by the shadow of the brim of her hat, with a warmer blood in her dark cheek from the exertion of the walk, with the deep darkness of her hair and the rich redness of her lips, she did, for the moment, seem to wear something of a gipsy favour. The very laughter that curled her mouth gave to her face an air of exquisite mockery that might well have become one of the daughters of the mysterious race.

Swift made her a salutation of solemn reverence, which was more of a tribute to her beauty than a concession to her jesting mood.

'If a gipsy,' he said, 'then, indeed, the queen of the gipsies.'

Her face suddenly grew grave.

'Perhaps I should make a good gipsy,' she said. 'But if so, I should certainly wish to be queen of the gipsies.'

The vehemence of her tone, the gravity of her voice, of her face, surprised him. He sat down beside her on another tree-root, holding in his hand the little bottle of claret, which he had taken out of the roomy pocket in which it had been resting.

'It would scarcely be difficult for you to queen it anywhere,' he said. 'But does sovereignty so greatly tempt you?'

' " Better the first man in the village than the second man in Rome," ' she answered.

She was merry again, and her eyes mocked him.

'The man who said that,' Swift commented, 'knew very well in his heart of hearts that he was going to be the first man in Rome.'

'Very well,' said Candida. 'Perhaps I know in my heart of hearts that I am going to be——'

'Queen of the gipsies?' Swift suggested.

He did not mean the words for a challenge, but she answered them with as much vivacity as if she took them for a challenge.

'Queen of the gipsies—queen of something—queen of anything—who knows? But now let us talk no more of queens and kings. Are we not democrats, you and I— or, at least, equal monarchs—here in this lonely woodland? Fellow-sovereign, may I offer you a sandwich?'

She had unfastened the package while she

was speaking, and now held it out to him
invitingly.

Swift took a sandwich and placed it by his
side on a piece of paper while he proceeded
to draw the little bottle of wine. When he
had done it he drew from another pocket—
that yellow coat of his was a marvel of
pockets—two small glasses, one of which
fitted into the other, and both of which,
being of the flattened shape affected by the
travelled, took up but little room. Candida
meanwhile went on quietly munching her
sandwiches with the healthy appetite of a
well-organized young woman who is hungry
after walking.

Swift filled the larger of the two glasses
with the red wine, and handed it to his
companion. Then he filled his own.

'I drink,' he said, 'to the queen of the
gipsies.'

And he pledged Candida with his eyes as
he drank his wine.

'And I,' said Candida, 'I drink as the old

Romans would have drunk, to the genius of
this place, to the kindly spirit that lingers
in these woods and grasses, and watches
benignly over the wanderers who come
within its domain.'

And as she spoke she sipped her wine and
her eyes laughed at Swift over the edge of
the glass.

'By all means,' said Swift. 'Genio loci—
to the genius of this place. I dare swear it
has never been so saluted before.' And as
he spoke he inverted his almost empty glass
and allowed a few crimson drops to trickle
down its sides and drop in small splashes
upon the dusty soil. 'You see,' he said, 'I
make libation.'

Candida followed his example.

They were silent for a little while. Then,
'This is very pleasant,' Candida said softly
to herself.

It certainly was very pleasant, Swift
thought, to sit there in that green place with
Candida by his side, sharing their bread and

wine like two tramps out of a dream. He
stretched himself out on the soft grass and
looked up at her. She was gazing across the
glade, but she was gazing vaguely, as if her
thoughts were otherwise than with what her
eyes beheld.

'This is delightful,' Swift said softly,
almost sighing for very pleasure. 'I feel as
if I should like to raise an altar in gratitude
to the rustic divinity.'

He looked around him again complacently,
and began to murmur to himself a few lines
of Greek verse. The girl turned sharply and
looked at him.

'What are you saying?' she asked
abruptly.

Swift looked up with a smile, somewhat
surprised to find her face so set.

'I was saying to myself,' he answered,
'some lines from the Greek Anthology, lines
attributed to Plato, in which the singer bids
his hearers to "sit down by this high-leafed,
voiceful pine, that rustles her branches

beneath the western breezes, and beside my babbling waters the pipe of Pan shall bring drowsiness down upon thy enchanted eyelids." Are they not delightful?'

Candida moved her head impatiently, and there was the shadow of a frown upon her forehead.

'Why must you always quote things?' she asked. 'We seem to live in an age of quotations, unable to ʰe anything, to do anything, to enjoy anything, unless we can fortify ourselves first by repeating like a charm something that some Greek, or Roman, or Italian, or Frenchman, or German, or Chinese, said before us. Can we not admire a fine day in a fair place without dragging in Plato to bolster us up in our delight? We are so dreadfully unreal, all of us; we seem to live in the shades of others instead of casting shadows of our own.'

Swift had never seen Candida so nearly approach to being angry before, and he felt guilty at having annoyed her. So he answered her apologetically, with an uneasy laugh :

' Was it so dreadfully unreal to quote poor old Plato ? The words seemed to chime in my mind with the time and the place.'

' No, they didn't,' said the girl decisively. ' To begin with, we are not sitting under a pine-tree at all, but an honest English elm. In the next place, we don't believe in Pan even as your Plato might have believed in him; it's only an affectation. In the third place, we are not Greeks of Arcady at all, but an English man and an English woman sitting in a suburban park. It is so far, far better to be a real thing than a reflection.'

Her voice softened suddenly as she saw how her little gust of anger had brought a troubled look into Swift's face.

' I dare say I don't express what I mean very well,' she said. ' But I do know what I mean, and that at least is something.'

' I think I understand your meaning very
well,' said Swift. ' But I do not think,
surely, that either of us is much to blame.
We are ourselves, we two ; we live our own
lives after our own fashion, free and straightforward. It is not a line from a Greek poet
that will turn us into hypocrites.'

The girl's face was turned away from
Swift, and he did not see the sadness on it.
But as she looked round at him now her lips
and her eyes were smiling.

' You are quite right,' she said, ' my dear
friend, and I am a peevish imp to-day. You
are as honest as the day—and I am as
honest as the night—and between us we
may perhaps succeed a little in remoulding
the world nearer to the heart's desire. Who
knows ?'

Swift's heart beat like drum-taps. He
raised himself upon one arm and looked
eagerly into her eyes.

' What do you mean ?' he said.

' I mean many things, nothing, everything.

I don't know what I mean to-day. Come, shall we tramp again?'

And Candida rose lightly to her feet; Swift sprang up, too, and stood beside her.

'Do you mean that perhaps——' he began, but the girl checked him.

'Remember,' she said, and laid her finger upon her lips. Swift inclined his head in a mute repentance. His pulses, that had begun to beat so hotly, flagged again.

CHAPTER XVII.

THE HOLLOW PLACE.

Even Arcady
Is still a portion of our common earth,
And those that dwell therein, however blessed,
Must not be counted as immortal gods,
But mortals set by danger everywhere,
Even where the world is greenest.

Alcibiades: A Comedy.

THERE was, however, only a momentary silence between them. If Candida's face had grown grave for a moment, it now smiled as gaily as ever, and her smile dispelled the chill that came over Swift's heart at the fear of offending her. Briskly he set himself to dissipate all signs of the feast—to roll up the brown paper into the smallest possible compass, and to bury it and the friendly flagon carefully under a clump of nettles. Candida watched his activity with an approving glance.

'Where shall we go now?' said Candida, after Swift had finished his task and restored the glasses to his pocket.

'If you are not tired——' Swift began.

'I am never tired!' Candida interrupted.

'Very well, then, I propose that we go along the Park towards Ham Gate, and so by the Common to the towing-path and back to Richmond for the train. It is a delightful way to walk.'

'Excellent. Onward!' Candida answered, and in another moment they were moving quickly through the trees in the direction that Swift had proposed.

Soon the ground sloped a little into a kind of gentle hill. Near the top a tall tree stretched a great curved branch across their path. Candida gave a little cry of joy.

'How delightful!' she said; 'I can just reach it.' And before Swift could understand

her intention she had swung herself lightly
into the seat that the great bough afforded,
and began to swing herself up and down,
pushing the ground with her foot every time
that the rustling bough came low enough to
allow her to do so.

'Oh, this is delightful!' she cried, looking
with a flushed, laughing face at Swift's somewhat amazed one. 'I feel like a little child
again. Swing me, please. "Hush-a-bye,
baby, on the tree-top; when the wind
blows, the cradle will rock."'

'"If the bough breaks, the cradle will
fall,"' said Swift, completing the quotation
anxiously, as he caught hold of one end
of the bough and scanned it to test its
strength. 'Are you sure the bough is strong
enough?'

'To bear my weight? Thanks for the
compliment. Don't be afraid. It is strong
enough—and if it breaks it breaks. "Down
will come cradle, baby and all."'

And Candida laughed again as Swift, in

obedience to her wish, swung his end of the
bough, and the girl rose and dipped among
the green leaves like a boat dancing on a
green sea.

It came to Swift, suddenly, that she had
never seemed so beautiful as she seemed
now, swaying with a kind of childish rapture
with the swaying bough, and laughing in
harmony with the music that the tree made
as the motion caused its branches to quiver
and its leaves to rustle up to the very
pinnacle of its woodland pride. She might
be a nymph of the woods, he thought—something less and more than human, one of
those mystical creatures who haunt the
hearts of German forests, and break the
hearts of hunters, and craze the brains of
lonely charcoal-burners. He felt a wild
longing to clasp her in his arms and kiss her,
kiss her again and again, while he cried out
a passion that filled his veins with flame.
And yet, even with the thought, he felt a
greater fear of her, a greater hopelessness

of ever quickening any love for him in her strange, wild heart. She may have read something of his thoughts, for she leaped lightly off the bough and stood, flushed, panting, but imperious, by his side.

'There!' she said, 'enough of that. I am tired of swinging.'

She looked around her with a sudden curiosity. At the point where they stood, on a crest of the rising ground, they could see over the Park wall in front of them the roofs and gables of a house. It was one of the many villas of Kingston Vale, and it lay so deep in the little valley that their eyes were on a level with its highest towers, and could look down upon as much of the roof as was visible amidst the trees of its garden. It was a picturesque house, mainly red in colour, and it seemed to have been put together whimsically, in an amalgamation of many orders and many periods of architecture. There was a wing that would have welcomed a gentleman of the Augustan

age of Anne.   There was a belfry that might
have sheltered the head of a sixteenth-
century Flemish burgher. 'There was a sham
classic colonnade that would have tickled the
taste of a Georgian recluse.   Yet the whole
thing, in its quaint incongruity, was very
decidedly modern.   A great gilded weather-
cock swung on the top of a little turret and
glittered in the sun.

Candida laughed softly to herself as she
looked with evident interest at the place.
Swift, following the direction of her glance,
gazed too, and felt slightly offended at the
confusion of styles which the house displayed.

'How   odd!' Candida   said, seeming   to
speak rather to herself than with any idea
of directly addressing her companion. 'I
wonder if they could see us from that
house ?'

Swift imagined that Candida was unwilling
to have been seen swinging so unconven-
tionally in the bough of the tree, and though

he was a little surprised to find her paying any heed to such a chance, he hastened to reassure her.

'I really don't think anyone could see us,' he said, 'with so many trees between us. And even if they could, there does not seem to be a sign of anyone about. If there were anyone at any of those windows in the turret I think I should see them.'

Candida did not seem to heed Swift's re-assurances. She still kept her eyes fixed on the house, and she still smiled softly to herself, as if she was very much amused at some memory.

'It certainly would be very funny,' she said, still more to herself than to Swift, 'if he——'

'What would be funny?' Swift inquired, now fairly mystified; 'and who is "he"?'

Candida looked away from the house, looked at Swift's puzzled face, and laughed again.

'Oh, nothing,' she said, 'only that I once

knew—or, rather, my father once knew—
a man who lived in that house. He was a
soldier, a neighbour of ours in the country. I
was only amused at thinking how amazed he
would be if he were to look out and see the
little girl he knew jumping up and down in
the branch of a tree with the assistance of a
great Greek scholar !'

Swift was a little surprised, but only a
little. If now and then, as at this moment,
he was made aware of how little he knew of
the past life of the girl who had become his
so constant companion, the thought scarcely
troubled him. His admiration for her was so
complete, his devotion so absolute, his joy in
the living present so intense, that it never
occurred to him to question Candida about
her past, or, indeed, ever to think of that
past and its possibilities with any serious
speculation. Yet as she stood before him
now, laughing and looking at the strange
house that lay below them, he felt as he had
felt before, that a chasm lay between their

two lives which he had not the power to bridge.

Candida noticed the shade of gravity that had stolen over Swift's face, and she looked away from the house and stopped laughing, though she still smiled.

'Come,' she said, 'onward. We are lazy wayfarers, you and I, and seize every pretext for a halt.'

She turned, and began to climb higher up the slope, so quickly that Swift had to exert himself to keep by her side, while he admired the sylvan vigour of her movements, the elasticity of her splendid youth.

At the top of the slope there was a little coppice of young trees enclosed by a slight railing, and in the grass at the foot of these trees a quantity of bluebells were growing. When Candida saw them she gave a cry of delight, and declared that she must needs gather some. Swift offered to defy the forest laws by vaulting over the railing and getting some for her, but Candida would not hear of this suggestion.

In another moment she had whisked her-self and her skirts dexterously and gracefully over the little paling, and was on her knees in the young grass, pulling with both hands at the bluebells. The whole purpose of her being seemed centred upon getting the flowers. Swift stared at her in some wonder —wonder at her shifting moods, at her strange alternations of jest and earnest, at her frequent gravity, her occasional air of weariness contrasting strangely with her fits of childlike frolicsomeness, of childlike pleasure in the easily attainable. She looked so young, so impulsive, so lightly happy as she stooped there in the coppice gathering her hyacinths, that she seemed to Swift more of an enigma than ever. Swift had known but few women in his time, and his know-ledge of those few did not help him to under-stand Candida.

Presently she came back to him, her eyes

bright with delight, and her cheeks flushed
by her exertions. She handed him a large
bunch of the pretty blue flowers over the
top of the paling.

'Hold these for a moment, please, while
I get over,' she said. 'Are they not beautiful?'

Swift had scarcely taken the bunch into
his hands before Candida had skimmed over
the fence, as easily and as gracefully as
before, and had taken the flowers from his
grasp.

'Ah!' she said, 'it is always delightful to
gather wild-flowers. You ought to write me
some verses—" To Candida gathering Bluebells "—something in the manner of Herrick,
you know, full of pretty phrases for me and
delicate regrets for the inevitable.'

'Ah!' said Swift, with a sigh, 'I am towards
myself of Touchstone's mind towards Audrey
—I would the Gods had made me poetical.'

Candida shrugged her shoulders.

'One may be poetical without writing

poetry,' she said. 'Would you love this scene any the more dearly because you were trying to shape a sonnet in its honour?'

They were now on the summit of the rising ground, and the park stretched away before them—a green plain dotted with clumps of trees, and traversed by a white ribbon of road.

'It is good to look at, is it not?' said Swift. 'And all within such a little distance of squares and streets and slums. We could almost hear the roar of London. But if we pleased, we could gain a greater quiet in this quiet place. You see how flat the ground looks before us?'

Candida nodded.

'Well,' Swift went on, 'there is, almost at our feet as it were, a spot wherein fifty men might lie concealed, and no one who walked on yonder road be ever the wiser.'

'Where?' Candida asked, looking all round her with surprise. 'I see no place where a cat could hide.'

'Come a little farther and you will,' Swift said. 'Do you see where those tufts of grass seem to grow a little thicker than the rest? Well, just beyond them there is a great hollow in the earth, so deep and wide that, as I said, I am sure fifty men could lie there unseen. I have lain there myself by the hour together, delighting in the sense that I was alone in the world, and that if an army was marching by on yonder highway I should be invisible to them.'

'It sounds most romantic,' Candida said. 'Show me your cave, gentle hermit.'

'Come,' Swift answered, 'let us imagine that we are seeking shelter in a strange land.'

He walked forward for a few yards in silence, Candida keeping close by his side. Suddenly the green seemed to yawn, and in another moment they were standing on the edge of the chasm of which Swift had spoken. It was a sloping, irregular, sandy pit, partly overgrown with coarse grass and gorse bushes. As Swift had said, it would have easily sheltered half a hundred men from the observation of anyone who did not come to its immediate edge.

At the moment, however, when Candida and Swift approached it, it only served to shelter one man. But it sheltered him so effectively that the pair had got to the very lip of the pit before they perceived that it had an occupant. A man was lying in the hole, lying on his stomach, on the slope of the pit which was nearest to the wall of the Park and farthest from the road. His face was raised a very little above the level of the pit's mouth, but it was concealed by the low bushes, through whose branches he seemed to be peering as if he were watching very intently something in the direction of the wall. He was so intent upon his watching, and Swift and Candida had come so quietly to the edge of the hole, that he had not heard their approach.

Now, however, Swift, startled to find his lair in the possession of a stranger, gave an involuntary sound of surprise, which roused the man's attention. He swung round for a moment on his side and glanced up at the new-comers, shading his eyes with his hand as he did so, for the sun was strong and beat hotly on the pit. The sight seemed to cause him more surprise than his presence had caused to the new-comers, for he immediately fell on to his face again and lay so for a second or two quite still, as if he had been shot. Then suddenly he swung himself to his left side, so as to present his back to them, and, leaping to his feet, scrambled quickly up the further side of the pit and proceeded to run away across the grass as fast as his legs could carry him.

Swift and Candida stared at each other for a moment in amazement, and then, with one accord, they burst out laughing heartily.

' Well,' said Candida, pointing to the man, who was still running as if for dear life among the trees, ' we seem to have startled one cave man a good deal.'

' Yes, indeed,' said Swift ; ' he must be some confirmed solitary, who resented our intrusion.'

' Or who, perhaps, was repelled by our personal appearance,' Candida suggested. ' He was evidently in so great a hurry to depart that he did not notice that he had left some of his property behind him.'

And Candida pointed to where, on the ground of the pit, a small object lay.

The object at which Candida pointed was a small piece of paper, folded square. Swift went down into the pit and picked it up. It was a curious yellowish colour and of thin texture, so that Swift could see through the folds that it was covered with some kind of black characters. Swift's first idea was to signal to the man, but when he looked up for this purpose the man was out of sight.

' Where has he vanished to ?' Swift asked of Candida, who had come down and was standing by his side.

' The man ?' Candida answered. ' He dis-

appeared behind those trees ;' and she pointed
to a clump of trees at the other side of the
road.

'What odd paper this is !' said Swift,
showing it to his companion. 'And it seems
to be full of writing.'

'Open it and see,' Candida suggested ;
and, as Swift was really curious, he obeyed
the suggestion and unfolded the paper.

It was a large piece of paper when it was
unfolded—of an oblong shape and a faded
yellow tinge. It was covered with large
characters that conveyed no meaning to
Swift, and appeared to be printed by some
common process, as in many places the ink
was very pale.

'Well,' said Swift, as he showed it to
Candida, 'I am no wiser than before.'

'Oh, I am so sorry,' sighed Candida ; 'I
felt sure that you would know, and I am
dying of curiosity.'

'I think it is some Eastern script,' Swift
said. 'But I am sorry to say that my

limited education does not include Eastern tongues.'

'And is there no way of finding out?' Candida asked.

'Oh yes,' said Swift, 'I can easily find out what it means if you wish.'

'Why, of course I wish,' she said. 'Who would not wish to know what those mysterious symbols mean? I am sure it must be something interesting.'

'I know a man,' said Swift, 'who is a great linguist. I believe he can read and write every language under heaven. He does a great deal of work for the Museum, and he lives quite near to me. I will take it to him for elucidation.'

'And then you will tell me all about it.'

'I will, indeed,' Swift answered, and then he folded up the paper and put it carefully into his pocket-book.

CHAPTER XVIII.

THE TURN OF HASSAN DRASS.

Although I most devoutly disbelieve
In necromancers' nonsense, and the web
Of glamour that your wizard tries to weave,
There is a kind of softness at my heart
For all the juggling fellowship.

The Devil's Comedy.

As a matter of fact, however, Swift forgot all about the mysterious paper. He had laid it between the leaves of the book he was carrying that day, which happened to be Shakespeare's 'Sonnets,' and on the following day he chose another book for his companion, and the little volume of Shakespeare lay on his table unheeded. Swift forgot many things in those delightful days of dawning

summer that were of greater moment than a
scrap of paper with strange signs upon it.
He forgot, or he neglected, which came to
the same thing, the claims of friendship, the
claims of politics, the claims of business.
The Windovers might never have existed;
the Cordeliers might have been transplanted
to Cloud-Cuckoo-Town, Cripple and Co.
have been no better than a solar myth, for
all the heed Swift paid to them.

It was Candida, Candida, and always
Candida. Since their expedition to Richmond Park their friendship seemed to have
grown closer, stronger, dearer, more delightful than before. The fine weather persisted,
and the example of their first adventure was
persistently followed. The British Museum
was abandoned, and the careless couple went
wandering, day after day, in the green and
gracious places which girdle London, as
happy and as heedless as if they were
indeed what they called themselves in jest
—a pair of tramps. And as their bodies

had broken away from the Museum, their
minds no longer occupied themselves with
antiquity.   The Gods of Greece were suffered to sleep undisturbed on the summits
of Olympus ; the man and the woman
busied themselves, very youthfully, with
problems.

Swift was always in earnest ; Candida
was always curious.   She told him one day
that she had read the 'Cry for Liberty,'
and she questioned him as to the various
doctrines laid down in that remarkable
volume with a closeness and a quickness
that Swift at times found perplexing.   The
sonorous phrases seemed to be less convincing to Swift after Candida had repeated
them to him and asked him for interpreta-
tion.   The 'Cry' did not seem so complete
a body of social philosophy as Swift had
hitherto believed it to be after some of these
examinations.   He had formulated certain
theories, which he believed to be very broad
theories, of the relationships between man

and woman ; had advocated and had felt delighted to advocate a system of free love. He had felt very sure at the time that these views were very sensible ; he was not quite so sure now, when Candida, divinely smiling and divinely frank, interrogated him as to the permanent applicability of his ideas. But he stuck to his guns gallantly, defended himself and his opinions as well as he could, and fell deeper and deeper in love with his companion every day.

And yet in all that time they talked no word of love. If Swift felt the sweet ache at his heart, outwardly the alliance was only friendship. Candida had laid down her conditions, and Swift had accepted them, and he meant to keep his promise. It was at times a kind of torture to him to be thus incessantly in the company of a woman he loved so well, and never to say word and never to look look that should betray his passion. But his honour was at stake, not merely in his promise to Candida, but in his adhesion to the great theory of the 'Cry for Liberty,' the theory of the possibility of friendship between a man and a woman as absolute as between a man and a man. So he thought of his love as of the genie in the Arabian tale, that it must be shut down in the compass of its little jar by virtue of the seal of Solomon.

And so through the golden days of that golden prime he saw Candida daily, and walked with her and talked with her as he would have walked and talked with any man who was his friend, when all the while he was longing to tell her that he loved her; and he shook hands with her at meeting and at parting in the manliest way, when his whole being was eager to catch her in his arms and kiss her on the lips. Even as to the shaking of hands Candida had reminded him that in the 'Cry for Liberty' he had derided these and the like ceremonies as antiquated conventionalities hampering to the intelligent intercourse of humanity. And

Swift, embarrassed, had said that some conventionalities were comparatively harmless, and that the shaking of hands was excusable as a sign of friendship. So they went on shaking hands at meeting and parting, and Swift went on being exquisitely happy and exquisitely unhappy.

Candida, on her side, took the friendship with the sweet gravity, the smiling composure, which seemed to be her attitude towards life. Her hand, when she gave it, rested as calmly in Swift's hand as if no thought of anything but friendship could ever come into their lives ; her eyes looked into his with an untroubled calm ; and the frankness of her speech, when she argued out the questions of the ' Cry for Liberty ' with its distinguished author, made her serenity, made her indifference to what might be, the more convincing and the more tantalizing. She went about with Swift as tranquilly as if she and he were doing the most ordinary thing in the world, as if young flesh never took fire, as if young blood never mutinied.

She seemed so sure of herself, so sure of him, so independent of and heedless of the ordinary rules that regulate the relations of free men with free women, that Swift, whose business it had been to defy conventionality in season and out of season, whose ' Cry ' was the very counterblast to all accepted things, was surprised at her absolute unconventionality—so surprised that once or twice he was startled to find himself suggesting to her, in a diffident, half-hearted way, that, perhaps, she didn't know how unconventional their actions were.

She silenced these suggestions by felicitous and apt quotations from the ' Cry for Liberty,' and by assuring him that she meant to live her life in her own way, that she believed in freedom, and that she was content for the present to be governed by her own theories of right and wrong and by the admirable views of the ' Cry.' So Swift had nothing more to say, and the amazing friendship prospered.

Since their essays in the sylvan life they were more together than ever. They almost always made their middle meal now like true gipsies, under a tree in some green woodland or in some tranquil reach of the river, for Swift, who loved boating, had soon discovered that Candida could pull an oar as well as he. And when they came back to town they would dine together very simply, but very pleasantly, at a little Italian restaurant which Swift had discovered long ago, a tranquil place in a quiet street out of a very crowded street, a kind of backwater from a roaring main current of London life, a place which, when you entered it, seemed to transport you at once to the Continent and to Continental ways. Candida made no demur to dining daily with Swift ; the only thing she insisted upon was that if he paid for the dinner one day she should pay for it on the next. At first Swift was for protest-

ing, but Candida was decided. If he agreed
to that she would dine with him as often as
he liked. If he did not agree to it she would
not dine with him at all. So Swift could
not choose but consent, and so it came about
that they dined together daily, very joyously
and very modestly, on the principle of
alternate host, in the quiet, kindly little
restaurant, whose people at last got to know
them and to expect their coming and salute
them cheerily. After these dinners Swift
would escort Candida home to Bury Street,
and at Bury Street he always parted from
her. She never asked him to come in, and
he never asked to be allowed to come in.
They always shook hands in the doorway,
and Swift always waited till the last sound
of Candida's ascending footsteps had died
away, and then he went on to Queen Square
to read himself sleepy over Plato, and so
to dream of Candida and the next day's
joy.

One day towards the end of May, on a

return from one of their expeditions, Swift's
attention was arrested by an advertisement
in the railway-station. It was one of the
many large coloured posters with which the
Imperial Theatre of Varieties adorned the
walls of London, posters which presented a
number of pictorial representations of per
formers of all kinds, from dancing girls to
dancing elephants. The particular picture
which caught Swift's eye represented a man
in Eastern costume encircled by gigantic
snakes, and the legend announced the un-
paralleled performances of Hassan Drass,
the great Indian snake-charmer. This could
be no other than his mysterious host, and
Swift immediately resolved that he would go
and see him. A study of the column in an
evening newspaper devoted to the music-
halls informed him that Mr. Drass's turn
came late in the evening's entertainment.
So after Candida and he had dined together,
and after he had seen her home to Bury
Street, instead of going on to his own rooms

in Queen Square, he turned back towards town and steered for the Imperial Theatre of Varieties.

The Imperial Theatre of Varieties was London's largest, London's latest music-hall. It was the stateliest temple that had yet been erected to the grotesque Muse; it was a splendid shrine for the great goddess. It gave the completest expression to that passion for the variety entertainment which was London's dominant enthusiasm. Swift did not share the enthusiasm, though he had often gone to music-halls with Budget, and even on occasion with the Windovers. But the Imperial Theatre was new to him, and he admired its magnificence ironically as he entered its glittering vestibule. He was anxious to get a seat as near to the front as possible. But the Imperial Theatre was popular, the evening was half over; there was not a seat left. So Swift, on the suggestion of the man in the box-office, took a ticket for the promenade, which allowed him to walk all round the stalls and to stand where he pleased in the space allotted for promenaders.

He took up his position by a pillar quite near to the stage, and waited. He had bought a programme as he came in, and the programme informed him that the turn of the snake-charmer was number sixteen. The number now displayed at the sides was fourteen, and was, as he learned from his programme, the number of the turn of the Sisters Aaron. The Sisters Aaron were four young ladies of a showily handsome, obviously Jewish favour, who were singing in chorus a song that informed the listeners that they were 'the models, yes, the models of the English aristocracy.' Swift did not approve of the English aristocracy, but he did not think that such specimens of its womenkind as he had seen at all resembled the Sisters Aaron, who, however, asserted their theory with much noise and persistence. They did not amuse Swift, and his glance wandered over the full house with the interest he always felt in crowds.

It was not at all the habitual music-hall audience. The Imperial Theatre of Varieties affected grandeur ; most of the visitors to the more expensive places came in evening dress ; there were a quantity of women in the boxes, and even in the stalls, who looked obviously smart. Some of the people Swift knew by sight. Lord Lancelot was in the stage-box with a number of handsome women ; in the stalls he recognised one of the younger members of the Government, who seemed to be entertaining a party of friends. Close to him in a corner stall sat someone he knew personally—Theocritus Marlowe, the writer of rhymes. He was not surprised to find Marlowe there.

He knew that Marlowe, tired of being overshadowed by Jack Harris in the propagation of the Higher Culture, had constituted himself the Apostle of the Music-Hall, the preacher, in melodious verse, of the

New Gospel of the Variety Show. Marlowe,
who was listening with an intent air of
rapture to the utterances of the Sisters
Aaron, sighed a faint sigh, half of pleasure,
half of regret, as that remarkable turn came
to an end. Then, as he glanced away from
the stage, he saw Swift standing by the
pillar, and immediately got up and came over
to talk to him. Swift had a kind of interest
for Theocritus Marlowe. A man who could
do without so many of the things which
seemed to him to be essential to the accept-
ance of life was a curious problem, a host
as worthy of attention as a contortionist,
a performing dog, or a Mammoth Comique.
Also Theocritus felt that it would look rather
nice for him to be seen in the carefully
harmonized black and white of his evening
dress, standing in speech with a big man in a
cheap yellow suit. So he saluted Swift with
that air of languor which, in his mind, lent a
piquancy to his chosen part as patron of the

music-hall, and Swift accepted his salutation with composure.

'What have you come here for, Swift?' he asked. 'Does this sort of thing'—and he waved his hand vaguely in the direction of the stage, where an energetic gentleman was doing an imitation of a brass band—'does this sort of thing come within the range of practical politics, or are you an emissary of the County Council come to mark us down for judgment?'

'For none of these reasons,' Swift answered composedly. 'I have come to see the man with the snakes.'

'Oh yes, the Serpent King,' Marlowe said. 'He is quite interesting—quite nice. You come in the nick of time, too; it is just his turn.'

For already the gentleman who simulated the brass band had, as it were, blown himself off the stage, and the attendants were slipping the number sixteen into the spaces. The great curtains of yellow brocade had fallen, and remained down for some appreciable seconds, during which Marlowe amiably pointed out to Swift various celebrities who were present in the house. Then the curtains were drawn aside for the entertainment of the Serpent King.

There was a kind of enclosure set up on the stage—an enclosure formed of solid brass railings. In the middle of this enclosure sat the performer, habited like a dervish. Behind him were two large boxes strongly bound with iron. For a few seconds the man sat quite still with his gaze bent on the ground ; then he slowly lifted his face and gazed steadfastly at the audience. Swift's curiosity was satisfied. The Serpent King was certainly his host of Camden Town. The persistent gaze, that was so intent that it seemed like the stare of a seeker, travelled quickly over the audience. For a moment it rested on that part of the house where Swift stood by the pillar, and Swift felt certain that the snake-charmer had seen him, had

recognised him.   It was but the briefest
glance, and yet Swift saw, or thought he
saw, in it a suggestion of displeasure at his
presence, which he was at a loss to account for.

The man began his performance.   He
opened the great coffers that stood behind
him on their trestles, and he drew out from
them great coils of monstrous shining snakes
that he laid about him on the floor within the
enclosure.   Swift could not avoid giving a
kind of shudder as he thought of the circum-
stances under which he had first seen those
terrible beasts who now crawled and wriggled
round and round their master as if something
in his very presence invincibly attracted
them.   When the enclosure was alive with
snakes the man began to play with them,
winding the hugest of the beasts round his
body, twisting smaller ones round his arms,
till it was hardly possible to see anything of
his body for the mass of serpents that encircled him.   Their weight alone must have
been enormous, but he seemed to support it

with ease. If those awful coils had tightened a little more they would inevitably have squeezed out the man's life, but the creatures seemed to be entirely under his domination, and to obey his slightest word or wish. At some sign from him they all uncurled themselves and left him free; then he began to play to them on a little pipe that he plucked from his girdle, and all the snakes, big and little, began to move about the enclosure rhythmically to the fantastic music that came with the piper's breath. There was something curiously attractive in seeing the man standing there blowing plaintive, alluring sounds from his reed, and the striped and spotted beasts swaying to the music and gliding about in a kind of ecstasy of fascination. After he had played for a few minutes, he stopped and began tossing the snakes about again, tying them into knots, winding them in and out of the bars of the enclosure, and in other ways showing his absolute command over his fantastic satellites. Then

the Indian began to put the reptiles back
into their boxes. His turn was only a brief
one—it was just at an end—but it fascinated
while it lasted, and the audience was prodigal
of applause.

Swift turned hurriedly to Marlowe.

' I wonder,' he said, ' if there is any way
by which I could get a word with that
man. If I went round to the stage-door, I
suppose I could send in my name to him.
Do you know the way to the stage-door ?'

' Do I know the way to the stage-door ?'
Theocritus answered with an amused smile.
' Of course I do ; but by the time you got
there the fellow might be gone, and waiting
at a stage-door is a slow business, any way.
If you want to see him at once, I can manage
it for you.'

Swift answered that he should be very
much obliged, whereupon Marlowe told him
to come with him, and led him down to a
door at the end of the promenade, a door
which was marked ' Private.' The curtains,

which had fallen, lifted again just as they reached it, and showed the snake-charmer standing gravely on the stage with his arms folded, accepting with inclined head the plaudits of the public.

Marlowe opened the private door, which led directly to the stage. A servant in the sumptuous livery affected by the Imperial Theatre stood on the other side. He looked at Marlowe, and immediately drew aside and let him pass through. Swift followed him on the stage.

'I am one of the directors,' Marlowe said to Swift, 'so I can come and go as I please. Ah, there is our Indian friend looking after his precious worms. Come along.'

Another turn was already on—a lady with an extravagant voice and exuberant carriage whom the house greeted rapturously as a popular serio-comic. Swift, as he hurriedly followed Marlowe's lead, noted quickly and curiously the details of the environment: the great gaunt stage, of which only a little

piece seemed necessary for the purposes of
representation ; the performers who waited
dressed and ready for their turn ; the men in
evening-dress, friends of the management or
of the stars, who talked to the performers
and each other ; the little group that clustered
at the sides to watch for the fiftieth time a
popular turn ; the bewildering lights and
shades ; the trained activity of the stage
hands ; the rapid movements of the dressing-
women ; the muffled forms of the girls who
were to go in the series of living pictures,
and who sheltered their slightly-clad bodies
from the draughts in garments that looked
like loose bathing-wrappers.

Any new sights interested Swift, but he
had not time for more than the rapidest im-
pression. Marlowe, who knew the whole
thing by heart, was already at the farthest
corner of the back of the stage, where the
Indian was superintending the removal of
his two boxes of snakes. Marlowe touched
him on the arm, and said, as he turned

round : 'Mr. Drass, here is a friend of mine who wants to congratulate you on your performance.'

Mr. Drass fixed his eyes on Swift's face, and Swift felt again the same sense of fascination that he had experienced before.

'Your friend and I are friends already,' the Indian said in his slow soft voice. 'I hope you are well, Mr. Swift.'

He made an Oriental salutation, but Swift put out his hand in the English fashion, and Mr. Drass, after what seemed to Swift like a second of hesitation, did the like, and laid his small brown hand in Swift's large hand. Swift shook it cordially, as a man should shake the hand of one to whom he owes a service. Mr. Drass accepted the pressure without returning it, and yet his touch convinced Swift that if the fingers that rested so idly in his clasp chose, they could close upon his with a grip that he might not be able to shake off.

'Well,' said Swift cordially, 'I am de-

lighted to see you again. I thought that
you had vanished for ever.'

Mr. Drass inclined his head gravely.

'You are very good,' he answered, 'to
take an interest in the stranger from across
the great water. But I knew very well
that we should meet again and again, and
my heart is not big with joy at the knowledge.'

There was certainly no sound of satisfaction in Mr. Drass's smooth monotonous voice;
there was certainly no sign of satisfaction in
Mr. Drass's shining snake-like eyes. It was
perfectly plain that he was not at all glad to
see Swift, and Swift, wondering why, acted,
as he usually acted, upon impulse, and asked
for a reason.

'How did you know that we should meet
again?' Swift said. 'And why should it
matter to you one way or another?'

They were standing alone at the moment
in that farther corner of the stage. Marlowe
had turned aside to talk to the manager,

an elderly gentleman who looked like a Cabinet Minister. There was some kind of little play being played now, and the stage behind the scene was quiet and almost deserted.

The snake-charmer slipped his hand for a moment inside his silken vest, and drew it out again closed closely over some small object. He stretched out his clenched fist towards Swift, and slowly opened it. Swift saw that a small crystal ball lay on the Indian's extended palm.

'I see you there,' Mr. Drass said, 'I see you there dimly, and I know that your presence is not propitious to me. I cannot read very clearly in the crystal since I came to this strange land and these cold skies. But I know that the way I see you is a warning, though I know not of what danger, and I am willing to be warned.'

Swift felt a disposition to smile, but the speaker's face was perfectly grave, and his manner was not the manner of the charlatan,

so Swift restrained his inclination. He said
quietly :

'I do not see why the wizard's crystal
should warn you against me. I do not see
how I can cross your path. I am not a
member of your profession. I am not a
rival snake-charmer.'

'That is quite true,' said Mr. Drass. He
spoke as calmly as if he were talking over
the most ordinary matter, instead of treating
of thoughts beyond the reaches of the soul.
'That is quite true.   There is no reason why
you should be called upon to interfere with
my '—he paused for a moment as if to find
the suitable word, and then went on—'with
my business in Europe.'

'Not the slightest,' Swift answered, smiling.
'On the contrary, I should be glad to assist
you in any way in my power, as I said before,
in return for your kindness to me.'

The Indian looked at the sphere again,
and shook his head as he slipped it back
again into his vest.

'I do not think you can help me,' he said,
'but I trust that you will not hinder me. I
cannot see clearly in the sphere; there is a
mist. Will you allow me to look at your
hand ?'

'My hand?' Swift questioned in some
surprise, and then, as the snake-charmer
nodded, he said, 'Oh, certainly,' and held
out his right hand. The Indian took it,
and looked anxiously at the lines on the
palm.

'Let me see the other hand,' he said
eagerly, and Swift gave him the left hand,
which he scanned as carefully. He had a
hand of Swift's in each of his, and his eyes
travelled backwards and forwards from one
to the other rapidly, as if he were reading in
the pages of a book.

'You are lucky,' he said, after a pause.
'You are lucky; you are very lucky.'

'It is very good of you to say so,' said
Swift, who began to find the situation a
little absurd. 'But I ought to tell you that

I do not believe in the least in this sort of thing.'

The snake-charmer let go Swift's hands, and drew himself up gravely.

'In this instance,' he said quietly, 'what you believe or do not believe is of no moment. It is what I believe that is of importance to me, and I believe that your luck is opposed to mine.'

'I'm sure I hope not,' Swift said cordially ; 'and I am sure that I should be sorry in any way to offend against your beliefs. There may be more things between heaven and earth——'

' "Than are dreamt of in your philosophy," ' Mr. Drass went on quietly, completing the quotation. Then, seeing the look of surprise on Swift's face, he added :

'Does it surprise you that the poor snake-charmer should know "Hamlet"? But I learned English at the college at Madras, and I got a prize for English literature. I owe much to the English Raj.'

'You certainly speak English very well,' Swift said. He thought that Mr. Drass was a very curious person, with his snakes and his sorceries, and his prize for English literature.

'It is good for the slave that he speak the tongue of his master,' the Indian said softly to himself. Then, in a louder tone, he added : 'It would be bad for me in my business if I did not speak English. And now, with your permission, I will wish you good-night.'

'Good-night,' said Swift. He held out his hand again, and the man took it for a moment, and quickly released it. 'You are sure that I cannot be of any service to you ?'

'Quite sure,' said Mr. Drass decisively.

He turned away and disappeared just as Marlowe, who had finished his conversation with the manager, came up and joined Swift.

'Well,' said Marlowe, 'how did you like your Indian Johnny ?'

'He is very curious,' Swift said, more to himself than to his companion.

'Yes,' said Marlowe, 'he is a queer old bird. Well, will you come back to the front again? Totty Crumpet's turn is coming on, and I don't want to miss it.'

But Swift had no desire to hear Totty Crumpet, and he said so with his habitual straightforwardness, while Marlowe eyed him with disdain. But the disdain was tempered with pity, and Marlowe conducted Swift to the stage-door as a quicker means of getting out than by returning to the front of the house. Under its flaring gas-lamp Swift thanked Marlowe for his friendly offices, and Marlowe wished him good-night and they parted, Marlowe returning to applaud Miss Crumpet and to meditate upon a new poem for his coming volume, 'Variety Verses,' and Swift speeding to Queen Square with his mind as usual occupied with Candida and his heart rejoicing at the thought of seeing her next day.

Swift found little to envy in the life of Theocritus Marlowe, but he did feel inclined

to envy him that facility in the framing of
verses which enabled him to make his
homages wear pretty shapes like well-placed
posies of flowers. He would have liked to
write rhymes to Candida, but the game was
not for him, and so he contented himself in
that spring night by repeating to himself all
the fairest lines he could remember from a
book that contains such a wonder of sweet
words, the Sonnets of Shakespeare. His talk
with Mr. Drass had brought Shakespeare
into his mind, and so had led to the Sonnets
and their application to love. There was a
line he could not remember, do what he
would ; so when he got home and lit his gas,
he looked for the little volume of the
Sonnets where it had lain unheeded on his
table for many days.

As he took it up, a bit of paper fell from
between its pages. Swift picked it up, and
saw that it was the curious fragment which
he had found in Richmond Park, and had
promised to get deciphered and had for-

gotten all about. He made a resolve to see about it on the morrow, and on that resolve he went to bed and to sleep and to dreams of Candida.

CHAPTER XIX.

LONELY.

Ask of the wind as it wails in the heather,
  Ask of the sea-bird that strains to the sea,
Ask of the roses that cluster together,
  Where my Aminta is hiding from me.
              A Pastoral in Pink.

HE awoke, as he always awoke now, with
the thought of her in his mind, and her name
was now as always on his lips as he turned
to look at her likeness. For she had given
him a photograph of herself in the early days
of their friendship, and the picture was his
idol and he its devotee; he had made a kind
of ritual for it, a ritual which he regularly
observed with a kind of pleasure and a kind
of pain at his own sentimentality. The

photograph stood in its silver frame on his
table all day, the exquisite despot of those
volumes of wisdom which now lay figuratively,
at least—for Swift's landlady was a tidy
woman, and deft with the brush—under the
dust of disdain. At night he always carried
it reverently into his bedroom, as one might
carry some sacred image, and hooked it to
a nail in the wall near his bed, so that it
might be the first thing he should see on
waking. And he was always buying flowers
to stand near it in a Chinese jar, and, in
fact, behaved about it and towards it after a
fashion that would have made Budget burst
with laughter and have brought a frown of
disapproval to the faces of the majority of
the Cordeliers.

Every day as he looked for the first time
at Candida's portrait he said to himself with
the same rapture, ' I shall see her to-day.'
And he had seen her every day through all
those divine weeks of spring, and now this
morning he repeated the dear familiar phrase,

and while he rejoiced in the immediate past, he looked forward with longing to the immediate future. They had arranged on the previous evening that he was to call for her as usual the next day. If it was fine they would wander afield. In the event, unlikely that year, of its not being fine, they would return for a time to the learned dusk of the British Museum.

Swift was in that happy madness of love when the longest hours with the beloved pass with the speed of smiling seconds, and the shortest absences seem to stretch into measureless æons. So Swift's pulses beat joyously at the thought that the new day would be blessed with the sight and the sound of Candida.

But when he went into his workroom he found some letters on his table, and one of them, as he saw at once, to his great surprise, was from Candida. He knew her handwriting, though she had never written to him before, and the letter was sealed with a seal that he had given to her—a Greek gem that represented a head of Pallas. He opened it with an apprehension that its contents justified.

'My dear Friend,' Candida wrote,

'I shall not be able to see you for a little while. It will, I hope and believe, only be a short while, and, indeed, it grieves me much that there should be even this break in our comradeship. You will hear from me again as soon as it is possible for us to meet. I shall be as glad of the meeting as you, for I hold our friendship dear, and shall miss your companionship. But you will remember that you consented to take me on my own imperious terms, and you must accept my disappearance as unquestioningly as you accepted the other conditions which made our alliance so delightful. I will not ask you not to miss me, for I am vain enough to think that you will miss me, but at least you will not have to miss me for long.

Believe in me and trust me as I believe in you and trust you.' Then, with no further formalities, came her bold signature,

'CANDIDA.'

Swift put the letter down with a groan. In a moment all the merry world was withered with sadness, the sunny day seemed as gray as winter. He had never suffered himself to think during all those enchanted weeks what life would be like without Candida, and now the question was cruelly forced upon him, and he was compelled to learn the answer. What did it all mean? Why was she going away? Where was she going to? Why had she told him so suddenly—taking him at all adventure? Perhaps he might never see her again; she might pass out of his life as strangely as she had passed into it, leaving nothing behind but an exquisite memory and an abiding heartache. It was true that her letter spoke only of a brief absence, but did she really

mean that—could he count upon that?
How little, after all, he knew of her! That
thought assailed him insistently. He knew
as little of where she came from as he now
knew of where she had gone to. He had met
her by chance, and now chance seemed to
carry her away, and all that he knew was
the name of a girl who lived by herself and
liked to read books and to walk walks, and
who was very beautiful and whom he loved.
But what she had been in the days before
he met her, how she had lived her life,
whom she had known, liked, disliked, perhaps loved—all this was as much of a
mystery to him as her sudden and fantastic
disappearance.

Swift sat for awhile silently, stupidly,
like a man nearly stunned. The intensity of
his devotion to the beautiful girl was made
plainer to him than ever by the pain he now
felt. He sat there in an agony of heart-
sickness, only able to realize how horribly
lonely, how horribly lost, he felt. She had

given a meaning to his life, and now all meaning seemed to be taken out of it. It was in vain that he tried to console himself by dwelling on her promise that the parting should not be for long. He felt too wretched to hope, too wretched to think, too wretched to be conscious of anything except a sense of despair. The passion which he had been compelled to keep to himself, to bind with silence, as the body of the Trusty John in the tale was bound with iron, had forced his fancy to a kind of exaltation in which it was defenceless against fact. He stared with weary eyes at her portrait, and murmured her name again and again. Candida, Candida, Candida! The beautiful face seemed to smile back at him with the girl's enchanting smile, but the sight only made his misery more flagrant, more helpless. To think that he might never see her again, and that he had never told her that he loved her! Why had he not told her, he asked himself angrily, and then his conscience answered the question, reminding him of his promise, and appealing to his honour. He took up her letter again and read the words in which she assured him that she believed in him and trusted him. He made a gallant effort to regain his self-possession.

There were two other letters on his table, and he opened them mechanically and read them without interest. The first was from the secretary of the Cordeliers' Club, calling his attention to the fact that he had not attended a single meeting of the committee for some time past, and pointing out that this was an infringement of one of the principal rules of the association. It added that another meeting was to be held on the following day, at which his presence was requested to consider a matter of much importance. The second was a hurried scrawl in Budget's large, loose hand, saying that he wanted to see Swift as soon as possible on urgent business, but not saying what the urgent business was. Swift pushed

both the letters from him with a sigh, and
stared at the picture of Candida.

'Well,' he said to himself with a dreary
effort to be courageous, 'the world goes on,
whatever happens, and if love flies out of the
window business walks in at the door. If
you go away, my dear'—he was addressing
himself to the picture—' you have, no doubt,
the wisest of reasons for what you do, and I
must try and make the best of it, and act as
you would have me act, and not go on as if
the world had come to an end because I shall
not see you for a few days. Courage, man,
courage! Don't play the fool! Pull yourself together, and remember that work is the
purpose of a man's life.'

Somewhat cheered by these edifying reflections, although he felt that they sounded
a little hollow and unreal, Swift set himself
steadily to make the best of the loneliness
that had been forced upon him. He turned
to some of his long-abandoned volumes, and
struggled heroically with the mutilators of

Homer. He worked away doggedly for some time, trying hard to forget the name that was sighing in his ears, trying hard to ignore the ache at his heart. But at last he gave it up as a bad job. What he read wearied him. What he wrote sickened him. He closed his books and put them by. He took up the few pages on which he had tried to write coherent sentences, and slowly and deliberately tore them into little strips and dropped them into the waste-paper basket. Then he flung on his hat and went out into the open air, with the volume of Shakespeare's Sonnets in his pocket, and the mysterious paper inside the volume. Here was a momentary way of killing time which might possibly have some gleam of interest in it. The new Homeric commentators had none. Not, at least, that morning.

CHAPTER XX.

MR. HEMPLETT.

> Here is one
> That can decipher any kind of speech—
> Runes, hieroglyphics, Oghams, cuneiforms,
> The symbols of the Aztecs, what you will;
> One that can talk a hundred different tongues,
> And read in every language in the world
> Not worth the reading. Oh, a marvellous man,
> A proper pedant!
>
> *The Wish of the World.*

THE British Museum attracts scholarship to its vicinity as Rhodian oil attracts rats. Swift had lived so long under its shadow that he knew a good deal about the wise men who came from all parts of the world to live also under its shadow, and to suck more learning from its fountains. One such wise man he had now in his mind, and he steered for that wise man's dwelling.

On the side of an open doorway in Great Russell Street were several small bell-handles, and by the side of each bell-handle was a strip of brass presenting the name of the person to whom the bell belonged. The door always stood open in the day-time, because its hall conducted directly to the door of the book-shop that occupied the ground-floor of the premises. It was a very learned book-shop — a book-shop that Swift knew well, for it was here that all the most erudite works of German critics were to be found, here that the results of foreign scholarship in all parts of the world were most surely and most easily to be ascertained. The bookseller himself, an ingenious German, lived on the floor over the shop. The second-floor was occupied by a British Museum official. The strip of brass that accompanied the third bell bore the inscription

'S. Hemplett.' It was S. Hemplett that Swift had come to see.

Mr. Septidecimus Hemplett was one of the most learned of living linguists. He came of a learned stock, to whose learning he owed the eccentricity of his name. For it had pleased a Hemplett in the latter years of the last century — the very Hemplett whose Latin Grammar enjoyed considerable favour in scholastic circles well on into the present century—to christen his children, of whom he had three, by the Roman numerals. His first boy was Primus Hemplett, his first girl was Prima Hemplett. The excellent grammarian had thought at first of calling her Secunda, but he decided, upon mature reflection, that it would be better to allow the sexes to have independent lines. His third child, a boy, became, duly, Secundus Hemplett. The pedagogic humour established a hereditary custom in the Hemplett family. Those of the Hempletts who married and had issue observed the system

of nomenclature as a tradition, and thus it
came to pass that in the last decade of
the nineteenth century Mr. Hemplett, the
learned linguist, found himself favoured witn
the sonorous name of Septidecimus. He was
the seventeenth male Hemplett since the
illustrious author of the Latin Grammar set
the joke going, and he was decidedly proud
of the fact. Also he was the last of his line,
and as he was unmarried, and did not seem
to be at all a marrying man, there was every
likelihood that the arithmetical jest would
come to an end with him.

Mr. Septidecimus Hemplett enjoyed the
reputation, in a limited circle of scholars, of
being the greatest linguist in the world. He
was believed to know all the languages that
there were to know, and not merely all the
languages, but all the various dialects of
each of those languages. His erudition was
immense, but then, as he always used to
say modestly of himself, since he had done
nothing all his life but learn languages, it

would be a strange thing indeed if he had not managed to pick up a word or two while he was about it. It was in the reading of languages that he excelled. He could write them, or most of them, too; but the speaking of languages was not in his way at all, for he seldom or never travelled, and, as he readily admitted, he did not possess at all the courier's gift of speaking glibly a foreign tongue. But for reading them he was unrivalled.

Swift went slowly up the three flights of stairs, and knocked at the door on the third landing. As he did so he thought with a sigh of the stairs he had hoped to climb that day, the stairs that led to Candida.

After a moment he heard the sound of shuffling feet; then the drawing of a latch. The door opened, and Mr. Septidecimus Hemplett stood in the doorway peering at his visitor.

Mr. Septidecimus Hemplett was a tall, thin man, of a somewhat stork-like build,

and with a long, beak-shaped nose that
heightened his resemblance to the bird of
the North. His dome-like head was largely
bald, and long wisps of a dust-coloured hair
were brushed up around it to form a thin
veil for its bareness. His skin was dry and
parchment-coloured; his chin was as peaked
as his nose; he was smooth-shaven, and he
wore spectacles over his pale blue eyes. His
lean, angular body was clothed in a suit of
a pale-gray stuff, which looked dusty as he
looked dusty. Books were bulging out of
the pockets of his coat; he had a book under
his arm, and another in his hand. At first
he did not seem to recognise Swift.

'How are you?' said Swift gloomily, and
extended his hand in greeting.

The sound of his voice seemed to quicken
the scholar's consciousness. His lank face
animated into a smile; his pale eyes gleamed
with recognition.

'My dear Mr. Swift,' he said, 'is it you?
I am delighted to see you. Pray walk in.'

And, retiring from the doorway, he ushered Swift into his apartment with an awkward but affable wave of his bony hand. Swift accepted the invitation, and preceded the scholar into his familiar study.

There never was such a room for books. The place overflowed with them. The whole of the walls from floor to ceiling were covered with bookshelves. Even the space between and around the two windows that looked out into Great Russell Street, even the space above and around the fireplace, were all shelved off; and every shelf in the place was not merely filled, but loaded with books. On the heads of the decorous ranks of books that had taken up their natural position on the shelves their owner had piled other books, filling up in this way the space left between their tops and the bottom of the shelf immediately above them. Books bulged from the choking shelves, books lay in little mountains upon the floor, books were stacked in heaps in all the corners,

books littered every available chair. The
place was a kind of delirious dream of books.
Swift, who knew the room well, was familiar
with greater places that held vaster quantities of books, but he knew of no other
small room, no other one man's den, which
was so gorged and glutted with volumes.

And all these books were books upon
languages. There were grammars, dictionaries, vocabularies, studies, histories of every
language spoken by man upon the face of
the earth, of every language that has ever
been spoken by man since he first framed his
crude ideas in almost formless sound. Here
were treatises on Egyptian hieroglyphics
cheek by jowl with pamphlets upon the
Chinook jargon; speculations upon early
Etruscan lay side by side with volumes on
Pigeon English and the tongue of the
gipsies. A volume on French theatrical
slang rested in whimsical companionship
with a dictionary of the speech of the Sioux
Red Indians.

'Pray be seated,' said Mr. Hemplett
affably, with a wave of his long hand.

Swift could not help smiling, for all his
gloom, as he looked around him, knowing as
he did, from former experiences of that cave
of wisdom, that every chair would be converted into a camel carrying his own pack
across the desert of difficult languages. It
was as he expected. Selecting the chair
that appeared to bear the lightest load, he
lifted from it some pamphlets on cuneiform
inscriptions, a Basque dictionary, and a
grammar of the Mandarin dialect of Chinese,
which he added with careful balancement to
the pile that already seemed to totter on
another chair. Then he sat down and smiled
cheerfully at his host.

'Will you excuse me for one moment?'
Mr. Hemplett said apologetically. 'I just
want to finish this page of notes on some
resemblances that I am tracing between the
Icelandic of the days of Erik the Red and
the remains of the aboriginal languages of

the New England tribes. I have a line of argument to conclude, and it is of great importance.'

Swift nodded assent, and Mr. Hemplett plunged his adust face into the books and papers on his table, while Swift allowed his gaze to wander from the books on the chairs and the books on the ground to the books on the groaning shelves all around him.

'Was there ever such a library before since the world began ?' he asked himself as he surveyed the hundreds, the thousands of books that were massed together, and that all bore only on the one topic of the tongues that men speak, or the tongues that men have spoken, or the tongues that man yet shall speak. For there were not a few volumes in Mr. Hemplett's library which dealt with ideal languages, with Volapuk and the made-up languages that rivalled Volapuk, not a few volumes devoted to speculations on the evolution of the speech of humanity. Indeed, it was reported amongst the learned in such lore, that Mr. Hemplett occupied his moments of leisure in putting together the materials for a great work upon the language of the future, a subject for which his extraordinary knowledge would seem, indeed, to equip him with authority.

It seemed to the poet in Swift to be a somewhat arid library, and a somewhat arid life that it overshadowed. Among all those masses of volumes, if his glance occasionally discovered the book of some poet, the book of some writer of living prose, he knew very well that it was not there for its own sake, but solely because of the assistance it might render to the settlement of some linguistic problem. Homer only interested Mr. Hemplett because he was written in Ionic Greek, and he only read the Pentamerone because it was composed in Neapolitan.

Presently Mr. Hemplett raised his head, pushed his papers from him, closed a big book with a sigh of satisfaction, and turned his spectacles upon Swift.

'Well,' he said, 'what can I do for you, my young friend?'

Swift took the paper out of his pocket. 'I wanted to ask you,' he said, 'if you would be kind enough to tell me what is written on this paper. It came by chance into my possession, and I must confess to being curious to know its meaning. It seems to me to be Oriental, and I know nothing of Eastern languages. But I felt sure that you would be able to pluck out the heart of its mystery for me. Do you not know all languages?'

Mr. Hemplett shook his head. 'I wish I did,' he said, 'I wish I did. But let me see your paper. Perhaps I may be able to read it.'

Swift got up and handed the paper to him.

Mr. Hemplett took the paper, unfolded it, and glanced at it through his carefully adjusted spectacles.

'There is certainly no great difficulty about this,' he said. 'It is printed in Hindostani, and though the type is cramped and bad, there need be no delay in deciphering it.'

'That's all right,' said Swift, trying to assume an interest he did not feel. 'Well, what is it all about?'

Mr. Hemplett, who had lifted his eyes from the paper as soon as he had ascertained the language it was couched in, smiled at Swift's impatience amiably, and returned to his study of the document. In a second or two Swift saw him give a little start of surprise.

'Ah!' said Mr. Hemplett, 'this is curious, this is interesting—very curious and interesting indeed.'

'What is it?' said Swift languidly; but for another few seconds Mr. Hemplett read on without answering him. Then the linguist again lifted his spectacled face and looked at Swift.

'This paper,' he said, 'is, or purports to be, a copy of a very extraordinary appeal made by an Indian soldier who was executed for murder during the Mutiny.'

'An appeal?' said Swift. 'What sort of appeal—an appeal for mercy?'

Mr. Hemplett shook his head.

'An appeal for vengeance,' he said gravely.

'An appeal for vengeance!' Swift echoed in surprise.

'Yes,' said Mr. Hemplett; 'it is, as it were, a kind of voice from the grave calling for vengeance. This is what it says.'

And Hemplett began to read in his slow, monotonous voice the words of the paper, words that appeared all the grimmer from the quiet, colourless way in which the reader read them.

'This is the imprecation cried out to Heaven by Ram Hassan Ali, Duffadar of the Second Regiment of Light Cavalry, who was executed at the slaughter-house in Cawnpore

on July 24, 1857, for the killing of infidel
women and children.

'O Mahommed, only Prophet of the only
God, the merciful, the compassionate, vouch-
safe in thy clemency and thy pity to receive
into Paradise the soul of thy slave whose
tongue has been defiled by licking of infidel
blood from the floor of the slaughter-house,
whose body, defiled by the blows of the
infidel, is shortly to be blown from a gun.
O Mahommed, only Prophet of the only
God, in the days yet to be, inspire my son,
Rassan Ali, who is now an infant at Meerut,
with the spirit of vengeance that he may
revenge his father's death upon his murderer,
and the children of his murderer, until blood
has atoned for blood. And I, now at the
door of death, bequeath my blessing to my
son if he obey my prayer, and my curse here
and hereafter if he disobey me. And the
name of my murderer is the commander of
my regiment.'

Mr. Hemplett came to a stop, and looked

meditatively at Swift, who had listened to the reading with much wonder.

'Is that all?' Swift asked.

Mr. Hemplett nodded his head.

'That is all,' he answered. 'What more do you want?'

'I certainly don't understand it,' said Swift. 'It seems to me a very incoherent document.'

'No,' said Mr. Hemplett; 'I don't think it is that. I understand it very well, but then'—he added this apologetically, as if to avoid hurting Swift's feelings—'you see, I am familiar with Eastern documents. I see the whole thing plainly enough. This man, who was about to be executed, no doubt called out this message to the crowd. It was, no doubt, written down by some pious fakir who would conceive it to be his duty to carry it to the son. It was probably printed and distributed through all the bazaars. It may have reached the son, or it may not.'

'I wonder,' said Swift, 'how one could

find out what was the name of the officer in command at the time, to whom the denunciation refers.'

'That ought not to be difficult,' said Mr. Hemplett. 'You would find the name, no doubt, in any history of the Mutiny, if the man happened to be prominent, or, in any case, you could find it out in the volume of the Army List for that year.'

'I suppose,' said Swift dubiously, as he looked around him at the loaded shelves, 'you don't happen to possess the Army List for that particular year.'

Mr. Hemplett shook his head and smiled.

'No,' he answered; 'that would not be much in my line. But you will find a set, of course, in the British Museum.'

'Of course I shall,' said Swift. 'Thank you very much for your kindness. I will go over to the Reading-room at once.'

'There is very little to thank me for,' said Mr. Hemplett. 'Hindostani is a very easy tongue. It is I who have to thank you for a pleasant interlude in my work. You have not been to see me for a long time. I was beginning to wonder what had become of you.'

Swift felt that he was blushing under the kindly gaze of Mr. Hemplett's spectacles. It was quite true that he had not been near the old scholar, that he had not been near any of his old friends, for quite a long time. The companionship of Candida had made him indifferent to and forgetful of all other companionship. Now he felt that the blush on his cheeks deepened while he stammered out something about having been exceedingly busy, while all the while his guilty conscience reminded him of the shut books, the dusty papers, the neglected task on his table at home.

Perhaps Mr. Hemplett's studies had not altogether dried the sap of humanity in his withered body. Perhaps he noted the flush on Swift's face, and perhaps he understood it aright. For he smiled a little as he said :

'Well, well! young men must be busy as well as old ones.' Then he added somewhat irrelevantly : ' I was young myself once.'

And as he spoke he looked away from Swift, and around him on the crowded shelves, and heaved a little sigh that was only slightly melancholy, and that was not at all bitter. If Mr. Hemplett wished for a moment to be young again, he did not at all regret the course that his life had taken, and the glance that beamed upon the books through his big spectacles was a glance of affection.

Swift noted the glance and understood it, and it set him thinking, wondering if in later days he should find as much content in the companionship of books as Mr. Hemplett seemed to find. Only a few short weeks ago he should have answered ' Yes ' without the slightest hesitation. As far as he had permitted himself to plan out a future, he had always pictured himself as working at his favourite work, acquiring a little more know-

ledge, a little more credit for his knowledge,
a little more reward for his knowledge, and
growing wiser in growing older, content with
his lot. But now a woman's face had shone
upon his life, and by that light he seemed
to read its meaning quite differently, and to
be stirred by all manner of hopes and fears,
agitations and desires, which had left him
unvexed before. He had thought that it
was the best thing in the world to be a
scholar ; now he was learning that it was the
best thing in the world to be a lover, and
the worst thing in the world to be away from
the beloved.

He had always liked Mr. Hemplett, but
he now felt a sudden sense of affection for
the old scholar, an affection inspired partly
and principally by the contrast between the
romantic colours in which his own life was
now painted and the neutral gray of Mr.
Hemplett's bookish existence. So it was
with a kind of tenderness that he took the
linguist's hand, and it seemed to him that it

was with a kind of tenderness that Mr. Hemplett returned the grasp. The scholar and the student, the master and the pupil, ceased for a moment to be scholars, and were content to be men. The one rich with a passionate present, the other rich, perhaps, with some golden memory that glowed, pure ore, out of the shadows of the past, stood for a moment with clasped hands linked by a subtle sympathy. In another moment the link was broken, the hands unclasped; Mr. Hemplett dropped back into his books again, and Swift went slowly down the stairs, trying to keep his mind interested in the contents of the piece of paper.

He resolved at once to visit the British Museum. He hurried across the street and across the great courtyard. He had not been to the Reading-room for many a day, for, even before he met Candida, he much preferred, whenever he could, to work at home in his own quiet room instead of adding another unit to the toilers in that human

hive. Luckily for him, his work was chiefly
of a kind that could be as well despatched
in his own study as elsewhere, and so his
visits to the great storehouse of books were
comparatively few, and were almost in-
variably brief, rapid visits for the consultation of some rare Greek book or some
colossal treatise upon ancient art or
archæology.

CHAPTER XXI.

THE COMING MAN.

It is a great art to make the mind up wisely and well. It is even something, at a pinch, to make it up unwisely and ill. At least the mind is made up. Some people never make up their minds at all, all through life, but seem to pause, perpetually irresolute, on the brink of possibility.

The Letters of Pertinax.

SWIFT's sense of loneliness deepened as he crossed the courtyard of the Museum and noted the flying pigeons. For the place and time recalled irresistibly the dear companionship that he missed, and the day when that companionship first began. The British Museum, which had for so long seemed the shrine of romance, now loomed upon his fancy as a temple dedicated to melancholy. Swift

· was furious with himself for feeling his loneliness so much, for making so poor a fight against the strokes of disappointment. He felt that his weakness was unworthy of a Cordelier, unworthy of the author of the ' Cry for Liberty,' but he yielded to the weakness none the less, and his spirit sighed for Candida. Where was she now? he wondered, and immediately after he chid himself for vain speculatious, and reminded himself with some acerbity that his immediate business was to consult an old volume of the Army List, and that the sooner he despatched that business the better.

But it was fated that he was not to consult the Army List that day. For at the top of the steps, just as he was going in, he ran against Windover, who was just coming out. Windover greeted him with an enthusiasm which Swift perceived to have a quality of subdued excitement in it unusual to Windover—an enthusiasm which made him feel slightly ashamed as he reflected upon his neglect, both physical and mental, of his dear friends through all those late enchanted weeks.

Windover caught Swift eagerly by the arm.

' I am so glad to have met you. I thought there might be a chance of finding you in the Museum, where I had to go to look up some facts for a paper that I wanted to finish before—— Well, I will tell you before what if you can spare the time to walk part of the way with me.'

Swift was really glad to see Windover, and the Army List could keep. He saw by his friend's manner that there was something which he wished to talk about, and even if Swift's errand to the Museum had been more important than it was, he would have given it the go-by to make amends, to salve in some degree his own conscience, sore at his neglect of the Windovers. So he assured his friend that his business in the Museum was not in the least ressing, and, turning round, he walked by Windover's side down the steps and across the courtyard back into Great Russell Street.

The first few seconds of their conversation Windover devoted to playfully upbraiding Swift for having left him and Lucilla in the cold for so long.

'What has become of you? Where have you been?' he asked. 'I began to fear that you had emigrated or married, or perhaps both. Now I perceive that you have not emigrated. Is it by chance the other trifle, actually or potentially?'

Swift felt his cheeks grow hotter, but he laughed an assertive denial.

'No, no, nothing of the kind! I have no wish to bid my native land good-night— at least, for the present; and as for the other, why, my life so far resembles heaven that there is no marrying or giving in marriage in it.'

'Then, what have you been doing to treat us so shamefully?' Windover persevered.

Swift murmured a stumbling explanation about being very busy, translating an especially important and unusually difficult book that took up all his time and absorbed all his attention. The sense that he was not speaking truth stung him sharply till he reflected that, after all, a human life was by a figure of speech a book, and that he had been occupied entirely with a human life of late, and had been overpoweringly interested in the attempt to translate it. Thus he solaced himself internally. Externally he reminded Windover, by way of turning the conversation, that there was something he promised to tell him.

Windover seemed pleased that Swift had by his reminder allowed him to turn to that topic without appearing unduly eager to push his own affairs.

'It's rather curious,' he said, 'and I know you will be surprised ; but the fact is that I have definitely decided to go into Parliament—at least, I am going to try,' he added,

as a deferential protest to the Fates against
Rockielaw's certainty.

Swift stared at him in considerable surprise. He had forgotten all about the offer
that had been made to Windover. It was
curious to think of him as coming forward,
with his cool air of agreeable scholarship,
into the heat and the dust of political life.
That Windover should direct the course of
Ministers in a column of prose as elegant as
Bolingbroke's, that he should reprimand
revolution with austere grace in learned
periodicals, was fitting, was natural, was
even inevitable. But that he should leave
his desk and his books and his green garden
and his pretty wife, to fling himself into the
scrimmage, seemed to Swift scarcely less
astounding than it would be to see him
suddenly pluck off his high hat and his
neatly-built frock-coat and jerk himself
joyously into a row at a street corner. He
looked carefully at his companion's face to
see if he could read there any lurking

humour, any half-hidden hint that Windover
was pleased to be merry.   But he saw no
such signs there, and Windover, who seemed
to guess what he was looking for, burst out
laughing.

'You are surprised,' he said—'very much
surprised.   Confess it.   I knew you would
be ; so did Lucilla.'

'Well,' said Swift slowly, 'I certainly
am surprised.   It seems a little sudden,
coming on one in this unexpected way.'

'It would not have come upon you in this
unexpected way,' Windover retorted, 'if
your friends had been fortunate enough to
see anything of you for the last six weeks.
At least, I could have told you that I was
gradually making up my mind to accept, if
the business ever took a definite shape.
The business has now taken a definite shape.
The other fellow has formally applied for the
Chiltern Hundreds.'

'Well,' said Swift, 'I am sure I hope you
will like it !'   He meant his tone to be

hearty, but it only succeeded in being half-hearted.

Windover's quick ear caught the dubiousness in the wish.

' Oh, of course it's a toss-up !' he admitted. ' I don't wish to pose as the Noble Roman, and that sort of thing ; but, to be honest with you, I should not dream of coming forward if it had not been made very plain to me that it was in a great degree my duty to do so.'

' I am sure of that !' Swift assented. And he was quite sure, for he knew Windover well enough to know that his honesty had no flaw in it.

' Of course, I know very well,' Windover went on, ' that my view of things is not your view of things. You are a Rad, and a Red, and all the rest of it, and you call me a re-actionary, and I am quite content to accept the title. But if I do get into that blessed place '—he gave a jerk of his head to suggest the direction of Westminster—' and as far as one can see it seems pretty certain that I shall get in, you may be sure that I shall try and do my best for the country, and not merely what is best for my party.'

'You are quite right; I wonder if you will be able to!' Swift said. He had a vague appreciation of the influence of party, and so had Windover, only more definitely, for he added :

'Well, I shall do my best, and I won't make any rash promises.'

There was a moment's silence between the two men, as they walked slowly along Gower Street. For a moment it came into Windover's mind to tell Swift of Budget's extraordinary overture to Rockielaw. But he immediately put the idea aside. Budget was a friend of Swift's as well as of himself, and, after all, it was no part of one friend's duty to speak of another friend's disloyalty to a third. It would be ungenerous to tell tales, Windover reflected. After all, Budget may not have appreciated the indecency of his action, and even if he did, nothing would be gained by betraying his conduct to Swift. So Windover held his peace on the subject; it did not occur to him as possible that anything in Swift's life could depend at all upon whether he spoke out or kept silence about Budget that afternoon.

Swift broke the brief silence with a question.

'Where are you going to stand for?' he asked. 'Tell us how, and all about it.'

Windover proceeded to satisfy Swift's curiosity by a rapid account of his and Lucilla's weighty deliberations ; of their final decision to accept a proposal which had come in the first place from Miss Dorothy Carteret.

'Miss Dorothy Carteret?' Swift queried. The name vaguely suggested some associations to him. He dimly recollected some remarks of Budget's at Windover's table.

Windover explained again, amiably and exhaustively. He told Swift of the Sylphs, that curious evanescent, incoherent, im-

palpable body, with its strange schemes, and
of the High-Priestess of the Sylphs, the
young lady who seemed to have taken it
into her pretty head that she was to re-
generate England—Miss Dorothy Carteret,
Lord Godolphin's eccentric daughter.

'I have not seen Miss Carteret yet,'
Windover said. 'She has been out of town,
but she is coming back for the election, and
Rockielaw thinks that her presence at Pine
Hill is enough to settle the matter. But I
don't expect that there will be any contest.
The place has been consistently one colour
for generations.'

'And that colour is Heaven's own blessed
blue,' said Swift with a smile, and Windover
answered him, smiling :

'Yes, indeed ; and blue is a brave colour,
my dear fellow, and pleases my fancy
better than scarlet. I am afraid your
friends wouldn't find much sympathy at
Bullford !'

'When do you begin ?' Swift asked. He

was so much interested at the idea of Windover's election that he almost forgot for the
moment how miserable he was.

'I am going down almost immediately,'
Windover answered; 'I and Lucilla—Lucilla
goes, of course. Rockielaw says that Lucilla
would make a splendid canvasser. We are
are all going to stop with Sir Charles Amber
at The Towers. The Ambers have been
Miss Carteret's closest friends since her
mother died. They are, I believe, delightful
people.'

'Do you know,' said Swift, 'I have it in
my heart to wish that I could turn Con-
servative for a fortnight, that I might go
down to Bullford with you, and help you to
carry Pine Hill. I should love to see Lucilla
canvassing, and to hear you thunder from
political platforms.'

'I wish you could, with all my heart,'
Windover said; 'but I am afraid you are
incorrigible. Still, there is one thing you
can do for me.'

'What is that?' asked Swift.

'You can come on to luncheon with me now. I will not ask you to drink success to my adventure, but we can at least pledge a persistent friendship. Besides, you owe Lucilla an apology for having neglected her all this great while. So! Will you come?'

'With all my heart,' Swift answered. He felt that it would be better for him than moping alone and moodily longing for the lost Candida. So the two friends walked across the Park, and discussed the political life in the abstract, away from party questions, and Swift agreed with Windover that it was a man's life, after all. His interest in the subject, and in any subject, was listless just then. He was in that dejected phase of the sentimental life when to love seems the only business, and the beloved the only woman, and when love's aches seem mortal and love's anxieties endless.

'Yes,' Windover said, unaware of his com-

panion's indifference, 'it is a man's life, of a
sort.   A real man ought to be a soldier or a
sailor, or an explorer or a gipsy, to be an
active, mobile, adventurous creature, not a
sluggard who stoops over a desk or squats
behind a counter.   But if a poor devil of a
man of letters can be none of these things,
he may find a kind of substitute in the
political hurly - burly, and give and take
some lusty strokes, and learn the joy of
eventful living, and, who knows? prove in
the end not wholly unserviceable to his
mother, the country.   Yes, yes, let us
assure ourselves that it is a man's life,
after all.'

They were skirting Primrose Hill as Windover was uttering these profound reflections,
and while Swift smiled a wistful agreement,
his glance travelled along the green shoulder
that sloped to the summer sky, and his mind
renewed his adventure.   Would he ever, he
wondered, learn the name of his rubicund
assailant, or the cause of the assault?   Was

it possible that the man was some friend of
Candida's, who had recognised the token ?
He wished that he had been able to ask
Candida that, to ask Candida other questions.
Now he might never see Candida again to
ask her any questions, to ask her the question.
He sighed wearily, and Windover, noting the
sigh, mistook it.

'Come,' he said, 'you live a man's life in
your way, with your " Cry for Liberty," and
your Cordeliers, and all the rest of it.'

To which Swift, disagreeing, agreed.

When they got to the house, Lucilla
welcomed Swift warmly, and upbraided him
with gracious severity for having dared to
neglect them for such a waste of weeks, and
made all sorts of sharp thrusts at the cause,
which Swift parried as well as he could.
The daintiness of Lucilla was a delight to
Swift in his vexed, lonely temper, and he
could have found it in his heart to tell her
all about his trouble, and perhaps he might
if he had been alone with her. But Anthony

was there, and Anthony's mind not un-
naturally ran on the election, and Lucilla's
mind kept him company, and so Swift held
his tongue as to his secret.

CHAPTER XXII.

VOX POPULI.

When the bonds of the earth are broken,
  When the fools of the time are free,
When the last of the lies is spoken,
The first of the truths awoken,
  When life shall begin to be ;
Then sorrow and sin and sadness
Shall turn to delight and gladness,
And life be no longer madness,
   But love of the trinity,
   Liberty,
   Equality,
   Fraternity.

Idylls of Insurrection.

THE Cordeliers' Club exerted some influence, and believed that it exerted an enormous influence, upon the political thought and the political action of its time. The extremely

advanced nature of its opinions won for it
the adhesion of all manner of wild, generous
and impetuous spirits, and when spirits are
wild, generous and impetuous, they must and
will count as erratic factors in the great
game of how things are not to be done. But
it did not depend for its existence merely
upon the irresponsible or the irreconcilable ;
it commanded solid men, earnest men, active
men. And Budget, who was adored by the
irresponsible for his glittering phrases and
his resonant republicanism, had managed
also to captivate the minds of the graver
spirits, and to convince them of two things.
The first thing was, that it was high time
that the Cordeliers' Club, which was beginning to establish affiliated bodies in all the
great provincial towns, and even in many of
the small ones, should have its own representative in Parliament. The second thing
was that the best possible man to be chosen
as the mouthpiece of the Cordeliers was
Stephen Budget himself. So when Swift

entered the committee-room of the Cordeliers that night, some surprises awaited him.

He had called for Budget in the afternoon, and had failed to find him at home. He had dined dismally enough at a place he used to haunt in the days before he knew Candida, and when his melancholy meal had ended, he had made his way due east to St. Ethelfreda's Without. The moment he entered the committee-room of the club, he was convinced that matter of importance was toward. He was a little late, only a few minutes, but the Cordeliers, most of whom lived in the neighbourhood, were habitually punctual, and the room was full when Swift made his appearance. He was greeted with a round of slightly ironical applause as he made his way to a vacant seat at the end of the long table directly facing a bust of Robespierre, which seemed to smile a thin-lipped smile of derisive welcome at him. Budget was sitting next to the chairman, with an air of satisfaction

and importance upon his face, and the
secretary of the club had just finished reading something aloud at the moment when
Swift came into the room.

As soon as he had finished, the chairman
addressed Swift, and put him in possession of
the business they were discussing. In half
a dozen clear, straightforward sentences he
managed to surprise Swift as much as Swift
had ever been surprised in his life. The
committee of the Cordeliers had decided that
it was for the interest of the cause and of
the club that they should seek to make their
influence felt at every election. There was
an election just about to take place, the
election for the Pine Hill Division of Surrey,
left vacant by the sitting member's application for the Chiltern Hundreds. The
Cordeliers had resolved to contest the seat,
not so much with any great confidence of
winning it, though they were by no means
without hope, as at once to assert themselves
as a serious factor in active political life.

The man whom they had unanimously resolved to select as their representative was Stephen Budget.

Here Stephen Budget drummed upon the table with his big fingers, and affected an air of statesmanlike modesty. Swift stared at the chairman in amazement, but he was destined to be yet more amazed. For the chairman went on to say that after due deliberation the committee had resolved to send with Budget, as his lieutenant in what must prove a memorable campaign, one of the ablest, the most illustrious, of their members, one who had endeared himself to advanced thought all over the country, one whose name was dear to every Cordelier in the kingdom, the eminent author of the ' Cry for Liberty,' Brander Swift.

A storm of applause greeted the conclusion of the chairman's words. As he sat down Swift leaped to his feet amidst renewed and more vehement cheering. It was evident that Swift's long absence from their deliberations had not diminished his popularity with the leading spirits of the Cordeliers, and it was with something as nearly approaching to a thrill of pleasure as he had experienced that day that Swift listened to the applause, and waited until it had died away into silence. But what he had to say was not of a nature to rekindle applause in the committee-room of the Cordeliers' Club. Swift was generally a ready and an easy speaker ; he was always classed among the orators of whom the Cordeliers were most proud, and he was always listened to with enthusiasm, and interrupted by approval. But now he was unready, embarrassed, apologetic, full of protestations, and his apologies and his protestations were made to listeners who grew more and more unfavourable as Swift went on.

Swift's purpose was to decline the mission that had been so unexpectedly put upon him, and as the Cordeliers regarded the offer as an honour and as a signal proof of their

forgiveness of Swift's late indifference to his
political duties, they were moved to an early
resentment of his attitude. But their resentment increased when Swift went on to
explain the reason for his unwillingness to
accept the unexpected honour. This was,
forsooth, that the candidate whom the
Cordeliers were about to oppose, the re-
actionary, the champion of aristocracy, was a
personal friend of Swift's against whom Swift
would find it painful, if not impossible, to
work. For the first time in the history of
the club words spoken by the author of ' A
Cry for Liberty' were received with sounds
of angry disapproval. Swift sat down, pale
and excited, with very distasteful cries
ringing in his ears. The smile on the bust
of Robespierre seemed, as he glanced up at
it, to be more derisive than ever.

Several members of the committee rose to
their feet in angry reprobation of what they
regarded as Swift's treason to the principles
of the organization. But while each of

Swift's accusers was appealing vociferously to the chairman for audience, Budget upreared his massive form from the table, and made it plain that he proposed to speak. The sight of his uplifted bulk, the sound of his tremendous voice, as it bellowed through the room a demand which was rather a command for silence, converted the sudden disorder into a no less sudden tranquillity. Everyone present felt that Budget, as the hero of the coming contest, was the man with the most right to speak of any man in the room ; everyone felt that no one was better qualified to give Swift his deserts for his perfidy.

Budget began by glancing in dignified silence at the busts of the revolutionary heroes which adorned the walls, as if he offered to each of their memories in turn a mute apology for the backsliding of one who had professed, and professed so ardently, their opinions. Then, turning his gaze full upon Swift, he began by expressing his regret and his surprise at the words which had just fallen from his friend, and as he spoke the committee supported him with a sullen undertone of applause.   But the speaker immediately went on to say that he could not help feeling much sympathy for Swift in the peculiar position in which Swift was placed, a position of whose extreme difficulty he himself was better qualified to judge than any other man there present. For he confessed that he shared with Swift a feeling of personal friendship for the man he was about to oppose, for the Apostle of Reaction, Anthony Windover.   At this the members of the committee, to whom the orator had never before mentioned any acquaintanceship with Windover, looked astonished, but Budget, disregarding their astonishment, continued his speech. He, too, had struggled with himself, had communed with his spirit, had wrestled with the angel of human affection like Jacob, and like Jacob had not been overthrown.   Biblical allusions of a somewhat obvious kind lent their perennial charm to all Stephen's discourses, and in this instance, as always, had their stimulative effect. When the prompt applause had faded, Budget asserted that one of the first principles on which an advanced movement such as theirs was based was to ignore all ties, all intimacies, all friendships, for the common good.

'I love Anthony Windover,' he declared with a voice that was shaken as if by well-nigh unconquerable sobs; 'I love Anthony Windover the man, but not Anthony Windover the oppressor, and the more I love the one the more it is my duty, and the duty of every loyal Cordelier, to oppose the other.'

And then, after an eloquent address to the austere Roman virtues, he turned to Swift and appealed to him, in an appeal that had a kind of wild eloquence in it, to play the Roman too, to show his unswerving, unalterable devotion to the cause that he adorned by obeying the behest of the institution they loved and served, even though that obedience should force him to run counter to a commendable human instinct.

' Would the soldier on the brink of battle,' he asked, ' betray his flag because he knew that in the opposite camp someone very dear to him had taken service ?' And with a last entreaty to Swift to be stanch to the principles of Eighty-Nine and Ninety-Four, Budget sat down, while the committee raved at him in hysterical raptures.

The lead which had been so ingeniously given was promptly followed. Member after member of the committee rose and added the weight of his personal appeal to a trusted and honoured brother not to abandon the cause he served and the theories he illuminated. Every speaker intensified the importance of the occasion, the austere grandeur of the sacrifice, until at last it seemed to the object of all this oratory that no more momentous matter was recorded in the chronicle of the age.

What was Swift to do? Dazed by the whirling words, irritated at the sudden and unwelcome disfavour in which he found himself, bewildered by the importance attached to his action by a body of men in whom he had long believed, Swift saw no other courses open to him but surrender or secession. He had no wish to secede from the Cordeliers; they represented his opinions, they championed his creed; they had often been led by him, and it might well seem stubborn on his part to refuse their lead now in a case where, after all, he felt that they were in the right. If he believed in the principles that he professed, it was plain that he ought not to allow himself to swerve from the course of duty merely because a personal friend stood in the path of progress and sought to bar the way. There was, too, something in all the Roman father business which touched the sentimentalism in Swift and flattered him against his will.

Candida ought to admire him, he thought,

for this splendid sacrifice of friendship upon the altar of patriotism, even if her sense of irony tempted her to smile at the proportions to which the concession sought to inflate itself. So, with the image of Candida in his mind, Swift rose and in a few brief words announced to the committee that he placed himself at their disposition.

The revulsion of feeling was complete. Swift had scarcely finished his sentence of concession before he found that he had not merely conquered his new unpopularity, but regained all, and more than all, his old popularity. The chairman metaphorically wept tears of joy over him ; Budget eulogized him in glowing periods, in which he declared that Swift's earlier hesitation was only one degree less admirable and less honourable than the manner in which he had overcome that hesitation.

'So long,' he said, 'as the Cordeliers boasted the services of such single-minded men, they might proudly assert that all was

well for them and for the country.' And
he concluded, as it was common for speakers
in that room to conclude their speeches,
with an apposite quotation from the ' Cry
for Liberty,' which brought the blood to
Swift's cheeks, because it reminded him
of Candida, who had once cited to him
that very sentence and asked him what it
meant.

After such an emotional episode, even the
austerity of the Cordeliers felt itself unsuited
to a struggle with further business. For-
tunately, there was little further business to
discuss, and so they broke up. Every
member of the committee in turn pressed
up to Swift before leaving, and wrung his
hand, assuring him at the same time, in
language of identical fervour and of almost
identical phrase, that he had deserved well
of the country, and that the Cordeliers were
proud of their gifted son. All of which Swift
took in good part, with that not unpleasing
sense of exaltation which usually accompanies

the reaction of compliment upon condemna-
tion. It was hard indeed not to believe his
friends when they assured him that he was
indeed a very fine fellow who would have
adorned the proudest period of the Revolution.

But that exhilaration of the sense which
flattery fans in the impressionable fell away
sensibly when the stimulating influence was
removed. At Budget's request Swift waited
for him, that they might make their way
home together. Budget had a few words to
say to the chairman; he was one of those
politicians who have always a few words to
say to somebody after everybody else has
gone; and while he whispered with him in a
corner, Swift looked round upon the almost
deserted room with a revived melancholy.
The place looked gaunt and cold, with its
whitewashed walls and glaring gaslights.
The busts on their brackets—Marat, Robespierre, Danton and St. Just, one for each
side of the room—did not seem so inspirit-

ing as he had found them of old time. He
thought of Candida, and sighed to himself,
and wondered if it was right and wise for a
patriot ever to fall in love. He felt un-
nerved, irresolute, and he shivered as if the
world had suddenly grown cold.

He and Budget walked home together all
the way from St. Ethelfreda's Without to
Bloomsbury. It was a long walk, but it did
not seem too long to Swift, who was very
willing to kill time, and it did not seem too
long to his companion, who talked the whole
time about himself, and his prospects and his
ambitions. He had no serious expectation
of winning the election, but it cost him
nothing; the campaign was paid for by
those in the background who filled the
exchequer of the party. It would put
him prominently before the country; it
was the first decisive step on the way to
Westminster. He decided to go down the
next day to the seat of war. Swift promised
to follow him in a day or two, pleading that

he had business to look after which must be settled before he left London. On that understanding they parted at the door of Budget's lodging.

Swift did not rejoice at the duty that had been put upon him. It had grown plainer than ever of late to him, under the influence of his romantic passion, that he did not respect Budget, and it was portion and parcel of Swift's theory of life that it was unfitting to like that which one could not respect. Even apart from his theories, however, Swift had felt of late that his lack of respect for his friend was accompanied by an independent lack of liking for him. He did not merely dislike him because he did not respect him : he found that he was growing to dislike him apart from any question of respect. The coarseness of Stephen's view of life disgusted him — a coarseness that not merely saw meanness and baseness in everything, but avowed meanness and baseness itself. He was tired of his eternal

farthing philosophy of the vicious, of his
nauseous disbelief in all the qualities of
courage, of honour, of truth, of devotion to
principle, of loyalty to a cause or a creed
which Swift believed to be the impulses of
life.

In this scheme of things no man was
brave except for his own advantage; no
woman was chaste except through fear or
force; the word of no human creature was
worth the air it wasted; man was dominated
by greed, by lust, and by greed and lust
alone; and religion, patriotism, heroism,
were but so many battered masks which
cunning men put on to entrap the wisest.

Swift guessed, and, indeed, Budget
scarcely attempted to conceal, that his
extreme views were adopted by him as the
best means of advancing his own interests
and giving him an opportunity for self-asser-
tion otherwise denied to him. After he left
his colleague he felt a strong impulse to
write to the Cordeliers and say that, after

all, and in spite of all, he could not go to
Pine Hill.

But at the same time he recognised, or
thought that he recognised, that he had no
right to set his private judgment of a man
against the judgment of those whom he con-
sidered to be in this regard his chiefs. If it
would do any good to the cause for Budget
to stand for Pine Hill, then it seemed to
Swift that it was his duty to respond with
readiness, if not with cheerfulness, to the call
made upon him to go to the assistance of
the candidate. After all, much of Budget's
avowed unscrupulousness might be an affectation ; men often loved to be the fanfarons of
vices that were not their own, and in any
case Stephen was a man of great ability,
whose qualities as a free companion had
better be enlisted under the banners of
progress than allowed to drift into the camp
of the reactionaries.

It came to pass, therefore, that Swift,
after a wakeful night passed in considera-

tion of the question, decided that he would go to Pine Hill and do the best he could for the Cordeliers' choice, and he prepared reluctantly for his departure. The advantage of contesting the district did not seem so obvious to him as it did to Budget, and not merely to Budget, but to the tireless wire-pullers who approved of the proposed step, and who financed it. He did not think that there would be the least chance of winning the seat, and he could by no means force his mind into the unshakable conviction that if by any strange influence of the unexpected Stephen did get elected, it would prove to be at all a good thing for the party to whose principles Swift was so loyally pledged. But at least it would be a good thing for him to get away from London, and to seek in action some nepenthe for the absence of Candida.

END OF VOL. II.

BILLING AND SONS, PRINTERS, GUILDFORD.

A List of Books Published by
CHATTO & WINDUS
214, Piccadilly, London, W.

ABOUT.—THE FELLAH: An Egyptian Novel. By EDMOND ABOUT. Translated by Sir RANDAL ROBERTS. Post 8vo, illustrated boards, **2s.**

ADAMS (W. DAVENPORT), WORKS BY.
A DICTIONARY OF THE DRAMA: The Plays, Playwrights, Players, and Playbouses of the United Kingdom and America. Cr. 8vo, half-bound, **12s. 6d.** [*Preparing.*
QUIPS AND QUIDDITIES. Selected by W. D. ADAMS. Post 8vo, cloth limp, **2s. 6d.**

AGONY COLUMN (THE) OF "THE TIMES," from 1800 to 1870. Edited, with an Introduction, by ALICE CLAY. Post 8vo, cloth limp, **2s. 6d.**

AIDE (HAMILTON), WORKS BY. Post 8vo, illustrated boards, **2s.** each.
CARR OF CARRLYON. | CONFIDENCES.

ALBERT.—BROOKE FINCHLEY'S DAUGHTER. By MARY ALBERT. Post 8vo, picture boards, **2s.**; cloth limp, **2s. 6d.**

ALDEN.—A LOST SOUL. By W. L. ALDEN. Fcap. 8vo, cl. bds., **1s. 6d.**

ALEXANDER (MRS.), NOVELS BY. Post 8vo, illustrated boards, **2s.** each.
MAID, WIFE, OR WIDOW? | VALERIE'S FATE.

ALLEN (F. M.).—GREEN AS GRASS. By F. M. ALLEN, Author of "Through Green Glasses." Frontispiece by J. SMYTH. Cr. 8vo, cloth ex., **3s. 6d.**

ALLEN (GRANT), WORKS BY. Crown 8vo, cloth extra, **6s.** each.
THE EVOLUTIONIST AT LARGE. | COLIN CLOUT'S CALENDAR.
POST-PRANDIAL PHILOSOPHY. Crown 8vo, linen, **3s. 6d.**

Crown 8vo, cloth extra, **3s. 6d.** each; post 8vo, illustrated boards, **2s.** each.

PHILISTIA.	IN ALL SHADES.	DUMARESQ'S DAUGHTER.
BABYLON.	THE DEVIL'S DIE.	THE DUCHESS OF
STRANGE STORIES.	THIS MORTAL COIL.	POWYSLAND.
BECKONING HAND.	THE TENTS OF SHEM.	BLOOD ROYAL.
FOR MAIMIE'S SAKE.	THE GREAT TABOO.	

Crown 8vo, cloth extra, **3s. 6d.** each.
IVAN GREET'S MASTERPIECE, &c. With a Frontispiece by STANLEY L. WOOD.
THE SCALLYWAG. With a Frontispiece.
DR. PALLISER'S PATIENT. Fcap. 8vo, cloth extra, **1s. 6d.**
AT MARKET VALUE. Two Vols., crown 8vo, cloth, **10s.** net.

ARCHITECTURAL STYLES, A HANDBOOK OF. By A. ROSENGARTEN. Translated by W. COLLETT-SANDARS. With 639 Illusts. Cr. 8vo, cl. ex., **7s. 6d.**

ART (THE) OF AMUSING: A Collection of Graceful Arts, GAMES, Tricks, Puzzles, and Charades. By FRANK BELLEW. 300 Illusts. Cr. 8vo, cl. ex., **4s. 6d.**

ARNOLD (EDWIN LESTER), WORKS BY.
THE WONDERFUL ADVENTURES OF PHRA THE PHŒNICIAN. With 12 Illust by H. M. PAGET. Crown 8vo, cloth extra, **3s. 6d.**; post 8vo, illust. boards, **2s.**
THE CONSTABLE OF ST. NICHOLAS. With a Frontispiece by STANLEY WOOD. Crown 8vo, cloth, **3s. 6d.**

ARTEMUS WARD'S WORKS. With Portrait and Facsimile. Crown 8vo, cloth extra, **7s. 6d.**—Also a POPULAR EDITION, post 8vo, picture boards, **2s.**
THE GENIAL SHOWMAN: Life and Adventures of ARTEMUS WARD. By EDWARD P. HINGSTON. With a Frontispiece. Crown 8vo, cloth extra, **3s. 6d.**

ASHTON (JOHN), WORKS BY. Crown 8vo, cloth extra, **7s. 6d.** each.
HISTORY OF THE CHAP-BOOKS OF THE 18th CENTURY. With 334 Illusts.
SOCIAL LIFE IN THE REIGN OF QUEEN ANNE. With 85 Illustrations.
HUMOUR, WIT, AND SATIRE OF SEVENTEENTH CENTURY. With 82 Illusts.
ENGLISH CARICATURE AND SATIRE ON NAPOLEON THE FIRST. 115 Illusts.
MODERN STREET BALLADS. With 57 Illustrations.

BACTERIA, YEAST FUNGI, AND ALLIED SPECIES, A SYNOPSIS
OF. By W. B. Grove, B.A. With 87 Illustrations, Crown 8vo, cloth extra, **3s. 6d.**

BARDSLEY (REV. C. W.), WORKS BY.
ENGLISH SURNAMES: Their Sources and Significations. Cr. 8vo, cloth, **7s. 6d.**
CURIOSITIES OF PURITAN NOMENCLATURE. Crown 8vo, cloth extra, **6s.**

BARING GOULD (S., Author of "John Herring," &c.), NOVELS BY.
Crown 8vo, cloth extra, **3s. 6d.** each; post 8vo, illustrated boards, **2s.** each.
RED SPIDER. | EVE.

BARR (ROBERT: LUKE SHARP), STORIES BY. Cr. 8vo, cl., **3s. 6d.** ea.
IN A STEAMER CHAIR. With Frontispiece and Vignette by Demain Hammond.
FROM WHOSE BOURNE, &c. With 47 Illustrations.

BARRETT (FRANK, Author of "Lady Biddy Fane,") NOVELS BY.
Post 8vo, illustrated boards, **2s.** each; cloth, **2s. 6d.** each.

FETTERED FOR LIFE.	A PRODIGAL'S PROGRESS.
THE SIN OF OLGA ZASSOULICH.	JOHN FORD; and HIS HELPMATE.
BETWEEN LIFE AND DEATH.	A RECOILING VENGEANCE.
FOLLY MORRISON.	HONEST DAVIE.	LIEUT. BARNABAS.	FOUND GUILTY.
LITTLE LADY LINTON.	FOR LOVE AND HONOUR.

THE WOMAN OF THE IRON BRACELETS. Crown 8vo, cloth, **3s. 6d.**

BEACONSFIELD, LORD. By T. P. O'Connor, M.P. Cr. 8vo, cloth, **5s.**

BEAUCHAMP (S).—GRANTLEY GRANGE. Post 8vo, illust. boards, **2s.**

BEAUTIFUL PICTURES BY BRITISH ARTISTS: A Gathering from
the Picture Galleries, engraved on Steel. Imperial 4to, cloth extra, gilt edges, **21s.**

BECHSTEIN.—AS PRETTY AS SEVEN, and other German Stories.
Collected by Ludwig Bechstein. With Additional Tales by the Brothers Grimm,
and 98 Illustrations by Richter. Square 8vo, cloth extra, **6s. 6d.**; gilt edges, **7s. 6d.**

BEERBOHM.—WANDERINGS IN PATAGONIA; or, Life among the
Ostrich Hunters. By Julius Beerbohm. With Illusts. Cr. 8vo, cl. extra, **3s. 6d.**

BENNETT (W. C., LL.D.), WORKS BY. Post 8vo, cloth limp, **2s.** each.
A BALLAD HISTORY OF ENGLAND. | SONGS FOR SAILORS.

BESANT (WALTER), NOVELS BY.
Cr. 8vo, cl. ex., **3s. 6d.** each; post 8vo, illust. bds., **2s.** each; cl. limp, **2s. 6d.** each.
ALL SORTS AND CONDITIONS OF MEN. With Illustrations by Fred. Barnard.
THE CAPTAINS' ROOM, &c. With Frontispiece by E. J. Wheeler.
ALL IN A GARDEN FAIR. With 6 Illustrations by Harry Furniss.
DOROTHY FORSTER. With Frontispiece by Charles Green.
UNCLE JACK, and other Stories. | CHILDREN OF GIBEON.
THE WORLD WENT VERY WELL THEN. With 12 Illustrations by A. Forestier.
HERR PAULUS: His Rise, his Greatness, and his Fall.
FOR FAITH AND FREEDOM. With Illustrations by A. Forestier and F. Waddy.
TO CALL HER MINE, &c. With 9 Illustrations by A. Forestier.
THE BELL OF ST. PAUL'S.
THE HOLY ROSE, &c. With Frontispiece by F. Barnard.
ARMOREL OF LYONESSE: A Romance of To-day. With 12 Illusts. by F. Barnard.
ST. KATHERINE'S BY THE TOWER. With 12 page Illustrations by C. Green.
VERBENA CAMELLIA STEPHANOTIS, &c. | THE IVORY GATE: A Novel.
Crown 8vo, cloth extra, **3s. 6d.** each.
THE REBEL QUEEN. | IN DEACON'S ORDERS. [Shortly.
BEYOND THE DREAMS OF AVARICE. Three Vols., cr. 8vo, **15s.** net. [Shortly.
FIFTY YEARS AGO. With 144 Plates and Woodcuts. Crown 8vo, cloth extra, **5s.**
THE EULOGY OF RICHARD JEFFERIES. With Portrait. Cr. 8vo, cl. extra, **6s.**
THE ART OF FICTION. Demy 8vo, **1s.**
LONDON. With 125 Illustrations. New Edition. Demy 8vo, cloth extra, **7s. 6d.**
SIR RICHARD WHITTINGTON. Frontispiece. Crown 8vo, Irish Linen, **3s. 6d.**
GASPARD DE COLIGNY. With a Portrait. Crown 8vo, Irish linen, **3s. 6d.**
AS WE ARE: AS WE MAY BE: Social Essays. Crown 8vo, cloth, **6s.** [Shortly.

BESANT (WALTER) AND JAMES RICE, NOVELS BY.
Cr. 8vo. cl. ex., **3s. 6d.** each ; post 8vo, illust. bds., **2s.** each; cl. limp, **2s. 6d.** each.

READY-MONEY MORTIBOY.	BY CELIA'S ARBOUR.
MY LITTLE GIRL.	THE CHAPLAIN OF THE FLEET.
WITH HARP AND CROWN.	THE SEAMY SIDE.
THIS SON OF VULCAN.	THE CASE OF MR. LUCRAFT, &c.
THE GOLDEN BUTTERFLY.	'TWAS IN TRAFALGAR'S BAY, &c.
THE MONKS OF THELEMA.	THE TEN YEARS' TENANT, &c.

*** There is also a LIBRARY EDITION of the above Twelve Volumes, handsomely set in new type, on a large crown 8vo page, and bound in cloth extra. **6s.** each.

BEWICK (THOMAS) AND HIS PUPILS. By AUSTIN DOBSON. With 95 Illustrations. Square 8vo, cloth extra, **6s.**

BIERCE.—IN THE MIDST OF LIFE: Tales of Soldiers and Civilians.
By AMBROSE BIERCE. Crown 8vo, cloth extra, **6s.**; post 8vo, illustrated boards, **2s.**

BILL NYE'S HISTORY OF THE UNITED STATES. With 146 Illustrations by F. OPPER. Crown 8vo, cloth extra, **3s. 6d.**

BLACKBURN'S (HENRY) ART HANDBOOKS.

ACADEMY NOTES, 1875, 1877-86, 1889, 1890, 1892-1894, each **1s.**	**GROSVENOR NOTES**, Vol. III., 1888-90. With 230 Illusts. Demy 8vo, cloth, **3s. 6d.**
ACADEMY NOTES, 1875-79. Complete in One Vol., with 600 Illusts. Cloth, **6s.**	**THE NEW GALLERY**, 1888-1894. With numerous Illustrations, each **1s.**
ACADEMY NOTES, 1880-84. Complete in One Vol., with 700 Illusts. Cloth, **6s.**	**THE NEW GALLERY**, Vol. I., 1888-1892. With 250 Illustrations. Demy 8vo, cloth, **6s.**
GROSVENOR NOTES, 1877. **6d.**	**ENGLISH PICTURES at the NATIONAL GALLERY.** With 114 Illustrations. **1s.**
GROSVENOR NOTES, separate years, from 1878-1890, each **1s.**	**OLD MASTERS AT THE NATIONAL GALLERY.** With 128 Illustrations. **1s. 6d.**
GROSVENOR NOTES, Vol. I., 1877-82. With 300 Illusts. Demy 8vo, cloth, **6s.**	**ILLUSTRATED CATALOGUE TO THE NATIONAL GALLERY.** 242 Illusts., cl., **3s.**
GROSVENOR NOTES, Vol. II., 1883-87. With 300 Illusts. Demy 8vo, cloth, **6s.**	

THE PARIS SALON, 1894. With Facsimile Sketches. **3s.**
THE PARIS SOCIETY OF FINE ARTS, 1894. With Sketches. **3s. 6d.**

BLAKE (WILLIAM): India-proof Etchings from his Works by WILLIAM BELL SCOTT. With descriptive Text. Folio, half-bound boards, **21s.**

BLIND (MATHILDE). Poems by. Crown 8vo, cloth extra, **5s.** each.
THE ASCENT OF MAN.
DRAMAS IN MINIATURE. With a Frontispiece by FORD MADOX BROWN.
SONGS AND SONNETS. Fcap. 8vo, vellum and gold.

BOURNE (H. R. FOX), WORKS BY.
ENGLISH MERCHANTS: Memoirs in Illustration of the Progress of British Commerce. With numerous Illustrations. Crown 8vo, cloth extra, **7s. 6d.**
ENGLISH NEWSPAPERS: The History of Journalism. Two Vols., demy 8vo, cl., **25s.**
THE OTHER SIDE OF THE EMIN PASHA RELIEF EXPEDITION. Cr. 8vo, **6s.**

BOWERS.—LEAVES FROM A HUNTING JOURNAL. By GEORGE BOWERS. Oblong folio, half-bound. **21s.**

BOYLE (FREDERICK), WORKS BY. Post 8vo, illustrated boards, **2s.** each.
CHRONICLES OF NO-MAN'S LAND. | CAMP NOTES. | SAVAGE LIFE.

BRAND'S OBSERVATIONS ON POPULAR ANTIQUITIES; chiefly illustrating the Origin of our Vulgar Customs, Ceremonies, and Superstitions. With the Additions of Sir HENRY ELLIS, and Illustrations. Cr. 8vo, cloth extra, **7s. 6d.**

BREWER (REV. DR.), WORKS BY.
THE READER'S HANDBOOK OF ALLUSIONS, REFERENCES, PLOTS, AND STORIES. Fifteenth Thousand. Crown 8vo, cloth extra, **7s. 6d.**
AUTHORS AND THEIR WORKS, WITH THE DATES: Being the Appendices to "The Reader's Handbook," separately printed. Crown 8vo, cloth limp, **2s.**
A DICTIONARY OF MIRACLES. Crown 8vo, cloth extra, **7s. 6d.**

BREWSTER (SIR DAVID), WORKS BY. Post 8vo, cl. ex., **4s. 6d.** each.
MORE WORLDS THAN ONE: Creed of Philosopher and Hope of Christian. Plates.
THE MARTYRS OF SCIENCE: GALILEO, TYCHO BRAHE, and KEPLER. With Portraits.
LETTERS ON NATURAL MAGIC. With numerous Illustrations.

BRILLAT-SAVARIN.—GASTRONOMY AS A FINE ART. By BRILLAT-SAVARIN. Translated by R. E. ANDERSON, M.A. Post 8vo, half-bound, **2s.**

BRET HARTE, WORKS BY.

LIBRARY EDITION. In Seven Volumes, crown 8vo, cloth extra, 6s. each.
BRET HARTE'S COLLECTED WORKS. Arranged and Revised by the Author.
Vol. I. COMPLETE POETICAL AND DRAMATIC WORKS. With Steel Portrait.
Vol. II. LUCK OF ROARING CAMP—BOHEMIAN PAPERS—AMERICAN LEGENDS.
Vol. III. TALES OF THE ARGONAUTS—EASTERN SKETCHES.
Vol. IV. GABRIEL CONROY. | Vol. V. STORIES—CONDENSED NOVELS, &c.
Vol. VI. TALES OF THE PACIFIC SLOPE.
Vol. VII. TALES OF THE PACIFIC SLOPE—II. With Portrait by JOHN PETTIE, R.A.
Vol. VIII. TALES OF THE PINE AND THE CYPRESS.

THE SELECT WORKS OF BRET HARTE, in Prose and Poetry. With Introductory Essay by J. M. BELLEW, Portrait of Author, and 50 Illusts. Cr. 8vo, cl. ex., 7s. 6d.
BRET HARTE'S POETICAL WORKS. Hand-made paper & buckram. Cr. 8vo, 4s. 6d.
THE QUEEN OF THE PIRATE ISLE. With 28 original Drawings by KATE GREENAWAY, reproduced in Colours by EDMUND EVANS. Small 4to, cloth, 5s.

Crown 8vo, cloth extra, 3s. 6d. each.
A WAIF OF THE PLAINS. With 60 Illustrations by STANLEY L. WOOD.
A WARD OF THE GOLDEN GATE. With 59 Illustrations by STANLEY L WOOD.
A SAPPHO OF GREEN SPRINGS, &c. With Two Illustrations by HUME NISBET.
COLONEL STARBOTTLE'S CLIENT, AND SOME OTHER PEOPLE. With a Frontispiece by FRED. BARNARD.
SUSY: A Novel. With Frontispiece and Vignette by J. A. CHRISTIE.
SALLY DOWS, &c. With 47 Illustrations by W. D. ALMOND, &c.
A PROTÉGÉE OF JACK HAMLIN'S. With 26 Illustrations by W. SMALL, &c.
THE BELL-RINGER OF ANGEL'S, &c. 39 Illusts. by DUDLEY HARDY, &c. [Shortly.

Post 8vo, illustrated boards, 2s. each.
GABRIEL CONROY. | THE LUCK OF ROARING CAMP, &c.
AN HEIRESS OF RED DOG, &c. | CALIFORNIAN STORIES.

Post 8vo, illustrated boards, 2s. each; cloth limp, 2s. 6d. each.
FLIP. | MARUJA. | A PHYLLIS OF THE SIERRAS.

Fcap. 8vo, picture cover, 1s. each.
SNOW-BOUND AT EAGLE'S. | JEFF BRIGGS'S LOVE STORY.

BRYDGES.—UNCLE SAM AT HOME. By HAROLD BRYDGES. Post 8vo, illustrated boards, 2s.; cloth limp, 2s. 6d.

BUCHANAN'S (ROBERT) WORKS. Crown 8vo, cloth extra, 6s. each.

SELECTED POEMS OF ROBERT BUCHANAN. With Frontispiece by T. DALZIEL.
THE EARTHQUAKE; or, Six Days and a Sabbath.
THE CITY OF DREAM: An Epic Poem. With Two Illustrations by P. MACNAB.
THE WANDERING JEW: A Christmas Carol. Second Edition.
THE OUTCAST: A Rhyme for the Time. With 15 Illustrations by RUDOLF BLIND, PETER MACNAB, and HUME NISBET. Small demy 8vo, cloth extra, 8s.
ROBERT BUCHANAN'S COMPLETE POETICAL WORKS. With Steel-plate Portrait. Crown 8vo, cloth extra, 7s. 6d.

Crown 8vo, cloth extra, 3s. 6d. each; post 8vo, illustrated boards, 2s. each.
THE SHADOW OF THE SWORD. | LOVE ME FOR EVER. Frontispiece.
A CHILD OF NATURE. Frontispiece. | ANNAN WATER. | FOXGLOVE MANOR.
GOD AND THE MAN. With 11 Illus- | THE NEW ABELARD.
trations by FRED. BARNARD. | MATT: A Story of a Caravan. Front.
THE MARTYRDOM OF MADELINE. | THE MASTER OF THE MINE. Front.
With Frontispiece by A. W. COOPER. | THE HEIR OF LINNE.

Crown 8vo, cloth extra, 3s. 6d. each.
WOMAN AND THE MAN. | RED AND WHITE HEATHER.
RACHEL DENE. Two Vols., crown 8vo, cloth, 10s. net. [Shortly.

BURTON (CAPTAIN).—THE BOOK OF THE SWORD. By RICHARD F. BURTON. With over 400 Illustrations. Demy 4to, cloth extra, 32s.

BURTON (ROBERT).

THE ANATOMY OF MELANCHOLY. Demy 8vo, cloth extra, 7s. 6d.
MELANCHOLY ANATOMISED. Abridgment of BURTON'S ANAT. Post 8vo, 2s. 6d.

CAINE (T. HALL), NOVELS BY. Crown 8vo, cloth extra, 3s. 6d. each; post 8vo, illustrated boards, 2s. each; cloth limp, 2s. 6d. each.

SHADOW OF A CRIME. | A SON OF HAGAR. | THE DEEMSTER.

CAMERON (COMMANDER). — THE CRUISE OF THE "BLACK PRINCE" PRIVATEER. By V. LOVETT CAMERON, R.N. Post 8vo, boards, 2s.

CAMERON (MRS. H. LOVETT), NOVELS BY. Post 8vo, illust. bds., 2s. each.

JULIET'S GUARDIAN. | DECEIVERS EVER.

CARLYLE (THOMAS) ON THE CHOICE OF BOOKS. With Life
by R. H. SHEPHERD, and Three Illustrations. Post 8vo, cloth extra, **1s. 6d.**
CORRESPONDENCE OF THOMAS CARLYLE AND R. W. EMERSON, 1834 to 1872.
Edited by C. E. NORTON. With Portraits. Two Vols., crown 8vo, cloth, **24s.**

CARLYLE (JANE WELSH), LIFE OF. By Mrs. ALEXANDER IRELAND.
With Portrait and Facsimile Letter. Small demy 8vo, cloth extra, **7s. 6d.**

CHAPMAN'S (GEORGE) WORKS.—Vol. I., Plays.—Vol. II., Poems and
Minor Translations, with Essay by A. C. SWINBURNE.—Vol. III., Translations of
the Iliad and Odyssey. Three Vols., crown 8vo. cloth, **6s.** each.

CHATTO AND JACKSON.—A TREATISE ON WOOD ENGRAVING.
By W. A. CHATTO and J. JACKSON. With 450 fine Illusts. Large 4to. hf.-bd., **28s.**

CHAUCER FOR CHILDREN ; A Golden Key. By Mrs. H. R. HAWEIS.
With 8 Coloured Plates and 30 Woodcuts. Small 4to, cloth extra, **3s. 6d.**
CHAUCER FOR SCHOOLS. By Mrs. H. R. HAWEIS. Demy 8vo. cloth limp. **2s. 6d.**

CLARE (A).—FOR THE LOVE OF A LASS. Post 8vo, 2s. ; cl., 2s. 6d.

CLIVE (MRS. ARCHER), NOVELS BY. Post 8vo, illust. boards **2s.** each.
PAUL FERROLL. | WHY PAUL FERROLL KILLED HIS WIFE.

CLODD.—MYTHS AND DREAMS. By EDWARD CLODD, F.R.A.S.
Second Edition. Revised. Crown 8vo, cloth extra, **3s. 6d.**

COBBAN (J. MACLAREN), NOVELS BY.
THE CURE OF SOULS. Post 8vo, illustrated boards, **2s.**
Crown 8vo, cloth extra, **3s. 6d.** each.
THE RED SULTAN. | THE BURDEN OF ISABEL. [Shortly.

COLEMAN (JOHN), WORKS BY.
PLAYERS AND PLAYWRIGHTS I HAVE KNOWN. Two Vols., 8vo, cloth, **24s.**
CURLY: An Actor's Story. With 21 Illusts. by J. C. DOLLMAN. Cr. 8vo, cl., **1s. 6d.**

COLERIDGE.—THE SEVEN SLEEPERS OF EPHESUS. By M. E.
COLERIDGE. Fcap. 8vo, cloth, **1s. 6d.**

COLLINS (C. ALLSTON). -THE BAR SINISTER. Post 8vo, 2s.

COLLINS (MORTIMER AND FRANCES), NOVELS BY.
Crown 8vo, cloth extra, **3s. 6d.** each ; post 8vo, illustrated boards, **2s.** each.
FROM MIDNIGHT TO MIDNIGHT. | BLACKSMITH AND SCHOLAR.
TRANSMIGRATION. | YOU PLAY ME FALSE. | A VILLAGE COMEDY.
Post 8vo, illustrated boards, **2s.** each.
SWEET ANNE PAGE. | FIGHT WITH FORTUNE. | SWEET & TWENTY. | FRANCES.

COLLINS (WILKIE), NOVELS BY.
Cr. 8vo. cl. ex., **3s. 6d.** each ; post 8vo, illust. bds., **2s.** each ; cl. limp, **2s. 6d.** each.
ANTONINA. With a Frontispiece by Sir JOHN GILBERT, R.A.
BASIL. Illustrated by Sir JOHN GILBERT, R.A., and J. MAHONEY.
HIDE AND SEEK. Illustrated by Sir JOHN GILBERT, R.A., and J. MAHONEY.
AFTER DARK. Illustrations by A. B. HOUGHTON. | THE TWO DESTINIES.
THE DEAD SECRET. With a Frontispiece by Sir JOHN GILBERT, R.A.
QUEEN OF HEARTS. With a Frontispiece by Sir JOHN GILBERT, R.A.
THE WOMAN IN WHITE. With Illusts. by Sir J. GILBERT, R.A., and F. A. FRASER.
NO NAME. With Illustrations by Sir J. E. MILLAIS, R.A., and A. W. COOPER.
MY MISCELLANIES. With a Steel-plate Portrait of WILKIE COLLINS.
ARMADALE. With Illustrations by G. H. THOMAS.
THE MOONSTONE. With Illustrations by G. DU MAURIER and F. A. FRASER.
MAN AND WIFE. With Illustrations by WILLIAM SMALL.
POOR MISS FINCH. Illustrated by G. DU MAURIER and EDWARD HUGHES.
MISS OR MRS.? With Illusts. by S. L. FILDES, R.A., and HENRY WOODS, A.R.A.
THE NEW MAGDALEN. Illustrated by G. DU MAURIER and C. S. REINHARDT.
THE FROZEN DEEP. Illustrated by G. DU MAURIER and J. MAHONEY.
THE LAW AND THE LADY. Illusts. by S. L. FILDES, R.A., and SYDNEY HALL.
THE HAUNTED HOTEL. Illustrated by ARTHUR HOPKINS.
THE FALLEN LEAVES. | HEART AND SCIENCE. | THE EVIL GENIUS.
JEZEBEL'S DAUGHTER. | "I SAY NO." | LITTLE NOVELS.
THE BLACK ROBE. | A ROGUE'S LIFE. | THE LEGACY OF CAIN.
BLIND LOVE. With Preface by WALTER BESANT, and Illusts. by A. FORESTIER.
THE WOMAN IN WHITE. Popular Edition. Medium 8vo. 6d. : cloth. 1s.

COLLINS (JOHN CHURTON, M.A.), BOOKS BY.
ILLUSTRATIONS OF TENNYSON. Crown 8vo, cloth extra, **6s.**
JONATHAN SWIFT : A Biographical and Critical Study. Crown 8vo, cloth extra **8s.**

COLMAN'S (GEORGE) HUMOROUS WORKS: "Broad Grins," "My Nightgown and Slippers," &c. With Life and Frontis. Cr. 8vo, cl. extra, **7s. 6d.**

COLQUHOUN.—EVERY INCH A SOLDIER: A Novel. By M. J. COLQUHOUN. Post 8vo, illustrated boards, **2s.**

CONVALESCENT COOKERY: A Family Handbook. By CATHERINE RYAN. Crown 8vo, **1s.**; cloth limp, **1s. 6d.**

CONWAY (MONCURE D.), WORKS BY.
DEMONOLOGY AND DEVIL-LORE. 65 Illustrations. Two Vols., 8vo, cloth, **28s.**
GEORGE WASHINGTON'S RULES OF CIVILITY. Fcap. 8vo, Jap. vellum, **2s. 6d.**

COOK (DUTTON), NOVELS BY.
PAUL FOSTER'S DAUGHTER. Cr. 8vo, cl. ex., **3s. 6d.**; post 8vo, illust. boards, **2s.**
LEO. Post 8vo, illustrated boards, **2s.**

COOPER (EDWARD H.)—GEOFFORY HAMILTON. Cr. 8vo, **3s. 6d.**

CORNWALL.—POPULAR ROMANCES OF THE WEST OF ENG-LAND; or, The Drolls, Traditions, and Superstitions of Old Cornwall. Collected by ROBERT HUNT, F.R.S. Two Steel-plates by GEO. CRUIKSHANK. Cr. 8vo, cl., **7s. 6d.**

COTES.—TWO GIRLS ON A BARGE. By V. CECIL COTES. With 44 Illustrations by F. H. TOWNSEND. Post 8vo, cloth, **2s. 6d.**

CRADDOCK (C. EGBERT), STORIES BY.
PROPHET of the GREAT SMOKY MOUNTAINS. Post 8vo, illust. bds., **2s.**; cl., **2s. 6d.**
HIS VANISHED STAR. Crown 8vo, cloth extra, **3s. 6d.**   [Shortly.

CRELLIN (H. N.), BOOKS BY.
ROMANCES of the OLD SERAGLIO. 28 Illusts. by S. L. WOOD. Cr. 8vo, cl., **3s. 6d.**
THE NAZARENES: A Drama. Crown 8vo, **1s.**

CRIM.—ADVENTURES OF A FAIR REBEL. By MATT CRIM. With a Frontispiece. Crown 8vo, cloth extra, **3s. 6d.**; post 8vo, illustrated boards, **2s.**

CROKER (B.M.), NOVELS BY. Crown 8vo, cloth extra, **3s. 6d.** each; post 8vo, illustrated boards, **2s.** each; cloth limp, **2s. 6d.** each.
PRETTY MISS NEVILLE.   DIANA BARRINGTON.
A BIRD OF PASSAGE.   PROPER PRIDE.
A FAMILY LIKENESS.   "TO LET."
MR. JERVIS. Three Vols., crown 8vo, cloth, **15s.** nett.

CRUIKSHANK'S COMIC ALMANACK. Complete in TWO SERIES: The FIRST from 1835 to 1843; the SECOND from 1844 to 1853. A Gathering of the BEST HUMOUR of THACKERAY, HOOD, MAYHEW, ALBERT SMITH, A'BECKETT, ROBERT BROUGH, &c. With numerous Steel Engravings and Woodcuts by CRUIK-SHANK, HINE, LANDELLS, &c. Two Vols., crown 8vo, cloth gilt, **7s. 6d.** each.
THE LIFE OF GEORGE CRUIKSHANK. By BLANCHARD JERROLD. With 84 Illustrations and a Bibliography. Crown 8vo, cloth extra, **6s.**

CUMMING (C. F. GORDON), WORKS BY. Demy 8vo, cl. ex., **8s. 6d.** each.
IN THE HEBRIDES. With Autotype Facsimile and 23 Illustrations.
IN THE HIMALAYAS AND ON THE INDIAN PLAINS. With 42 Illustrations.
TWO HAPPY YEARS IN CEYLON. With 28 Illustrations.
VIA CORNWALL TO EGYPT. With Photogravure Frontis. Demy 8vo, cl., **7s. 6d.**

CUSSANS.—A HANDBOOK OF HERALDRY; with Instructions for Tracing Pedigrees and Deciphering Ancient MSS., &c. By JOHN E. CUSSANS. With 408 Woodcuts and 2 Coloured Plates. Fourth edition, revised, crown 8vo, cloth, **6s.**

CYPLES (W.)—HEARTS of GOLD. Cr. 8vo, cl., **3s. 6d.**; post 8vo, bds., **2s.**

DANIEL.—MERRIE ENGLAND IN THE OLDEN TIME. By GEORGE DANIEL. With Illustrations by ROBERT CRUIKSHANK. Crown 8vo, cloth extra, **3s. 6d.**

DAUDET.—THE EVANGELIST; or, Port Salvation. By ALPHONSE DAUDET. Crown 8vo, cloth extra, **3s. 6d.**; post 8vo, illustrated boards, **2s.**

DAVIDSON.—MR. SADLER'S DAUGHTERS. By HUGH COLEMAN DAVIDSON. With a Frontispiece. Crown 8vo, cloth extra, **3s. 6d.**

DAVIES (DR. N. E. YORKE-), WORKS BY. Cr. 8vo, **1s.** ea.; cl., **1s. 6d.** ea.
ONE THOUSAND MEDICAL MAXIMS AND SURGICAL HINTS.
NURSERY HINTS: A Mother's Guide in Health and Disease.
FOODS FOR THE FAT: A Treatise on Corpulency, and a Dietary for its Cure.
AIDS TO LONG LIFE. Crown 8vo, **2s.**; cloth limp, **2s. 6d.**

DAVIES' (SIR JOHN) COMPLETE POETICAL WORKS, for the first time Collected and Edited, with Memorial-Introduction and Notes, by the Rev. A. B. GROSART, D.D. Two Vols., crown 8vo, cloth boards, 12s.

DAWSON.—THE FOUNTAIN OF YOUTH. By ERASMUS DAWSON, M.B. Crown 8vo, cloth extra, 3s. 6d.; post 3vo, illustrated boards, 2s.

DE GUERIN.—THE JOURNAL OF MAURICE DE GUERIN. Edited by G. S. TREBUTIEN. With a Memoir by SAINTE-BEUVE. Translated from the 20th French Edition by JESSIE P FROTHINGHAM. Fcap. 8vo, half-bound, 2s. 6d.

DE MAISTRE.—A JOURNEY ROUND MY ROOM. By XAVIER DE MAISTRE. Translated by HENRY ATTWELL. Post 8vo, cloth limp, 2s. 6d.

DE MILLE.—A CASTLE IN SPAIN. By JAMES DE MILLE. With a Frontispiece. Crown 8vo, cloth extra, 3s. 6d.; post 8vo, illustrated boards, 2s.

DERBY (THE).—THE BLUE RIBBON OF THE TURF. With Brief Accounts of THE OAKS. By LOUIS HENRY CURZON. Cr. 8vo, cloth limp, 2s. 6d.

DERWENT (LEITH), NOVELS BY. Cr. 8vo. cl., 3s. 6d. ea.; post 8vo, bds., 2s. ea.
OUR LADY OF TEARS. | CIRCE'S LOVERS.

DEWAR.—A RAMBLE ROUND THE GLOBE. By T. R. DEWAR. With 220 Illustrations by W. L. WYLLIE, A.R.A., SYDNEY COWELL, A. S. FORREST, S. L. WOOD, JAMES GREIG, &c. Crown 8vo, cloth extra, 7s. 6d. [*Shortly.*

DICKENS (CHARLES), NOVELS BY. Post 8vo, illustrated boards, 2s. each.
SKETCHES BY BOZ. | NICHOLAS NICKLEBY.
THE PICKWICK PAPERS. | OLIVER TWIST.
THE SPEECHES OF CHARLES DICKENS, 1841-1870. With a New Bibliography. Edited by RICHARD HERNE SHEPHERD. Crown 8vo, cloth extra, 6s.
ABOUT ENGLAND WITH DICKENS. By ALFRED RIMMER. With 57 Illustrations by C. A. VANDERHOOF, ALFRED RIMMER, and others. Sq. 8vo, cloth extra, 7s. 6d.

DICTIONARIES.
A DICTIONARY OF MIRACLES: Imitative, Realistic, and Dogmatic. By the Rev. E. C. BREWER, LL.D. Crown 8vo, cloth extra, 7s. 6d.
THE READER'S HANDBOOK OF ALLUSIONS, REFERENCES, PLOTS, AND STORIES. By the Rev. E. C. BREWER, LL.D. With an ENGLISH BIBLIOGRAPHY. Fifteenth Thousand. Crown 8vo, cloth extra, 7s. 6d.
AUTHORS AND THEIR WORKS, WITH THE DATES. Cr. 8vo, cloth limp, 2s.
FAMILIAR SHORT SAYINGS OF GREAT MEN. With Historical and Explanatory Notes. By SAMUEL A. BENT, A M. Crown 8vo, cloth extra, 7s. 6d.
SLANG DICTIONARY: Etymological, Historical, and Anecdotal. Cr. 8vo, cl., 6s. 6d.
WOMEN OF THE DAY: A Biographical Dictionary. By F. HAYS. Cr. 8vo, cl., 5s.
WORDS, FACTS, AND PHRASES: A Dictionary of Curious, Quaint, and Out-of-the-Way Matters. By ELIEZER EDWARDS. Crown 8vo, cloth extra, 7s. 6d.

DIDEROT.—THE PARADOX OF ACTING. Translated, with Annotations, from Diderot's "Le Paradoxe sur le Comédien," by WALTER HERRIES POLLOCK. With a Preface by HENRY IRVING. Crown 8vo, parchment, 4s. 6d.

DOBSON (AUSTIN), WORKS BY.
THOMAS BEWICK & HIS PUPILS. With 95 Illustrations. Square 8vo, cloth, 6s.
FOUR FRENCHWOMEN. With 4 Portraits. Crown 8vo, buckram, gilt top, 6s.
EIGHTEENTH CENTURY VIGNETTES. Two SERIES. Cr. 8vo, buckram, 6s. each.

DOBSON (W. T.)—POETICAL INGENUITIES AND ECCENTRICITIES. Post 8vo, cloth limp, 2s. 6d.

DONOVAN (DICK), DETECTIVE STORIES BY.
Post 8vo, illustrated boards, 2s. each; cloth limp, 2s. 6d. each.
THE MAN-HUNTER. | WANTED! | A DETECTIVE'S TRIUMPHS.
CAUGHT AT LAST! | IN THE GRIP OF THE LAW.
TRACKED AND TAKEN. | FROM INFORMATION RECEIVED.
WHO POISONED HETTY DUNCAN? | LINK BY LINK.
SUSPICION AROUSED.
Crown 8vo, cloth, 3s. 6d. each; post 8vo, boards, 2s. each; cloth, 2s. 6d. each.
THE MAN FROM MANCHESTER. With 23 Illustrations.
TRACKED TO DOOM. With 6 full-page Illustrations by GORDON BROWNE.

DOYLE (CONAN).—THE FIRM OF GIRDLESTONE. By A. CONAN DOYLE, Author of "Micah Clarke." Crown 8vo, cloth extra, 3s. 6d.

DRAMATISTS, THE OLD. With Vignette Portraits. Cr.8vo, cl. ex., **6s.** per Vol.
BEN JONSON'S WORKS. With Notes Critical and Explanatory, and a Biographical Memoir by WM. GIFFORD. Edited by Col. CUNNINGHAM. Three Vols.
CHAPMAN'S WORKS. Complete in Three Vols. Vol. 1. contains the Plays complete; Vol. II., Poems and Minor Translations, with an Introductory Essay by A. C. SWINBURNE; Vol. III., Translations of the Iliad and Odyssey.
MARLOWE'S WORKS. Edited, with Notes, by Col. CUNNINGHAM. One Vol.
MASSINGER'S PLAYS. From GIFFORD's Text. Edit by Col.CUNNINGHAM. OneVol.

DUNCAN (SARA JEANNETTE), WORKS BY. Cr. 8vo. cl., **7s. 6d.** each.
A SOCIAL DEPARTURE: How Orthodocia and I Went round the World by Ourselves. With 111 Illustrations by F. H. TOWNSEND.
AN AMERICAN GIRL IN LONDON. With 80 Illustrations by F. H. TOWNSEND.
THE SIMPLE ADVENTURES OF A MEMSAHIB. Illustrated by F. H. TOWNSEND.
A DAUGHTER OF TO-DAY. Two Vols., crown 8vo, **10s.** net.
VERNON'S AUNT. With 47 Illusts. by HAL HURST. Cr.8vo,cl. ex., **3s 6d.** [Shortly.

DYER.—THE FOLK-LORE OF PLANTS. By Rev. T. F. THISELTON DYER, M.A. Crown 8vo, cloth extra, **6s.**

EARLY ENGLISH POETS. Edited, with Introductions and Annotations, by Rev. A. B. GROSART, D.D. Crown 8vo, cloth boards, **6s.** per Volume.
FLETCHER'S (GILES) COMPLETE POEMS. One Vol.
DAVIES' (SIR JOHN) COMPLETE POETICAL WORKS. Two Vols.
HERRICK'S (ROBERT) COMPLETE COLLECTED POEMS. Three Vols.
SIDNEY'S (SIR PHILIP) COMPLETE POETICAL WORKS. Three Vols.

EDGCUMBE.—ZEPHYRUS : A Holiday in Brazil and on the River Plate. By E. R. PEARCE EDGCUMBE. With 41 Illustrations. Crown 8vo, cloth extra, **5s.**

EDISON, THE LIFE & INVENTIONS OF THOMAS A. By W. K. L. and A. DICKSON. 250 Illusts. by R. F. OUTCALT, &c. Demy 4to, linen gilt, **18s.** [Shortly.

EDWARDES (MRS. ANNIE), NOVELS BY:
A POINT OF HONOUR. Post 8vo, illustrated boards, **2s.**
ARCHIE LOVELL. Crown 8vo, cloth extra, **3s. 6d.** ; post 8vo, illust. boards, **2s.**

EDWARDS (ELIEZER).—WORDS, FACTS, AND PHRASES : A Dictionary of Quaint Matters. By ELIEZER EDWARDS. Crown 8vo, cloth, **7s. 6d.**

EDWARDS (M. BETHAM-), NOVELS BY.
KITTY. Post 8vo, illustrated boards, **2s.**; cloth limp, **2s. 6d.**
FELICIA. Post 8vo, illustrated boards, **2s.**

EGERTON.—SUSSEX FOLK & SUSSEX WAYS. By Rev. J. C. EGERTON. With Introduction by Rev. Dr. H. WACE, and 4 Illustrations. Cr.8vo,cloth ex., **5s.**

EGGLESTON (EDWARD).—ROXY : A Novel. Post 8vo, illust. bds., **2s.**

ENGLISHMAN'S HOUSE, THE : A Practical Guide to all interested in Selecting or Building a House; with Estimates of Cost, Quantities, &c. By C. J. RICHARDSON. With Coloured Frontispiece and 600 Illusts. Crown 8vo, cloth, **7s. 6d.**

EWALD (ALEX. CHARLES, F.S.A.), WORKS BY.
THE LIFE AND TIMES OF PRINCE CHARLES STUART, Count of Albany (THE YOUNG PRETENDER). With a Portrait. Crown 8vo, cloth extra, **7s. 6d.**
STORIES FROM THE STATE PAPERS. With an Autotype. Crown 8vo, cloth, **6s.**

EYES, OUR : How to Preserve Them from Infancy to Old Age. By JOHN BROWNING, F.R.A.S. With 70 Illusts. Eighteenth Thousand. Crown 8vo, **1s.**

FAMILIAR SHORT SAYINGS OF GREAT MEN. By SAMUEL ARTHUR BENT, A.M. Fifth Edition. Revised and Enlarged. Crown 8vo, cloth extra, **7s. 6d.**

FARADAY (MICHAEL), WORKS BY. Post 8vo, cloth extra, **4s. 6d.** each.
THE CHEMICAL HISTORY OF A CANDLE: Lectures delivered before a Juvenile Audience. Edited by WILLIAM CROOKES F.C.S. With numerous Illustrations.
ON THE VARIOUS FORCES OF NATURE, AND THEIR RELATIONS TO EACH OTHER. Edited by WILLIAM CROOKES, F.C.S. With Illustrations.

FARRER (J. ANSON), WORKS BY.
MILITARY MANNERS AND CUSTOMS. Crown 8vo, cloth extra, **6s.**
WAR: Three Essays, reprinted from "Military Manners." Cr. 8vo, **1s.** ; cl., **1s. 6d.**

FENN (G. MANVILLE), NOVELS BY.
THE NEW MISTRESS. Cr. 8vo, cloth extra, **3s. 6d.**; post 8vo, illust. boards, **2s.**
Crown 8vo, cloth extra, **3s. 6d.** each.
WITNESS TO THE DEED. | THE TIGER LILY. | THE WHITE VIRGIN. [Shortly.

FIN-BEC.—THE CUPBOARD PAPERS: Observations on the Art of Living and Dining. By FIN-BEC. Post 8vo. cloth limp, 2s. 6d.

FIREWORKS, THE COMPLETE ART OF MAKING; or, The Pyrotechnist's Treasury. By THOMAS KENTISH. With 267 Illustrations. Cr. 8vo. cl., 5s.

FIRST BOOK, MY. By WALTER BESANT, J. K. JEROME, R. L. STEVENSON. and others. With a Prefatory Story by JEROME K. JEROME, and nearly 200 Illustrations. Small demy 8vo, cloth extra, 7s. 6d.

FITZGERALD (PERCY, M.A., F.S.A.), WORKS BY.
THE WORLD BEHIND THE SCENES. Crown 8vo, cloth extra, 3s. 6d.
LITTLE ESSAYS: Passages from Letters of CHARLES LAMB. Post 8vo, cl., 2s. 6d.
A DAY'S TOUR: Journey through France and Belgium. With Sketches. Cr. 4to. 1s.
FATAL ZERO. Crown 8vo, cloth extra, 3s. 6d.: post 8vo, illustrated boards, 2s.

Post 8vo, illustrated boards, 2s. each.
BELLA DONNA. | LADY OF BRANTOME. | THE SECOND MRS. TILLOTSON.
POLLY. | NEVER FORGOTTEN. | SEVENTY-FIVE BROOKE STREET.
LIFE OF JAMES BOSWELL (of Auchinleck). With an Account of his Sayings, Doings, and Writings; and Four Portraits. Two Vols., demy 8vo, cloth. 24s.
THE SAVOY OPERA. With 60 Illustrations and Portraits. Cr. 8vo, cloth, 3s. 6d.

FLAMMARION (CAMILLE), WORKS BY.
POPULAR ASTRONOMY: A General Description of the Heavens. Trans. by J. E. GORE, F.R.A.S. With 3 Plates and 288 Illusts. Medium 8vo, cloth, 16s. [Shortly.
URANIA: A Romance. With 87 Illustrations. Crown 8vo, cloth extra, 5s.

FLETCHER'S (GILES, B.D.) COMPLETE POEMS: Christ's Victorie in Heaven, Christ's Victorie on Earth, Christ's Triumph over Death, and Minor Poems. With Notes by Rev. A. B. GROSART, D.D. Crown 8vo, cloth boards, 6s.

FONBLANQUE (ALBANY).—FILTHY LUCRE. Post 8vo, illust. bds., 2s.

FRANCILLON (R. E.), NOVELS BY.
Crown 8vo, cloth extra, 3s. 6d. each: post 8vo, illustrated boards, 2s. each.
ONE BY ONE. | QUEEN COPHETUA. | A REAL QUEEN. | KING OR KNAVE?

Crown 8vo, cloth extra, 3s. 6d. each.
ROPES OF SAND. Illustrated. | JACK DOYLE'S DAUGHTER. [Shortly.
A DOG AND HIS SHADOW. |

OLYMPIA. Post 8vo, illust. bds., 2s. | ESTHER'S GLOVE. Fcap. 8vo, pict. cover, 1s.
ROMANCES OF THE LAW. Post 8vo, illustrated boards, 2s.

FREDERIC (HAROLD), NOVELS BY. Post 8vo, illust. bds., 2s. each.
SETH'S BROTHER'S WIFE. | THE LAWTON GIRL.

FRENCH LITERATURE, A HISTORY OF. By HENRY VAN LAUN. Three Vols., demy 8vo, cloth boards, 7s. 6d. each.

FRERE.—PANDURANG HARI; or, Memoirs of a Hindoo. With Preface by Sir BARTLE FRERE. Crown 8vo, cloth, 3s. 6d.: post 8vo, illust. bds., 2s.

FRISWELL (HAIN).—ONE OF TWO: A Novel. Post 8vo, illust. bds., 2s.

FROST (THOMAS), WORKS BY. Crown 8vo, cloth extra, 3s. 6d. each.
CIRCUS LIFE AND CIRCUS CELEBRITIES. | LIVES OF THE CONJURERS.
THE OLD SHOWMEN AND THE OLD LONDON FAIRS.

FRY'S (HERBERT) ROYAL GUIDE TO THE LONDON CHARITIES.
Edited by JOHN LANE. Published Annually. Crown 8vo, cloth, 1s. 6d.

GARDENING BOOKS. Post 8vo. 1s. each; cloth limp, 1s. 6d. each.
A YEAR'S WORK IN GARDEN AND GREENHOUSE. By GEORGE GLENNY.
HOUSEHOLD HORTICULTURE. By TOM and JANE JERROLD. Illustrated.
THE GARDEN THAT PAID THE RENT. By TOM JERROLD.
OUR KITCHEN GARDEN. By TOM JERROLD. Crown 8vo, cloth, 1s. 6d.
MY GARDEN WILD. By FRANCIS G. HEATH. Crown 8vo, cloth extra, 6s.

GARRETT.—THE CAPEL GIRLS: A Novel. By EDWARD GARRETT. Crown 8vo, cloth extra, 3s. 6d.: post 8vo, illustrated boards, 2s.

GAULOT.—THE RED SHIRTS: A Story of the Revolution. By PAUL GAULOT. Translated by J. A. J. DE VILLIERS. Crown 8vo, cloth, 3s. 6d.

GENTLEMAN'S MAGAZINE, THE. 1s. Monthly. Articles upon Literature, Science and Art, and "TABLE TALK" by SYLVANUS URBAN, appear monthly.
. Bound Volumes for recent years kept in stock, 8s. 6d. each. Cases for binding, 2s.

GENTLEMAN'S ANNUAL, THE. Published Annually in November. 1s.

GERMAN POPULAR STORIES. Collected by the Brothers GRIMM and Translated by EDGAR TAYLOR. With Introduction by JOHN RUSKIN, and 22 Steel Plates after GEORGE CRUIKSHANK. Square 8vo, cloth, **6s. 6d.**; gilt edges, **7s. 6d.**

GIBBON (CHARLES), NOVELS BY. Crown 8vo, cloth extra, **3s. 6d.** each; post 8vo, illustrated boards, **2s. each.**

ROBIN GRAY.	LOVING A DREAM.	THE GOLDEN SHAFT.
THE FLOWER OF THE FOREST.	OF HIGH DEGREE.

Post 8vo, illustrated boards. **2s.** each.

THE DEAD HEART.	IN LOVE AND WAR.
FOR LACK OF GOLD.	A HEART'S PROBLEM.
WHAT WILL THE WORLD SAY?	BY MEAD AND STREAM.
FOR THE KING.	A HARD KNOT.	THE BRAES OF YARROW.
QUEEN OF THE MEADOW.	FANCY FREE.	IN HONOUR BOUND.
IN PASTURES GREEN.	HEART'S DELIGHT.	BLOOD-MONEY.

GIBNEY (SOMERVILLE).—SENTENCED! Cr. 8vo, 1s. ; cl., 1s. 6d.

GILBERT (WILLIAM), NOVELS BY. Post 8vo, illustrated boards. **2s.** each.

DR. AUSTIN'S GUESTS.	JAMES DUKE, COSTERMONGER.
THE WIZARD OF THE MOUNTAIN.	

GILBERT (W. S.), ORIGINAL PLAYS BY. Two Series, 2s. 6d. each.
The FIRST SERIES contains: The Wicked World—Pygmalion and Galatea—Charity—The Princess—The Palace of Truth—Trial by Jury.
The SECOND SERIES: Broken Hearts—Engaged—Sweethearts—Gretchen—Dan'l Druce—Tom Cobb—H.M.S. "Pinafore"—The Sorcerer—Pirates of Penzance.

EIGHT ORIGINAL COMIC OPERAS written by W. S. GILBERT. Containing: The Sorcerer—H.M.S. "Pinafore"—Pirates of Penzance—Iolanthe—Patience—Princess Ida—The Mikado—Trial by Jury. Demy 8vo. cloth limp, **2s. 6d.**

THE **"GILBERT AND SULLIVAN" BIRTHDAY BOOK:** Quotations for Every Day in the Year, Selected from Plays by W. S. GILBERT set to Music by Sir A. SULLIVAN. Compiled by ALEX. WATSON. Royal 16mo, Jap. leather, **2s. 6d.**

GLANVILLE (ERNEST), NOVELS BY. Crown 8vo, cloth extra, **3s. 6d.** each; post 8vo, illustrated boards, **2s.** each.
THE LOST HEIRESS: A Tale of Love, Battle, and Adventure. With 2 Illusts.
THE FOSSICKER: A Romance of Mashonaland. With 2 Illusts. by HUME NISBET.
A FAIR COLONIST. With a Frontispiece. Cr. 8vo, cl. extra, **3s. 6d.**

GLENNY.—A YEAR'S WORK IN GARDEN AND GREENHOUSE: Practical Advice to Amateur Gardeners as to the Management of the Flower, Fruit, and Frame Garden. By GEORGE GLENNY. Post 8vo, **1s.**; cloth limp, **1s. 6d.**

GODWIN.—LIVES OF THE NECROMANCERS. By WILLIAM GODWIN. Post 8vo, cloth limp, **2s.**

GOLDEN TREASURY OF THOUGHT, THE: An Encyclopædia of QUOTATIONS. Edited by THEODORE TAYLOR. Crown 8vo, cloth gilt, **7s. 6d.**

GONTAUT, MEMOIRS OF THE DUCHESSE DE, Gouvernante to the Children of France, 1773-1836. With Photogravure Frontispieces. Two Vols., small demy 8vo, cloth extra, **21s.**

GOODMAN.—THE FATE OF HERBERT WAYNE. By E. J. GOODMAN, Author of "Too Curious." Crown 8vo, cloth, **3s. 6d.**

GRAHAM. — THE PROFESSOR'S WIFE: A Story By LEONARD GRAHAM. Fcap. 8vo, picture cover, **1s.**

GREEKS AND ROMANS, THE LIFE OF THE, described from Antique Monuments. By ERNST GUHL and W. KONER. Edited by Dr. F. HUEFFER. With 545 Illustrations. Large crown 8vo, cloth extra, **7s. 6d.**

GREENWOOD (JAMES), WORKS BY. Cr. 8vo. cloth extra, **3s. 6d.** each.

THE WILDS OF LONDON.	LOW-LIFE DEEPS.

GREVILLE (HENRY), NOVELS BY:
NIKANOR. Translated by ELIZA E. CHASE. With 8 Illustrations. Crown 8vo, cloth extra, **6s.**; post 8vo, illustrated boards, **2s.**
A NOBLE WOMAN. Crown 8vo, cloth extra, **5s.**; post 8vo. illustrated boards, **2s.**

GRIFFITH.—CORINTHIA MARAZION: A Novel. By CECIL GRIFFITH. Crown 8vo, cloth extra, **3s. 6d.**; post 8vo, illustrated boards, **2s.**

GRUNDY.—THE DAYS OF HIS VANITY: A Passage in the Life of a Young Man. By SYDNEY GRUNDY. Crown 8vo, cloth extra, **3s. 6d.**

HABBERTON (JOHN, Author of "Helen's Babies"), NOVELS BY.
Post 8vo, illustrated boards **2s.** each; cloth limp, **2s. 6d.** each.
BRUETON'S BAYOU. | COUNTRY LUCK.

HAIR, THE: Its Treatment in Health, Weakness, and Disease. Translated from the German of Dr. J. PINCUS. Crown 8vo. **1s.**; cloth, **1s. 6d.**

HAKE (DR. THOMAS GORDON), POEMS BY. Cr. 8vo, cl. ex., **6s.** each.
NEW SYMBOLS. | LEGENDS OF THE MORROW. | THE SERPENT PLAY.
MAIDEN ECSTASY. Small 4to, cloth extra, **8s.**

HALL.—SKETCHES OF IRISH CHARACTER. By Mrs. S. C. HALL.
With numerous Illustrations on Steel and Wood by MACLISE, GILBERT, HARVEY, and GEORGE CRUIKSHANK. Medium 8vo, cloth extra, **7s. 6d.**

HALLIDAY (ANDR.).—EVERY-DAY PAPERS. Post 8vo, bds., **2s.**

HANDWRITING, THE PHILOSOPHY OF. With over 100 Facsimiles and Explanatory Text. By DON FELIX DE SALAMANCA. Post 8vo, cloth limp, **2s. 6d.**

HANKY-PANKY: Easy Tricks, White Magic, Sleight of Hand, &c.
Edited by W. H. CREMER. With 200 Illustrations. Crown 8vo, cloth extra, **4s. 6d.**

HARDY (LADY DUFFUS).—PAUL WYNTER'S SACRIFICE. **2s.**

HARDY (THOMAS).—UNDER THE GREENWOOD TREE. By THOMAS HARDY, Author of "Tess." With Portrait and 15 Illustrations. Crown 8vo, cloth extra, **3s. 6d.**; post 8vo, illustrated boards, **2s.**; cloth limp, **2s. 6d.**

HARPER (CHARLES G.), WORKS BY. Demy 8vo, cloth extra, **16s.** each.
THE BRIGHTON ROAD. With Photogravure Frontispiece and 90 Illustrations.
FROM PADDINGTON TO PENZANCE: The Record of a Summer Tramp. 105 Illusts.

HARWOOD.—THE TENTH EARL. By J. BERWICK HARWOOD. Post 8vo, illustrated boards, **2s.**

HAWEIS (MRS. H. R.), WORKS BY. Square 8vo, cloth extra, **6s.** each.
THE ART OF BEAUTY. With Coloured Frontispiece and 91 Illustrations.
THE ART OF DECORATION. With Coloured Frontispiece and 74 Illustrations.
THE ART OF DRESS. With 32 Illustrations. Post 8vo, **1s.**; cloth, **1s. 6d.**
CHAUCER FOR SCHOOLS. Demy 8vo, cloth limp, **2s. 6d.**
CHAUCER FOR CHILDREN. 38 Illusts. (8 Coloured). Sm. 4to, cl. extra, **3s. 6d.**

HAWEIS (Rev. H. R., M.A.).—AMERICAN HUMORISTS: WASHINGTON IRVING, OLIVER WENDELL HOLMES, JAMES RUSSELL LOWELL, ARTEMUS WARD, MARK TWAIN, and BRET HARTE. Third Edition. Crown 8vo, cloth extra, **6s.**

HAWLEY SMART.—WITHOUT LOVE OR LICENCE: A Novel. By HAWLEY SMART. Crown 8vo cloth extra, **3s. 6d.**; post 8vo, illustrated boards, **2s.**

HAWTHORNE.—OUR OLD HOME. By NATHANIEL HAWTHORNE.
Annotated with Passages from the Author's Note-book, and Illustrated with 31 Photogravures. Two Vols., crown 8vo. buckram, gilt top, **15s.**

HAWTHORNE (JULIAN), NOVELS BY.
Crown 8vo, cloth extra, **3s. 6d.** each; post 8vo, illustrated boards, **2s.** each.
GARTH. | ELLICE QUENTIN. | BEATRIX RANDOLPH. | DUST.
SEBASTIAN STROME. | DAVID POINDEXTER.
FORTUNE'S FOOL. | THE SPECTRE OF THE CAMERA.
Post 8vo, illustrated boards, **2s.** each.
MISS CADOGNA. | LOVE—OR A NAME.
MRS. GAINSBOROUGH'S DIAMONDS. Fcap. 8vo. illustrated cover, **1s.**

HEATH.—MY GARDEN WILD, AND WHAT I GREW THERE.
By FRANCIS GEORGE HEATH. Crown 8vo, cloth extra, gilt edges, **6s.**

HELPS (SIR ARTHUR), WORKS BY. Post 8vo, cloth limp, **2s. 6d.** each.
ANIMALS AND THEIR MASTERS. | SOCIAL PRESSURE.
IVAN DE BIRON: A Novel. Cr. 8vo, cl. extra, **3s. 6d.**; post 8vo, illust. bds., **2s.**

HENDERSON.—AGATHA PAGE: A Novel. By ISAAC HENDERSON.
Crown 8vo, cloth extra, **3s. 6d.**

HENTY (G. A.), NOVELS BY. Crown 8vo, cloth extra, **3s. 6d.** each.
RUJUB THE JUGGLER. 8 Illusts. by STANLEY L. WOOD. PRESENTATION ED., **5s.**
DOROTHY'S DOUBLE. [Shortly.

HERMAN.—A LEADING LADY. By HENRY HERMAN, joint-Author of "The Bishops' Bible." Post 8vo, illustrated boards, **2s.**; cloth extra, **2s. 6d.**

HERRICK'S (ROBERT) HESPERIDES, NOBLE NUMBERS, AND COMPLETE COLLECTED POEMS. With Memorial-Introduction and Notes by the Rev. A. B. GROSART, D.D.; Steel Portrait, &c. Three Vols., crown 8vo, cl. bds., **18s.**

HERTZKA.—FREELAND: A Social Anticipation. By Dr. THEODOR HERTZKA. Translated by ARTHUR RANSOM. Crown 8vo, cloth extra, **6s.**

HESSE-WARTEGG.—TUNIS: The Land and the People. By Chevalier ERNST VON HESSE-WARTEGG. With 22 Illustrations. Cr. 8vo, cloth extra, **3s. 6d.**

HILL (HEADON).—ZAMBRA THE DETECTIVE. By HEADON HILL. Post 8vo, illustrated boards, **2s.**; cloth, **2s. 6d.**

HILL (JOHN, M.A.), WORKS BY.
TREASON-FELONY. Post 8vo, **2s.** | THE COMMON ANCESTOR. Cr. 8vo, **3s. 6d.**

HINDLEY (CHARLES), WORKS BY.
TAVERN ANECDOTES AND SAYINGS: Including Reminiscences connected with Coffee Houses, Clubs, &c. With Illustrations. Crown 8vo, cloth, **3s. 6d.**
THE LIFE AND ADVENTURES OF A CHEAP JACK. Cr. 8vo, cloth ex., **3s. 6d.**

HOEY.—THE LOVER'S CREED. By Mrs. CASHEL HOEY. Post 8vo, **2s.**

HOLLINGSHEAD (JOHN).—NIAGARA SPRAY. Crown 8vo, 1s.

HOLMES.—THE SCIENCE OF VOICE PRODUCTION AND VOICE PRESERVATION. By GORDON HOLMES, M.D. Crown 8vo, 1s.; cloth, **1s. 6d.**

HOLMES (OLIVER WENDELL), WORKS BY.
THE AUTOCRAT OF THE BREAKFAST-TABLE. Illustrated by J. GORDON THOMSON. Post 8vo, cloth limp **2s. 6d.**—Another Edition, post 8vo, cloth, **2s.**
THE AUTOCRAT OF THE BREAKFAST-TABLE and THE PROFESSOR AT THE BREAKFAST-TABLE. In One Vol. Post 8vo, half-bound, **2s.**

HOOD'S (THOMAS) CHOICE WORKS, in Prose and Verse. With Life of the Author, Portrait, and 200 Illustrations. Crown 8vo, cloth extra, **7s. 6d.**
HOOD'S WHIMS AND ODDITIES. With 85 Illusts. Post 8vo, half-bound, **2s.**

HOOD (TOM).—FROM NOWHERE TO THE NORTH POLE: A Noah's Arkæological Narrative. By TOM HOOD. With 25 Illustrations by W. BRUNTON and E. C. BARNES. Square 8vo, cloth extra, gilt edges, **6s.**

HOOK'S (THEODORE) CHOICE HUMOROUS WORKS; including his Ludicrous Adventures, Bons Mots, Puns, and Hoaxes. With Life of the Author, Portraits, Facsimiles, and Illustrations. Crown 8vo, cloth extra, **7s. 6d.**

HOOPER.—THE HOUSE OF RABY: A Novel. By Mrs. GEORGE HOOPER. Post 8vo, illustrated boards. **2s.**

HOPKINS.—"'TWIXT LOVE AND DUTY:" A Novel. By TIGHE HOPKINS. Post 8vo, illustrated boards, **2s.**

HORNE.—ORION: An Epic Poem. By RICHARD HENGIST HORNE. With Photographic Portrait by SUMMERS. Tenth Edition. Cr. 8vo, cloth extra, **7s.**

HUNGERFORD (MRS.), Author of "Molly Bawn," NOVELS BY.
Post 8vo, illustrated boards, **2s.** each; cloth limp, **2s. 6d.** each.
A MAIDEN ALL FORLORN. | IN DURANCE VILE. | A MENTAL STRUGGLE.
MARVEL. | A MODERN CIRCE.
Crown 8vo, cloth extra, **3s. 6d.** each.
LADY VERNER'S FLIGHT. | THE RED-HOUSE MYSTERY.

HUNT.—ESSAYS BY LEIGH HUNT: A TALE FOR A CHIMNEY CORNER, &c. Edited by EDMUND OLLIER. Post 8vo, printed on laid paper and half-bd., **2s.**

HUNT (MRS. ALFRED), NOVELS BY.
Crown 8vo, cloth extra, **3s. 6d.** each; post 8vo, illustrated boards, **2s.** each.
THE LEADEN CASKET. | SELF-CONDEMNED. | THAT OTHER PERSON.
THORNICROFT'S MODEL. Post 8vo, illustrated boards, **2s.**
MRS. JULIET. Crown 8vo, cloth extra, **3s. 6d.**

HUTCHISON.—HINTS ON COLT-BREAKING. By W. M. HUTCHISON. With 25 Illustrations. Crown 8vo, cloth extra, **3s. 6d.**

HYDROPHOBIA: An Account of M. PASTEUR'S System; Technique of his Method, and Statistics. By RENAUD SUZOR, M.B. Crown 8vo, cloth extra, **6s.**

IDLER (THE): A Monthly Magazine. Profusely Illustr. 6d. Monthly. The first FIVE VOLS. now ready, cl. extra, **5s.** each; Cases for Binding, **1s. 6d.** each.

INGELOW (JEAN).—FATED TO BE FREE. Post 8vo, illustrated bds., 2s.

INDOOR PAUPERS. By ONE OF THEM. Crown 8vo, 1s.; cloth, 1s. 6d.

INNKEEPER'S HANDBOOK (THE) AND LICENSED VICTUALLER'S MANUAL. By J. TREVOR-DAVIES. Crown 8vo, 1s.; cloth, 1s. 6d.

IRISH WIT AND HUMOUR, SONGS OF. Collected and Edited by A. PERCEVAL GRAVES. Post 8vo. cloth limp, 2s. 6d.

JAMES.—A ROMANCE OF THE QUEEN'S HOUNDS. By CHARLES JAMES. Post 8vo, picture cover, 1s.; cloth limp, 1s. 6d.

JAMESON.—MY DEAD SELF. By WILLIAM JAMESON. Post 8vo, illustrated boards, 2s.; cloth, 2s. 6d.

JAPP.—DRAMATIC PICTURES, SONNETS, &c. By A. H. JAPP, LL.D. Crown 8vo, cloth extra, 5s.

JAY (HARRIETT), NOVELS BY. Post 8vo, illustrated boards, 2s. each.
THE DARK COLLEEN. | THE QUEEN OF CONNAUGHT.

JEFFERIES (RICHARD), WORKS BY. Post 8vo, cloth limp, 2s. 6d. each.
NATURE NEAR LONDON. | THE LIFE OF THE FIELDS. | THE OPEN AIR.
. Also the HAND-MADE PAPER EDITION, crown 8vo, buckram, gilt top, 6s. each
THE EULOGY OF RICHARD JEFFERIES. By WALTER BESANT. Second Edition. With a Photograph Portrait. Crown 8vo, cloth extra, 6s.

JENNINGS (H. J.), WORKS BY.
CURIOSITIES OF CRITICISM. Post 8vo, cloth limp, 2s. 6d.
LORD TENNYSON: A Biographical Sketch. Post 8vo, 1s.; cloth, 1s. 6d.

JEROME.—STAGELAND. By JEROME K. JEROME. With 64 Illustrations by J. BERNARD PARTRIDGE. Square 8vo, picture cover, 1s.; cloth limp, 2s.

JERROLD.—THE BARBER'S CHAIR; & THE HEDGEHOG LETTERS. By DOUGLAS JERROLD. Post 8vo, printed on laid paper and half-bound, 2s.

JERROLD (TOM), WORKS BY. Post 8vo, 1s. each; cloth limp, 1s. 6d. each.
THE GARDEN THAT PAID THE RENT.
HOUSEHOLD HORTICULTURE: A Gossip about Flowers. Illustrated.
OUR KITCHEN GARDEN: The Plants, and How we Cook Them. Cr. 8vo, cl., 1s. 6d.

JESSE.—SCENES AND OCCUPATIONS OF A COUNTRY LIFE. By EDWARD JESSE. Post 8vo, cloth limp, 2s.

JONES (WILLIAM, F.S.A.), WORKS BY. Cr. 8vo, cl. extra, 7s. 6d. each.
FINGER-RING LORE: Historical, Legendary, and Anecdotal. With nearly 300 Illustrations. Second Edition, Revised and Enlarged.
CREDULITIES, PAST AND PRESENT. Including the Sea and Seamen, Miners, Talismans, Word and Letter Divination, Exorcising and Blessing of Animals, Birds, Eggs, Luck, &c. With an Etched Frontispiece.
CROWNS AND CORONATIONS: A History of Regalia. With 100 Illustrations.

JONSON'S (BEN) WORKS. With Notes Critical and Explanatory, and a Biographical Memoir by WILLIAM GIFFORD. Edited by Colonel CUNNINGHAM. Three Vols., crown 8vo, cloth extra, 6s. each.

JOSEPHUS, THE COMPLETE WORKS OF. Translated by WHISTON. Containing "The Antiquities of the Jews" and "The Wars of the Jews." With 52 Illustrations and Maps. Two Vols., demy 8vo. half-bound, 12s. 6d.

KEMPT.—PENCIL AND PALETTE: Chapters on Art and Artists. By ROBERT KEMPT. Post 8vo, cloth limp, 2s. 6d.

KERSHAW. — COLONIAL FACTS AND FICTIONS: Humorous Sketches. By MARK KERSHAW. Post 8vo, illustrated boards, 2s.; cloth, 2s. 6d.

KEYSER. — CUT BY THE MESS: A Novel. By ARTHUR KEYSER. Crown 8vo, picture cover, 1s.; cloth limp, 1s. 6d.

KING (R. ASHE), NOVELS BY. Cr. 8vo, cl., 3s. 6d. ea.; post 8vo, bds., 2s. ea.
A DRAWN GAME. | "THE WEARING OF THE GREEN."
Post 8vo, illustrated boards, 2s. each.
PASSION'S SLAVE. | BELL BARRY.

KNIGHT.—THE PATIENT'S VADE MECUM: How to Get Most Benefit from Medical Advice. By WILLIAM KNIGHT, M.R.C.S., and EDWARD KNIGHT, L.R.C.P. Crown 8vo, 1s.; cloth limp, 1s. 6d.

KNIGHTS (THE) OF THE LION : A Romance of the Thirteenth Century
Edited, with an Introduction, by the MARQUESS of LORNE, K.T. Cr. 8vo, cl. ex. **6s.**

LAMB'S (CHARLES) COMPLETE WORKS, in Prose and Verse,
including " Poetry for Children " and " Prince Dorus." Edited, with Notes and
Introduction, by R. H. SHEPHERD. With Two Portraits and Facsimile of a page
of the " Essay on Roast Pig." Crown 8vo, half-bound, **7s. 6d.**
THE ESSAYS OF ELIA. Post 8vo, printed on laid paper and half-bound, **2s.**
LITTLE ESSAYS: Sketches and Characters by CHARLES LAMB, selected from his
Letters by PERCY FITZGERALD. Post 8vo, cloth limp, **2s. 6d.**
THE DRAMATIC ESSAYS OF CHARLES LAMB. With Introduction and Notes
by BRANDER MATTHEWS, and Steel-plate Portrait. Fcap. 8vo, hf.-bd., **2s. 6d.**

LANDOR.—CITATION AND EXAMINATION OF WILLIAM SHAKS-
PEARE, &c., before Sir THOMAS LUCY, touching Deer-stealing, 19th September, 1582.
To which is added, **A CONFERENCE OF MASTER EDMUND SPENSER** with the
Earl of Essex, touching the State of Ireland, 1595. By WALTER SAVAGE LANDOR.
Fcap. 8vo, half-Roxburghe, **2s. 6d.**

LANE.—THE THOUSAND AND ONE NIGHTS, commonly called in
England THE ARABIAN NIGHTS' ENTERTAINMENTS. Translated from the
Arabic, with Notes, by EDWARD WILLIAM LANE. Illustrated by many hundred
Engravings from Designs by HARVEY. Edited by EDWARD STANLEY POOLE. With a
Preface by STANLEY LANE-POOLE. Three Vols., demy 8vo, cloth extra, **7s. 6d.** each.

LARWOOD (JACOB), WORKS BY.
THE STORY OF THE LONDON PARKS. With Illusts. Cr. 8vo, cl. extra, **3s. 6d.**
ANECDOTES OF THE CLERGY. Post 8vo, laid paper, half-bound, **2s.**
Post 8vo, cloth limp, **2s. 6d.** each.
FORENSIC ANECDOTES. | THEATRICAL ANECDOTES.

LEHMANN (R. C.) WORKS BY. Post 8vo, pict. cover, **1s.** ea. ; cloth, **1s. 6d.** ea.
HARRY FLUDYER AT CAMBRIDGE.
CONVERSATIONAL HINTS FOR YOUNG SHOOTERS: A Guide to Polite Talk.

LEIGH (HENRY S.), WORKS BY.
CAROLS OF COCKAYNE. Printed on hand-made paper, bound in buckram, **5s.**
JEUX D'ESPRIT. Edited by HENRY S. LEIGH. Post 8vo, cloth limp, **2s. 6d.**

LEYS (JOHN).—THE LINDSAYS : A Romance. Post 8vo, illust. bds., **2s.**

LINTON (E. LYNN), WORKS BY. Post 8vo, cloth limp, **2s. 6d.** each.
WITCH STORIES. | OURSELVES: ESSAYS ON WOMEN.
Crown 8vo, cloth extra, **3s. 6d.** each ; post 8vo, illustrated boards, **2s.** each.
PATRICIA KEMBALL. | IONE. | UNDER WHICH LORD?
ATONEMENT OF LEAM DUNDAS. | " MY LOVE!" | SOWING THE WIND.
THE WORLD WELL LOST. | PASTON CAREW, Millionaire & Miser.
Post 8vo, illustrated boards, **2s.** each.
THE REBEL OF THE FAMILY. | WITH A SILKEN THREAD.
THE ONE TOO MANY. Crown 8vo, cloth, **3s. 6d.** [Shortly.
FREESHOOTING: Extracts from Works of Mrs. LINTON. Post 8vo, cloth, **2s. 6d.**

LONGFELLOW'S POETICAL WORKS. With numerous Illustrations
on Steel and Wood. Crown 8vo, cloth extra, **7s. 6d.**

LUCY.—GIDEON FLEYCE : A Novel. By HENRY W. LUCY. Crown
8vo, cloth extra, **3s. 6d.** : post 8vo, illustrated boards, **2s.**

MACALPINE (AVERY), NOVELS BY.
TERESA ITASCA. Crown 8vo, cloth extra, **1s.**
BROKEN WINGS. With 6 Illusts. by W. J. HENNESSY. Crown 8vo, cloth extra, **6s.**

MACCOLL (HUGH), NOVELS BY.
MR. STRANGER'S SEALED PACKET. Post 8vo, illustrated boards, **2s.**
EDNOR WHITLOCK. Crown 8vo, cloth extra, **6s.**

MACDONELL.—QUAKER COUSINS : A Novel. By AGNES MACDONELL.
Crown 8vo, cloth extra, **3s. 6d.** ; post 8vo, illustrated boards, **2s.**

MACGREGOR. — PASTIMES AND PLAYERS: Notes on Popular
Games. By ROBERT MACGREGOR. Post 8vo, cloth limp, **2s. 6d.**

MACKAY.—INTERLUDES AND UNDERTONES; or, Music at Twilight.
By CHARLES MACKAY, L.L.D. Crown 8vo, cloth extra, **6s.**

MAGIC LANTERN, THE, and its Management: including full Practical
Directions. By T. C. HEPWORTH. 10 Illustrations. Cr. 8vo, **1s.** ; cloth, **1s. 6d.**

McCARTHY (JUSTIN, M.P.), WORKS BY.

A HISTORY OF OUR OWN TIMES, from the Accession of Queen Victoria to the General Election of 1880. Four Vols. demy 8vo, cloth extra, **12s.** each.—Also a POPULAR EDITION, in Four Vols., crown 8vo, cloth extra, **6s.** each.—And a JUBILEE EDITION, with an Appendix of Events to the end of 1886, in Two Vols., large crown 8vo, cloth extra, **7s. 6d.** each.

A SHORT HISTORY OF OUR OWN TIMES. One Vol., crown 8vo, cloth extra, **6s.**—Also a CHEAP POPULAR EDITION, post 8vo, cloth limp, **2s. 6d.**

A HISTORY OF THE FOUR GEORGES. Four Vols. demy 8vo, cloth extra, **12s.** each.   [Vols. I. & II. *ready.*

Cr. 8vo, cl. extra, **3s. 6d.** each; post 8vo, illust. bds., **2s.** each; cl. limp, **2s. 6d.** each.

THE WATERDALE NEIGHBOURS.	MISS MISANTHROPE.
MY ENEMY'S DAUGHTER.	DONNA QUIXOTE.
A FAIR SAXON.	THE COMET OF A SEASON.
LINLEY ROCHFORD.	MAID OF ATHENS.
DEAR LADY DISDAIN.	CAMIOLA: A Girl with a Fortune.

Crown 8vo, cloth extra, **3s. 6d.** each.

THE DICTATOR.	RED DIAMONDS.

"THE RIGHT HONOURABLE." By JUSTIN McCARTHY, M.P., and Mrs. CAMPBELL-PRAED. Fourth Edition. Crown 8vo, cloth extra, **6s.**

McCARTHY (JUSTIN H.), WORKS BY.

THE FRENCH REVOLUTION. Four Vols., 8vo, **12s.** each.   [Vols. I. & II. *ready.*
AN OUTLINE OF THE HISTORY OF IRELAND. Crown 8vo, **1s.**; cloth, **1s. 6d.**
IRELAND SINCE THE UNION: Irish History, 1798-1886. Crown 8vo, cloth, **6s.**
HAFIZ IN LONDON: Poems. Small 8vo, gold cloth, **3s. 6d.**
HARLEQUINADE: Poems. Small 4to, Japanese vellum, **8s.**
OUR SENSATION NOVEL. Crown 8vo, picture cover, **1s.**; cloth limp, **1s. 6d.**
DOOM! An Atlantic Episode. Crown 8vo, picture cover, **1s.**
DOLLY: A Sketch. Crown 8vo, picture cover, **1s.**; cloth limp, **1s. 6d.**
LILY LASS: A Romance. Crown 8vo, picture cover, **1s.**; cloth limp, **1s. 6d.**
THE THOUSAND AND ONE DAYS: Persian Tales. With 2 Photogravures by STANLEY L. WOOD. Two Vols., crown 8vo, half-bound, **12s.**

MACDONALD (GEORGE, LL.D.), WORKS BY.

WORKS OF FANCY AND IMAGINATION. Ten Vols., cl. extra, gilt edges, in cloth case, **21s.** Or the Vols. may be had separately, in grolier cl., at **2s. 6d.** each.
Vol. I. WITHIN AND WITHOUT.—THE HIDDEN LIFE.
"   II. THE DISCIPLE.—THE GOSPEL WOMEN.—BOOK OF SONNETS.—ORGAN SONGS.
"   III. VIOLIN SONGS.—SONGS OF THE DAYS AND NIGHTS.—A BOOK OF DREAMS.—ROADSIDE POEMS.—POEMS FOR CHILDREN.
"   IV. PARABLES.—BALLADS.—SCOTCH SONGS.
" V. & VI. PHANTASTES: A Faerie Romance. | Vol. VII. THE PORTENT.
" VIII. THE LIGHT PRINCESS.—THE GIANT'S HEART.—SHADOWS.
"   IX. CROSS PURPOSES.—THE GOLDEN KEY.—THE CARASOYN.—LITTLE DAYLIGHT.
"   X. THE CRUEL PAINTER.—THE WOW o' RIVVEN.—THE CASTLE.—THE BROKEN SWORDS.—THE GRAY WOLF.—UNCLE CORNELIUS.

POETICAL WORKS OF GEORGE MACDONALD. Collected and arranged by the Author. 2 vols., crown 8vo, buckram, **12s.**
A THREEFOLD CORD. Edited by GEORGE MACDONALD. Post 8vo, cloth, **5s.**
HEATHER AND SNOW: A Novel. Crown 8vo, cloth extra, **3s. 6d.**
PHANTASTES: A Faerie Romance. A New Edition. With 25 Illustrations by J. BELL. Crown 8vo, cloth extra. **3s. 6d.**   [*Shortly.*

MACLISE PORTRAIT GALLERY (THE) OF ILLUSTRIOUS LITER-

ARY CHARACTERS: **85 PORTRAITS**; with Memoirs — Biographical, Critical, Bibliographical, and Anecdotal—illustrative of the Literature of the former half of the Present Century, by WILLIAM BATES, B.A. Crown 8vo, cloth extra, **7s. 6d.**

MACQUOID (MRS.), WORKS BY. Square 8vo, cloth extra, **7s. 6d.** each.

IN THE ARDENNES. With 50 Illustrations by THOMAS R. MACQUOID.
PICTURES AND LEGENDS FROM NORMANDY AND BRITTANY. 34 Illustrations.
THROUGH NORMANDY. With 92 Illustrations by T. R. MACQUOID, and a Map.
THROUGH BRITTANY. With 35 Illustrations by T. R. MACQUOID, and a Map.
ABOUT YORKSHIRE. With 67 Illustrations by T. R. MACQUOID. Square 8vo, cloth extra, **6s.**

Post 8vo, illustrated boards, **2s.** each.

THE EVIL EYE, and other Stories.	LOST ROSE.

MAGICIAN'S OWN BOOK, THE: Performances with Eggs, Hats, &c

Edited by W. H. CREMER. 200 Illustrations. Crown 8vo, cloth extra, **4s.**

MAGNA CHARTA: An Exact Facsimile of the Original in the British Museum, 3 feet by 2 feet, with Arms and Seals emblazoned in Gold and Colours, **5s.**

MALLOCK (W. H.), WORKS BY.
THE NEW REPUBLIC. Post 8vo, picture cover, **2s.**; cloth limp, **2s. 6d.**
THE NEW PAUL & VIRGINIA: Positivism on an Island. Post 8vo, cloth, **2s. 6d.**
POEMS. Small 4to, parchment, **8s.**
IS LIFE WORTH LIVING? Crown 8vo, cloth extra, **6s.**
A ROMANCE OF THE NINETEENTH CENTURY. Crown 8vo, cloth, **6s.**; post 8vo, illustrated boards, **2s.**

MALLORY'S (SIR THOMAS) MORT D'ARTHUR: The Stories of King Arthur and of the Knights of the Round Table. (A Selection.) Edited by B. MONTGOMERIE RANKING. Post 8vo, cloth limp, **2s.**

MARK TWAIN, WORKS BY. Crown 8vo, cloth extra, **7s. 6d.** each.
THE CHOICE WORKS OF MARK TWAIN. Revised and Corrected throughout by the Author. With Life, Portrait, and numerous Illustrations.
ROUGHING IT, and INNOCENTS AT HOME. With 200 Illusts. by F. A. FRASER.
MARK TWAIN'S LIBRARY OF HUMOUR. With 197 Illustrations.
Crown 8vo, cloth extra (illustrated), **7s. 6d.** each; post 8vo, illust. boards, **2s.** each.
THE INNOCENTS ABROAD; or, New Pilgrim's Progress. With 234 Illustrations. (The Two-Shilling Edition is entitled MARK TWAIN'S PLEASURE TRIP.)
THE GILDED AGE. By MARK TWAIN and C. D. WARNER. With 212 Illustrations.
THE ADVENTURES OF TOM SAWYER. With 111 Illustrations.
A TRAMP ABROAD. With 314 Illustrations.
THE PRINCE AND THE PAUPER. With 190 Illustrations.
LIFE ON THE MISSISSIPPI. With 300 Illustrations.
ADVENTURES OF HUCKLEBERRY FINN. With 174 Illusts. by E. W. KEMBLE.
A YANKEE AT THE COURT OF KING ARTHUR. With 220 Illusts. by BEARD.
Post 8vo, illustrated boards, **2s.** each.
THE STOLEN WHITE ELEPHANT. | MARK TWAIN'S SKETCHES.
Crown 8vo, cloth extra, **3s. 6d.** each.
THE AMERICAN CLAIMANT. With 81 Illustrations by HAL HURST, &c.
THE £1,000,000 BANK-NOTE, and other New Stories.
TOM SAWYER ABROAD. Illustrated by DAN BEARD.
PUDD'NHEAD WILSON.

MARKS (H. S., R.A.), PEN AND PENCIL SKETCHES BY. With 4 Photogravures and 126 Illustrations. Two Vols., demy 8vo, cloth, **32s.** [Shortly.

MARLOWE'S WORKS. Including his Translations. Edited, with Notes and Introductions, by Col. CUNNINGHAM. Crown 8vo, cloth extra, **6s.**

MARRYAT (FLORENCE), NOVELS BY. Post 8vo, illust. boards, **2s.** each.
A HARVEST OF WILD OATS. | FIGHTING THE AIR.
OPEN! SESAME! | WRITTEN IN FIRE.

MASSINGER'S PLAYS. From the Text of WILLIAM GIFFORD. Edited by Col CUNNINGHAM Crown 8vo cloth extra, **6s.**

MASTERMAN.—HALF-A-DOZEN DAUGHTERS: A Novel. By J. MASTERMAN. Post 8vo, illustrated boards, **2s.**

MATTHEWS.—A SECRET OF THE SEA, &c. By BRANDER MATTHEWS. Post 8vo, illustrated boards, **2s.**; cloth limp, **2s. 6d.**

MAYHEW.—LONDON CHARACTERS AND THE HUMOROUS SIDE OF LONDON LIFE. By HENRY MAYHEW. With Illusts. Crown 8vo, cloth, **3s. 6d.**

MEADE (L. T.), NOVELS BY.
A SOLDIER OF FORTUNE. Crown 8vo, cloth, **3s. 6d.** [Shortly.
IN AN IRON GRIP. Two Vols., crown 8vo, cloth, **10s.** net. [Shortly.

MERRICK.—THE MAN WHO WAS GOOD. By LEONARD MERRICK, Author of "Violet Moses," &c. Post 8vo, illustrated boards, **2s.**

MEXICAN MUSTANG (ON A), through Texas to the Rio Grande. By A. E. SWEET and J. ARMOY KNOX. With 265 Illusts. Cr. 8vo, cloth extra, **7s. 6d.**

MIDDLEMASS (JEAN), NOVELS BY. Post 8vo, illust. boards, **2s.** each.
TOUCH AND GO. | MR. DORILLION.

MILLER.—PHYSIOLOGY FOR THE YOUNG; or, The House of Life. By Mrs. F. FENWICK MILLER. With Illustrations. Post 8vo, cloth limp, **2s. 6d.**

MILTON (J. L.), WORKS BY. Post 8vo, 1s. each; cloth, 1s. 6d. each.
THE HYGIENE OF THE SKIN. With Directions for Diet, Soaps, Baths, &c.
THE BATH IN DISEASES OF THE SKIN.
THE LAWS OF LIFE, AND THEIR RELATION TO DISEASES OF THE SKIN.
THE SUCCESSFUL TREATMENT OF LEPROSY. Demy 8vo, 1s.

MINTO (WM.)—WAS SHE GOOD OR BAD? Cr. 8vo, 1s. ; cloth, 1s. 6d.

MITFORD (BERTRAM), NOVELS BY. Crown 8vo, cloth extra, 3s. 6d. each.
THE GUN-RUNNER: A Romance of Zululand. With Frontispiece by S. L. Wood.
THE LUCK OF GERARD RIDGELEY. With a Frontispiece by Stanley L. Wood.
THE KING'S ASSEGAI. With Six full-page Illustrations.
RENSHAW FANNING'S QUEST. With Frontispiece by S. L. Wood.   [Shortly.

MOLESWORTH (MRS.), NOVELS BY.
HATHERCOURT RECTORY. Post 8vo, illustrated boards, 2s.
THAT GIRL IN BLACK. Crown 8vo, cloth, 1s. 6d.

MOORE (THOMAS), WORKS BY.
THE EPICUREAN; and ALCIPHRON. Post 8vo, half-bound, 2s.
PROSE AND VERSE. With Suppressed Passages from the MEMOIRS OF LORD
BYRON. Edited by R. H. Shepherd. With Portrait. Cr. 8vo, cl. ex., 7s. 6d.

MUDDOCK (J. E.), STORIES BY.
STORIES WEIRD AND WONDERFUL. Post 8vo, illust. boards, 2s.; cloth, 2s. 6d.
THE DEAD MAN'S SECRET; or, The Valley of Gold. With Frontispiece by
F. BARNARD. Crown 8vo, cloth extra, 5s.; post 8vo, illustrated boards, 2s.
FROM THE BOSOM OF THE DEEP. Post 8vo, illustrated boards, 2s.
MAID MARIAN AND ROBIN HOOD: A Romance of Old Sherwood Forest. With
12 Illustrations by Stanley L. Wood. Crown 8vo, cloth extra, 3s. 6d.

MURRAY (D. CHRISTIE), NOVELS BY.
Crown 8vo, cloth extra, 3s. 6d. each; post 8vo, illustrated boards, 2s. each.

A LIFE'S ATONEMENT.	WAY OF THE WORLD	BY THE GATE OF THE SEA.
JOSEPH'S COAT.	A MODEL FATHER.	A BIT OF HUMAN NATURE.
COALS OF FIRE.	OLD BLAZER'S HERO.	FIRST PERSON SINGULAR.
VAL STRANGE.	HEARTS.	CYNIC FORTUNE.	BOB MARTIN'S LITTLE

Crown 8vo, cloth extra, 3s. 6d. each.   [GIRL.
TIME'S REVENGES. | A WASTED CRIME. | IN DIREST PERIL. [Shortly.
THE MAKING OF A NOVELIST: An Experiment in Autobiography. With a
Collotype Portrait and Vignette. Crown 8vo, Irish linen, 6s.

MURRAY (D. CHRISTIE) & HENRY HERMAN, WORKS BY.
Crown 8vo, cloth extra, 3s. 6d. each; post 8vo, illustrated boards, 2s. each.
ONE TRAVELLER RETURNS. | PAUL JONES'S ALIAS. | THE BISHOPS' BIBLE.

MURRAY (HENRY), NOVELS BY. Post 8vo, illust. bds., 2s. ea.; cl., 2s. 6d. ea.
A GAME OF BLUFF. | A SONG OF SIXPENCE.

NEWBOLT.—TAKEN FROM THE ENEMY. By Henry Newbolt.
Fcap. 8vo, cloth boards, 1s. 6d.

NISBET (HUME), BOOKS BY.
"BAIL UP!" Crown 8vo, cloth extra, 3s. 6d.; post 8vo, illustrated boards, 2s.
DR. BERNARD ST. VINCENT. Post 8vo, illustrated boards. 2s.
LESSONS IN ART. With 21 Illustrations. Crown 8vo, cloth extra, 2s. 6d.
WHERE ART BEGINS. With 27 Illusts. Square 8vo, cloth extra, 7s. 6d.

NORRIS.—ST. ANN'S : A Novel. By W. E. Norris. Cr. 8vo, 3s. 6d. [Shortly.

O'HANLON (ALICE), NOVELS BY. Post 8vo, illustrated boards, 2s. each.
THE UNFORESEEN. | CHANCE? OR FATE?

OHNET (GEORGES), NOVELS BY. Post 8vo, illustrated boards, 2s. each.
DOCTOR RAMEAU. | A LAST LOVE.
A WEIRD GIFT. Crown 8vo, cloth, 3s. 6d., post 8vo, picture boards, 2s.

OLIPHANT (MRS.), NOVELS BY. Post 8vo, illustrated boards, 2s. each.
THE PRIMROSE PATH. | WHITELADIES.
THE GREATEST HEIRESS IN ENGLAND.

O'REILLY (HARRINGTON).—LIFE AMONG THE AMERICAN IN-
DIANS: Fifty Years on the Trail. 100 Illusts. by P. Frenzeny. Crown 8vo, 3s. 6d.

O'REILLY (MRS.).—PHŒBE'S FORTUNES. Post 8vo, illust. bds., 2s.

OUIDA, NOVELS BY. Cr. 8vo, cl., **3s. 6d.** each; post 8vo. illust. bds., **2s.** each.

HELD IN BONDAGE.	FOLLE-FARINE.	MOTHS.	PIPISTRELLO.
TRICOTRIN.	A DOG OF FLANDERS.	A VILLAGE COMMUNE.
STRATHMORE.	PASCAREL.	SIGNA.	IN MAREMMA.
CHANDOS.	TWO LITTLE WOODEN	BIMBI.	SYRLIN.
CECIL CASTLEMAINE'S	SHOES.	WANDA.
GAGE.	IN A WINTER CITY.	FRESCOES.	OTHMAR.
UNDER TWO FLAGS.	ARIADNE.	PRINCESS NAPRAXINE.
PUCK.	IDALIA.	FRIENDSHIP.	GUILDEROY.	RUFFINO.

Square 8vo, cloth extra, **5s.** each.

BIMBI. With Nine Illustrations by EDMUND H. GARRETT.
A DOG OF FLANDERS, &c. With Six Illustrations by EDMUND H. GARRETT.
SANTA BARBARA. &c. Square 8vo, cloth, **6s.**; crown 8vo, cloth, **3s. 6d.**; post 8vo, illustrated boards, **2s.**
TWO OFFENDERS. Square 8vo, cloth extra, **6s.**; crown 8vo, cloth extra, **3s. 6d.**
WISDOM, WIT, AND PATHOS, selected from the Works of OUIDA by F. SYDNEY MORRIS. Post 8vo, cloth extra, **5s.** CHEAP EDITION, illustrated boards, **2s.**

PAGE (H. A.), WORKS BY.
THOREAU: His Life and Aims. With Portrait. Post 8vo, cloth limp, **2s. 6d.**
ANIMAL ANECDOTES. Arranged on a New Principle. Crown 8vo, cloth extra, **5s.**

PASCAL'S PROVINCIAL LETTERS. A New Translation, with Historical Introduction and Notes by T. M'CRIE, D.D. Post 8vo, cloth limp, **2s.**

PAUL.—GENTLE AND SIMPLE. By MARGARET A. PAUL. With Frontispiece by HELEN PATERSON Crown 8vo, cloth, **3s. 6d.**; post 8vo, illust. boards, **2s.**

PAYN (JAMES), NOVELS BY.
Crown 8vo, cloth extra, **3s. 6d.** each; post 8vo, illustrated boards, **2s.** each.

LOST SIR MASSINGBERD.	A GRAPE FROM A THORN.
WALTER'S WORD.	FROM EXILE.	HOLIDAY TASKS.
LESS BLACK THAN WE'RE	THE CANON'S WARD.
PAINTED.	THE TALK OF THE TOWN.
BY PROXY.	FOR CASH ONLY.	GLOW-WORM TALES.
HIGH SPIRITS.	THE MYSTERY OF MIRBRIDGE.
UNDER ONE ROOF.	THE WORD AND THE WILL.
A CONFIDENTIAL AGENT.	THE BURNT MILLION.

Post 8vo, illustrated boards, **2s.** each.

HUMOROUS STORIES.	FOUND DEAD.
THE FOSTER BROTHERS.	GWENDOLINE'S HARVEST.
THE FAMILY SCAPEGRACE.	A MARINE RESIDENCE.
MARRIED BENEATH HIM.	MIRK ABBEY.	SOME PRIVATE VIEWS.
BENTINCK'S TUTOR.	NOT WOOED, BUT WON.
A PERFECT TREASURE.	TWO HUNDRED POUNDS REWARD.
A COUNTY FAMILY.	THE BEST OF HUSBANDS.
LIKE FATHER, LIKE SON.	HALVES.
A WOMAN'S VENGEANCE.	FALLEN FORTUNES.
CARLYON'S YEAR. CECIL'S TRYST.	WHAT HE COST HER.
MURPHY'S MASTER.	KIT: A MEMORY.
AT HER MERCY.	A PRINCE OF THE BLOOD.
THE CLYFFARDS OF CLYFFE.	SUNNY STORIES.

Crown 8vo, cloth extra, **3s. 6d.** each.
A TRYING PATIENT, &c. With a Frontispiece by STANLEY L. WOOD.
IN PERIL AND PRIVATION: Stories of MARINE ADVENTURE. With 17 Illusts.
NOTES FROM THE "NEWS." Crown 8vo, portrait cover, **1s.**; cloth, **1s. 6d.**

PENNELL (H. CHOLMONDELEY), WORKS BY. Post 8vo, cl., **2s. 6d.** each.
PUCK ON PEGASUS. With Illustrations.
PEGASUS RE-SADDLED. With Ten full-page Illustrations by G. DU MAURIER.
THE MUSES OF MAYFAIR. Vers de Société, Selected by H. C. PENNELL.

PHELPS (E. STUART), WORKS BY. Post 8vo **1s.** each; cloth **1s. 6d.** each.
BEYOND THE GATES. | OLD MAID'S PARADISE. | BURGLARS IN PARADISE.
JACK THE FISHERMAN. Illustrated by C. W. REED. Cr. 8vo, **1s.**; cloth, **1s. 6d.**

PIRKIS (C. L.), NOVELS BY.
TROOPING WITH CROWS. Fcap. 8vo, picture cover, **1s.**
LADY LOVELACE. Post 8vo, illustrated boards, **2s.**

PLANCHÉ (J. R.), WORKS BY.
THE PURSUIVANT OF ARMS. With Six Plates, and 209 Illusts. Cr. 8vo, cl. **7s. 6d.**
SONGS AND POEMS, 1819-1879. Introduction by Mrs. MACKARNESS. Cr. 8vo cl., **6s.**

PLUTARCH'S LIVES OF ILLUSTRIOUS MEN. With Notes and Life of Plutarch by J. and WM. LANGHORNE. Portraits. Two Vols., demy 8vo, 10s. 6d.

POE'S (EDGAR ALLAN) CHOICE WORKS, in Prose and Poetry. Introduction by CHAS. BAUDELAIRE, Portrait, and Facsimiles. Cr. 8vo, cloth, 7s. 6d.
THE MYSTERY OF MARIE ROGET, &c. Post 8vo, illustrated boards, 2s.

POPE'S POETICAL WORKS. Post 8vo, cloth limp. 2s.

PRAED (MRS. CAMPBELL), NOVELS BY. Post 8vo, illust. bds., 2s. ea.
THE ROMANCE OF A STATION. | THE SOUL OF COUNTESS ADRIAN.
Crown 8vo, cloth, 3s. 6d. each
OUTLAW AND LAWMAKER. | CHRISTINA CHARD. [Shortly.

PRICE (E. C.), NOVELS BY.
Crown 8vo, cloth extra, 3s. 6d. each; post 8vo, illustrated boards, 2s. each.
VALENTINA. | THE FOREIGNERS. | MRS. LANCASTER'S RIVAL.
GERALD. Post 8vo, illustrated boards, 2s.

PRINCESS OLGA.—RADNA. By Princess OLGA. Crown 8vo, cloth extra, 6s.

PROCTOR (RICHARD A., B.A.), WORKS BY.
FLOWERS OF THE SKY. With 55 Illusts. Small crown 8vo, cloth extra, 3s. 6d.
EASY STAR LESSONS. With Star Maps for Every Night in the Year. Cr. 8vo, 6s.
FAMILIAR SCIENCE STUDIES. Crown 8vo, cloth extra, 6s.
SATURN AND ITS SYSTEM. With 13 Steel Plates. Demy 8vo, cloth ex., 10s. 6d.
MYSTERIES OF TIME AND SPACE. With Illustrations. Cr. 8vo, cloth extra, 6s.
THE UNIVERSE OF SUNS. With numerous Illustrations. Cr. 8vo, cloth ex., 6s.
WAGES AND WANTS OF SCIENCE WORKERS. Crown 8vo, 1s. 6d.

PRYCE.—MISS MAXWELL'S AFFECTIONS. By RICHARD PRYCE. Frontispiece by HAL LUDLOW. Cr. 8vo, cl., 3s. 6d. ; post 8vo, illust. boards., 2s.

RAMBOSSON.—POPULAR ASTRONOMY. By J. RAMBOSSON, Laureate of the Institute of France. With numerous Illusts. Crown 8vo, cloth extra. 7s. 6d.

RANDOLPH.—AUNT ABIGAIL DYKES: A Novel. By Lt.-Colonel GEORGE RANDOLPH, U.S.A. Crown 8vo, cloth extra, 7s. 6d.

READE (CHARLES), NOVELS BY.
Crown 8vo, cloth extra, illustrated, 3s. 6d. each; post 8vo, illust. bds., 2s. each.
PEG WOFFINGTON. Illustrated by S. L. FILDES, R.A.—Also a POCKET EDITION, set in New Type, in Elzevir style, fcap. 8vo, half-leather, 2s. 6d.—And a Cheap POPULAR EDITION of PEG WOFFINGTON and CHRISTIE JOHNSTONE, the two Stories in One Volume, medium 8vo, 6d. ; cloth, 1s.
CHRISTIE JOHNSTONE. Illustrated by WILLIAM SMALL.—Also a POCKET EDITION, set in New Type, in Elzevir style, fcap. 8vo, half-leather, 2s. 6d.
IT IS NEVER TOO LATE TO MEND. Illustrated by G. J. PINWELL.—Also a Cheap POPULAR EDITION, medium 8vo, portrait cover. 6d. ; cloth, 1s.
COURSE OF TRUE LOVE NEVER DID RUN SMOOTH. Illust HELEN PATERSON.
THE AUTOBIOGRAPHY OF A THIEF, &c. Illustrated by MATT STRETCH.
LOVE ME LITTLE, LOVE ME LONG. Illustrated by M. ELLEN EDWARDS.
THE DOUBLE MARRIAGE. Illusts. by Sir JOHN GILBERT, R.A., and C. KEENE.
THE CLOISTER AND THE HEARTH. Illustrated by CHARLES KEENE.—Also a CHEAP POPULAR EDITION, medium 8vo, 6d. ; cloth, 1s.
HARD CASH. Illustrated by F. W. LAWSON.
GRIFFITH GAUNT. Illustrated by S. L. FILDES, R.A., and WILLIAM SMALL.
FOUL PLAY. Illustrated by GEORGE DU MAURIER.
PUT YOURSELF IN HIS PLACE. Illustrated by ROBERT BARNES.
A TERRIBLE TEMPTATION. Illustrated by EDWARD HUGHES and A. W. COOPER.
A SIMPLETON. Illustrated by KATE CRAUFURD.
THE WANDERING HEIR. Illust. by H. PATERSON, S. L. FILDES, C. GREEN, &c.
A WOMAN-HATER. Illustrated by THOMAS COULDERY.
SINGLEHEART AND DOUBLEFACE. Illustrated by P. MACNAB.
GOOD STORIES OF MEN AND OTHER ANIMALS. Illust. by E. A. ABBEY, &c.
THE JILT, and other Stories. Illustrated by JOSEPH NASH.
A PERILOUS SECRET. Illustrated by FRED. BARNARD.
READIANA. With a Steel-plate Portrait of CHARLES READE.
BIBLE CHARACTERS: Studies of David, Paul, &c. Fcap. 8vo, leatherette, 1s.
THE CLOISTER AND THE HEARTH. With an Introduction by WALTER BESANT. Elzevir Edition. 4 vols., post 8vo, each with Front., cl. ex., gilt top, 14s. the set.
SELECTIONS FROM THE WORKS OF CHARLES READE. Crown 8vo, with Portrait, buckram, 6s. ; post 8vo, cloth limp, 2s. 6d.

RIVES.—BARBARA DERING. By AMÉLIE RIVES, Author of "The Quick or the Dead?" Crown 8vo, cloth extra, 3s. 6d. ; post 8vo, illust. bds., 2s.

RIDDELL (MRS. J. H.), NOVELS BY.
Crown 8vo, cloth extra, **3s. 6d.** each; post 8vo, illustrated boards, **2s.** each.
THE PRINCE OF WALES'S GARDEN PARTY. | WEIRD STORIES.
Post 8vo, illustrated boards, **2s.** each.
THE UNINHABITED HOUSE. | HER MOTHER'S DARLING.
MYSTERY IN PALACE GARDENS. | THE NUN'S CURSE.
FAIRY WATER. | IDLE TALES.

RIMMER (ALFRED), WORKS BY. Square 8vo, cloth gilt, **7s. 6d.** each.
OUR OLD COUNTRY TOWNS. With 55 Illustrations.
RAMBLES ROUND ETON AND HARROW. With 50 Illustrations.
ABOUT ENGLAND WITH DICKENS. With 58 Illusts. by C. A. VANDERHOOF, &c.

ROBINSON CRUSOE. By DANIEL DEFOE. (MAJOR'S EDITION.) With
37 Illustrations by GEORGE CRUIKSHANK. Post 8vo, half-bound, **2s.**

ROBINSON (F. W.), NOVELS BY.
WOMEN ARE STRANGE. Post 8vo, illustrated boards, **2s.**
THE HANDS OF JUSTICE. Cr. 8vo, cloth ex., **3s. 6d.**; post 8vo, illust. bds., **2s.**

ROBINSON (PHIL), WORKS BY. Crown 8vo, cloth extra, **6s.** each.
THE POETS' BIRDS. | THE POETS' BEASTS.
THE POETS AND NATURE: REPTILES, FISHES, AND INSECTS.

ROCHEFOUCAULD'S MAXIMS AND MORAL REFLECTIONS. With
Notes, and an Introductory Essay by SAINTE-BEUVE. Post 8vo, cloth limp, **2s.**

ROLL OF BATTLE ABBEY, THE : A List of the Principal Warriors
who came from Normandy with William the Conqueror. Handsomely printed, **5s.**

ROWLEY (HON. HUGH), WORKS BY. Post 8vo, cloth, **2s. 6d.** each.
PUNIANA: RIDDLES AND JOKES. With numerous Illustrations.
MORE PUNIANA. Profusely Illustrated.

RUNCIMAN (JAMES), STORIES BY. Post 8vo, bds., **2s.** ea.; cl., **2s. 6d.** ea.
SKIPPERS AND SHELLBACKS. | GRACE BALMAIGN'S SWEETHEART.
SCHOOLS AND SCHOLARS.

RUSSELL (W. CLARK), BOOKS AND NOVELS BY :
Cr. 8vo, cloth extra, **6s.** each; post 8vo, illust. boards, **2s.** each; cloth limp, **2s. 6d.** ea.
ROUND THE GALLEY-FIRE. | A BOOK FOR THE HAMMOCK.
IN THE MIDDLE WATCH. | MYSTERY OF THE "OCEAN STAR."
A VOYAGE TO THE CAPE. | THE ROMANCE OF JENNY HARLOWE.
Cr. 8vo, cl. extra, **3s. 6d.** ea.; post 8vo, illust. boards, **2s.** ea.; cloth limp, **2s. 6d.** ea.
AN OCEAN TRAGEDY. | MY SHIPMATE LOUISE.
ALONE ON A WIDE WIDE SEA.
ON THE FO'K'SLE HEAD. Post 8vo, illust. boards, **2s.**; cloth limp, **2s. 6d.**
THE GOOD SHIP "MOHOCK." Two Vols., cr. 8vo, cloth, **10s.** net. [*Shortly.*

RUSSELL (DORA).—A COUNTRY SWEETHEART. Three Vols.,
crown 8vo, **15s.** net.

SAINT AUBYN (ALAN), NOVELS BY.
Crown 8vo, cloth extra, **3s. 6d.** each; post 8vo, illust. boards, **2s.** each.
A FELLOW OF TRINITY. Note by OLIVER WENDELL HOLMES and Frontispiece.
THE JUNIOR DEAN. | THE MASTER OF ST. BENEDICT'S.
Fcap. 8vo, cloth boards, **1s. 6d.** each.
THE OLD MAID'S SWEETHEART. | MODEST LITTLE SARA.
Crown 8vo, cloth extra, **3s. 6d.** each.
TO HIS OWN MASTER. | IN THE FACE OF THE WORLD. [*Shortly.*

SALA (G. A.).—GASLIGHT AND DAYLIGHT. Post 8vo, boards, 2s.

SANSON.—SEVEN GENERATIONS OF EXECUTIONERS : Memoirs
of the Sanson Family (1688 to 1847). Crown 8vo, cloth extra, **3s. 6d.**

SAUNDERS (JOHN), NOVELS BY.
Crown 8vo, cloth, **3s. 6d.** each; post 8vo, illustrated boards, **2s.** each.
GUY WATERMAN. | THE LION IN THE PATH. | THE TWO DREAMERS.
BOUND TO THE WHEEL. Crown 8vo, cloth extra, **3s. 6d.**

SAUNDERS (KATHARINE), NOVELS BY.
Crown 8vo, cloth extra, **3s. 6d.** each; post 8vo, illustrated boards, **2s.** each.
MARGARET AND ELIZABETH. | HEART SALVAGE.
THE HIGH MILLS. | SEBASTIAN.
JOAN MERRYWEATHER. Post 8vo, illustrated boards, **2s.**
GIDEON'S ROCK. Crown 8vo, cloth extra, **3s. 6d.**

SCOTLAND YARD, Past and Present : Experiences of 37 Years. By Ex-Chief Inspector CAVANAGH. Post 8vo, illustrated boards, 2s.; cloth, 2s. 6d.

SECRET OUT, THE: One Thousand Tricks with Cards; with Entertaining Experiments in Drawing-room or "White Magic." By W. H. CREMER. With 300 Illustrations. Crown 8vo, cloth extra, 4s. 6d.

SEGUIN (L. G.), WORKS BY.
THE COUNTRY OF THE PASSION PLAY (OBERAMMERGAU) and the Highlands of Bavaria. With Map and 37 Illustrations. Crown 8vo, cloth extra, 3s. 6d.
WALKS IN ALGIERS. With 2 Maps and 16 Illusts. Crown 8vo, cloth extra, 6s.

SENIOR (WM.).—BY STREAM AND SEA. Post 8vo, cloth, 2s. 6d.

SERGEANT (A.).—DR. ENDICOTT'S EXPERIMENT. 2 vols., 10s. net.

SHAKESPEARE FOR CHILDREN: LAMB'S TALES FROM SHAKE-
SPEARE. With Illusts., coloured and plain, by J. MOYR SMITH. Cr. 4to, 3s. 6d.

SHARP.—CHILDREN OF TO-MORROW: A Novel. By WILLIAM SHARP. Crown 8vo, cloth extra, 6s.

SHELLEY.—THE COMPLETE WORKS IN VERSE AND PROSE OF
PERCY BYSSHE SHELLEY. Edited, Prefaced, and Annotated by R. HERNE SHEPHERD. Five Vols., crown 8vo, cloth boards, 3s. 6d. each.
POETICAL WORKS, in Three Vols.:
Vol. I. Introduction by the Editor; Posthumous Fragments of Margaret Nicholson; Shelley's Correspondence with Stockdale; The Wandering Jew; Queen Mab, with the Notes; Alastor, and other Poems; Rosalind and Helen; Prometheus Unbound; Adonais, &c.
Vol. II. Laon and Cythna; The Cenci; Julian and Maddalo; Swellfoot the Tyrant; The Witch of Atlas; Epipsychidion; Hellas.
Vol. III. Posthumous Poems; The Masque of Anarchy; and other Pieces.
PROSE WORKS, in Two Vols.:
Vol. I. The Two Romances of Zastrozzi and St. Irvyne; the Dublin and Marlow Pamphlets; A Refutation of Deism; Letters to Leigh Hunt, and some Minor Writings and Fragments.
Vol. II. The Essays; Letters from Abroad; Translations and Fragments. Edited by Mrs. SHELLEY. With a Bibliography of Shelley, and an Index of the Prose Works.

SHERARD (R. H.).—ROGUES: A Novel. Crown 8vo, 1s.; cloth, 1s. 6d.

SHERIDAN (GENERAL). — PERSONAL MEMOIRS OF GENERAL
P. H. SHERIDAN. With Portraits and Facsimiles. Two Vols., demy 8vo, cloth, 24s.

SHERIDAN'S (RICHARD BRINSLEY) COMPLETE WORKS. With
Life and Anecdotes. Including his Dramatic Writings, his Works in Prose and Poetry, Translations, Speeches and Jokes. 10 Illusts. Cr. 8vo, hf.-bound, 7s. 6d.
THE RIVALS, THE SCHOOL FOR SCANDAL, and other Plays. Post 8vo, printed on laid paper and half-bound. 2s.
SHERIDAN'S COMEDIES: THE RIVALS and THE SCHOOL FOR SCANDAL.
Edited, with an Introduction and Notes to each Play, and a Biographical Sketch, by BRANDER MATTHEWS. With Illustrations. Demy 8vo, half-parchment, 12s. 6d.

SIDNEY'S (SIR PHILIP) COMPLETE POETICAL WORKS, including all those in "Arcadia." With Portrait, Memorial-Introduction, Notes, &c. by the Rev. A.B. GROSART, D.D. Three Vols., crown 8vo, cloth boards, 18s.

SIGNBOARDS: Their History. With Anecdotes of Famous Taverns and Remarkable Characters. By JACOB LARWOOD and JOHN CAMDEN HOTTEN. With Coloured Frontispiece and 94 Illustrations. Crown 8vo, cloth extra, 7s. 6d.

SIMS (GEO. R.), WORKS BY. Post 8vo, illust. bds., 2s. ea.; cl. limp, 2s. 6d. ea.
ROGUES AND VAGABONDS. | MARY JANE MARRIED.
THE RING O' BELLS. | TALES OF TO-DAY.
MARY JANE'S MEMOIRS. | DRAMAS OF LIFE. With 60 Illustrations.
TINKLETOP'S CRIME. With a Frontispiece by MAURICE GREIFFENHAGEN.
ZEPH: A Circus Story, &c. | MY TWO WIVES.
MEMOIRS OF A LANDLADY. | SCENES FROM THE SHOW. [Shortly.
Crown 8vo, picture cover, 1s. each; cloth, 1s. 6d. each.
HOW THE POOR LIVE; and HORRIBLE LONDON.
THE DAGONET RECITER AND READER: being Readings and Recitations in Prose and Verse, selected from his own Works by GEORGE R. SIMS.
THE CASE OF GEORGE CANDLEMAS. | DAGONET DITTIES.

SISTER DORA: A Biography. By MARGARET LONSDALE. With Four Illustrations. Demy 8vo, picture cover, 4d.; cloth, 6d.

SKETCHLEY.—A MATCH IN THE DARK, By ARTHUR SKETCHLEY,
Post 8vo, illustrated boards, 2s.

SLANG DICTIONARY (THE): Etymological, Historical, and Anecdotal. Crown 8vo, cloth extra, 6s. 6d.

SMITH (J. MOYR). WORKS BY.
THE PRINCE OF ARGOLIS. With 130 Illusts. Post 8vo, cloth extra. 3s. 6d.
THE WOOING OF TH; WATER WITCH. Illustrated. Post 8vo, cloth, 6s.

SOCIETY IN LONDON. Crown 8vo, 1s. ; cloth, 1s. 6d.

SOCIETY IN PARIS: The Upper Ten Thousand. A Series of Letters from Count PAUL VASILI to a Young French Diplomat. Crown 8vo. cloth, 6s.

SOMERSET. — SONGS OF ADIEU. By Lord HENRY SOMERSET. Small 4to, Japanese vellum, 6s.

SPALDING.—ELIZABETHAN DEMONOLOGY: An Essay on the Belief in the Existence of Devils. By T. A. SPALDING, LL.B. Crown 8vo, cloth extra, 5s.

SPEIGHT (T. W.), NOVELS BY.
Post 8vo, illustrated boards, 2s. each.

THE MYSTERIES OF HERON DYKE.	THE GOLDEN HOOP.
BY DEVIOUS WAYS, &c.	BACK TO LIFE.
HOODWINKED; and THE SANDY-	THE LOUDWATER TRAGEDY,
CROFT MYSTERY.	BURGO'S ROMANCE.

Post 8vo, cloth limp, 1s. 6d. each.

A BARREN TITLE.	WIFE OR NO WIFE?

THE SANDYCROFT MYSTERY. Crown 8vo, picture cover, 1s.
A SECRET OF THE SEA. Crown 8vo, cloth extra, 3s. 6d.

SPENSER FOR CHILDREN. By M. H. TOWRY. With Illustrations by WALTER J. MORGAN. Crown 4to, cloth extra, 3s. 6d.

STARRY HEAVENS (THE): A POETICAL BIRTHDAY BOOK. Royal 16mo, cloth extra, 2s. 6d.

STAUNTON.—THE LAWS AND PRACTICE OF CHESS. With an Analysis of the Openings. By HOWARD STAUNTON. Edited by ROBERT B. WORMALD. Crown 8vo, cloth extra, 5s.

STEDMAN (E. C.), WORKS BY. Crown 8vo. cloth extra, 9s. each.

VICTORIAN POETS.	THE POETS OF AMERICA.

STERNDALE. — THE AFGHAN KNIFE: A Novel. By ROBERT ARMITAGE STERNDALE. Cr. 8vo. cloth extra, 3s. 6d.; post 8vo, illust. boards, 2s.

STEVENSON (R. LOUIS), WORKS BY. Post 8vo, cl. limp, 2s. 6d. each.
TRAVELS WITH A DONKEY. Seventh Edit. With a Frontis. by WALTER CRANE.
AN INLAND VOYAGE. Fourth Edition. With a Frontispiece by WALTER CRANE.

Crown 8vo, buckram, gilt top, 6s. each.
FAMILIAR STUDIES OF MEN AND BOOKS. Sixth Edition.
THE MERRY MEN. Third Edition. | UNDERWOODS: Poems. Fifth Edition.
MEMORIES AND PORTRAITS. Third Edition.
VIRGINIBUS PUERISQUE, and other Papers. Seventh Edition. | BALLADS.
ACROSS THE PLAINS, with other Memories and Essays.
NEW ARABIAN NIGHTS. Eleventh Edition. Crown 8vo, buckram, gilt top, 6s.; post 8vo, illustrated boards, 2s.
THE SUICIDE CLUB; and THE RAJAH'S DIAMOND. (From NEW ARABIAN NIGHTS.) With 8 Illustrations by W. J. HENNESSY. Crown 8vo, cloth, 5s.
PRINCE OTTO. Sixth Edition. Post 8vo, illustrated boards, 2s.
FATHER DAMIEN: An Open Letter to the Rev. Dr. Hyde. Second Edition. Crown 8vo, hand-made and brown paper, 1s.
THE EDINBURGH EDITION OF THE WORKS OF ROBERT LOUIS STEVENSON. 20 Vols., demy 8vo, price £12 10s. net. Prospectuses and Specimens of this Edition (which is limited to 1,000 copies) may be had from any Bookseller. The Vols. will appear at the rate of one a month. beginning with Oct. 1894.

STODDARD. — SUMMER CRUISING IN THE SOUTH SEAS. By C. WARREN STODDARD. Illustrated by WALLIS MACKAY. Cr. 8vo, cl. extra, 3s. 6d.

STORIES FROM FOREIGN NOVELISTS. With Notices by HELEN and ALICE ZIMMERN. Crown 8vo, cloth extra, 3s. 6d.; post 8vo, illustrated boards, 2s.

STRANGE MANUSCRIPT (A) FOUND IN A COPPER CYLINDER. Cr. 8vo, cloth extra, with 19 Illusts. by GILBERT GAUL, 5s.; post 8vo, illust. bds., 2s.

STRANGE SECRETS. Told by CONAN DOYLE, PERCY FITZGERALD, FLORENCE MARRYAT, &c. Post 8vo, illustrated boards, 2s.

STRUTT'S SPORTS AND PASTIMES OF THE PEOPLE OF ENGLAND; including the Rural and Domestic Recreations, May Games, Mummeries, Shows, &c., from the Earliest Period to the Present Time. Edited by WILLIAM HONE. With 140 Illustrations. Crown 8vo, cloth extra, 7s. 6d.

SWIFT'S (DEAN) CHOICE WORKS, in Prose and Verse. With Memoir, Portrait, and Facsimiles of the Maps in "Gulliver's Travels." Cr. 8vo. cl., 7s. 6d.
GULLIVER'S TRAVELS, and A TALE OF A TUB. Post 8vo, half-bound, 2s.
JONATHAN SWIFT: A Study. By J. CHURTON COLLINS. Crown 8vo, cloth extra, 8s.

SWINBURNE (ALGERNON C.), WORKS BY.

SELECTIONS FROM POETICAL WORKS OF A. C. SWINBURNE. Fcap. 8vo, 6s.
ATALANTA IN CALYDON. Crown 8vo, 6s.
CHASTELARD: A Tragedy. Crown 8vo, 7s.
POEMS AND BALLADS. FIRST SERIES. Crown 8vo or fcap. 8vo, 9s.
POEMS AND BALLADS. SECOND SERIES. Crown 8vo or fcap. 8vo, 9s.
POEMS & BALLADS. THIRD SERIES. Cr. 8vo, 7s.
SONGS BEFORE SUNRISE. Crown 8vo, 10s. 6d.
BOTHWELL: A Tragedy. Crown 8vo, 12s. 6d.
SONGS OF TWO NATIONS. Crown 8vo, 6s.
GEORGE CHAPMAN. (See Vol. II. of G. CHAPMAN'S Works.) Crown 8vo, 6s.
ESSAYS AND STUDIES. Crown 8vo, 12s.
ERECHTHEUS: A Tragedy. Crown 8vo, 6s.

A NOTE ON CHARLOTTE BRONTE. Cr. 8vo, 6s.
SONGS OF THE SPRINGTIDES. Crown 8vo, 6s.
STUDIES IN SONG. Crown 8vo, 7s.
MARY STUART: A Tragedy. Crown 8vo, 8s.
TRISTRAM OF LYONESSE. Crown 8vo, 9s.
A CENTURY OF ROUNDELS. Small 4to, 8s.
A MIDSUMMER HOLIDAY. Crown 8vo, 7s.
MARINO FALIERO: A Tragedy. Crown 8vo, 6s.
A STUDY OF VICTOR HUGO. Crown 8vo, 6s.
MISCELLANIES. Crown 8vo, 12s.
LOCRINE: A Tragedy. Crown 8vo, 6s.
A STUDY OF BEN JONSON. Crown 8vo, 7s.
THE SISTERS: A Tragedy. Crown 8vo, 6s.
ASTROPHEL, &c. Crown 8vo, 7s.
STUDIES IN PROSE AND POETRY. Crown 8vo, 9s.

SYNTAX'S (DR.) THREE TOURS: In Search of the Picturesque, in Search of Consolation, and in Search of a Wife. With ROWLANDSON'S Coloured Illustrations, and Life of the Author by J. C. HOTTEN. Crown 8vo, cloth extra, 7s. 6d.

TAINE'S HISTORY OF ENGLISH LITERATURE. Translated by HENRY VAN LAUN. Four Vols., small demy 8vo, cl. bds., 30s.—POPULAR EDITION, Two Vols., large crown 8vo, cloth extra. 15s.

TAYLOR'S (BAYARD) DIVERSIONS OF THE ECHO CLUB: Burlesques of Modern Writers. Post 8vo, cloth limp, 2s.

TAYLOR (DR. J. E., F.L.S.), WORKS BY. Crown 8vo, cloth, 5s. each.
THE SAGACITY AND MORALITY OF PLANTS: A Sketch of the Life and Conduct of the Vegetable Kingdom. With a Coloured Frontispiece and 100 Illustrations.
OUR COMMON BRITISH FOSSILS, and Where to Find Them. 331 Illustrations.
THE PLAYTIME NATURALIST. With 366 Illustrations.

TAYLOR'S (TOM) HISTORICAL DRAMAS. Containing " Clancarty," "Jeanne Darc," "'Twixt Axe and Crown," "The Fool's Revenge," "Arkwright's Wife," "Anne Boleyn," "Plot and Passion." Crown 8vo, cloth extra, 7s. 6d.
. The Plays may also be had separately, at 1s. each.

TENNYSON (LORD): A Biographical Sketch. By H. J. JENNINGS. With a Photograph-Portrait. Crown 8vo, cloth extra, 6s.—Cheap Edition, post 8vo, portrait cover, 1s.; cloth, 1s. 6d.

THACKERAYANA: Notes and Anecdotes. Illustrated by Hundreds of Sketches by WILLIAM MAKEPEACE THACKERAY. Crown 8vo, cloth extra, 7s. 6d.

THAMES.—A NEW PICTORIAL HISTORY OF THE THAMES. By A. S. KRAUSSE. With 340 Illustrations Post 8vo, 1s.; cloth, 1s. 6d.

THIERS.—HISTORY OF THE CONSULATE & EMPIRE OF FRANCE UNDER NAPOLEON. By A. THIERS. Translated by D. FORBES CAMPBELL and JOHN STEBBING. With 36 Steel Plates. 12 vols., demy 8vo, cloth extra, 12s. each.

THOMAS (BERTHA), NOVELS BY. Cr. 8vo, cl., 3s. 6d. ea.; post 8vo, 2s. ea.
THE VIOLIN-PLAYER. | PROUD MAISIE.
CRESSIDA. Post 8vo, illustrated boards, 2s.

THOMSON'S SEASONS, and CASTLE OF INDOLENCE. With Introduction by ALLAN CUNNINGHAM, and 48 Illustrations. Post 8vo, half-bound, 2s.

THORNBURY (WALTER), WORKS BY.
THE LIFE AND CORRESPONDENCE OF J. M. W. TURNER. With Illustrations in Colours. Crown 8vo, cloth extra, 7s. 6d.
Post 8vo, illustrated boards, 2s. each.
OLD STORIES RE-TOLD. | TALES FOR THE MARINES.

TIMBS (JOHN), WORKS BY. Crown 8vo, cloth extra, **7s. 6d.** each.
THE HISTORY OF CLUBS AND CLUB LIFE IN LONDON: Anecdotes of its
Famous Coffee-houses, Hostelries, and Taverns. With 42 Illustrations.
ENGLISH ECCENTRICS AND ECCENTRICITIES: Stories of Delusions, Impos-
tures, Sporting Scenes, Eccentric Artists, Theatrical Folk, &c. 48 Illustrations.

TROLLOPE (ANTHONY), NOVELS BY.
Crown 8vo, cloth extra, **3s. 6d.** each; post 8vo, illustrated boards. **2s.** each.
THE WAY WE LIVE NOW. | MR. SCARBOROUGH'S FAMILY.
FRAU FROHMANN. | MARION FAY. | THE LAND-LEAGUERS.
Post 8vo, illustrated boards, **2s.** each.
KEPT IN THE DARK. | AMERICAN SENATOR.
GOLDEN LION OF GRANPERE. | JOHN CALDIGATE.

TROLLOPE (FRANCES E.), NOVELS BY.
Crown 8vo, cloth extra, **3s. 6d.** each: post 8vo, illustrated boards, **2s.** each.
LIKE SHIPS UPON THE SEA. | MABEL'S PROGRESS. | ANNE FURNESS.

TROLLOPE (T. A.).—DIAMOND CUT DIAMOND. Post 8vo, illust. bds., **2s.**

**TROWBRIDGE.—FARNELL'S FOLLY: A Novel. By J. T. Trow-
BRIDGE.** Post 8vo, illustrated boards, **2s.**

**TYTLER (C. C. FRASER-).—MISTRESS JUDITH: A Novel. By
C. C. Fraser-Tytler.** Crown 8vo, cloth extra, **3s. 6d.**; post 8vo, illust. boards, **2s.**

TYTLER (SARAH), NOVELS BY.
Crown 8vo. cloth extra, **3s. 6d.** each; post 8vo, illustrated boards, **2s.** each.
THE BRIDE'S PASS. | BURIED DIAMONDS.
LADY BELL. | THE BLACKHALL GHOSTS.
Post 8vo, illustrated boards. **2s.** each.
WHAT SHE CAME THROUGH. | BEAUTY AND THE BEAST.
CITOYENNE JACQUELINE | DISAPPEARED. | NOBLESSE OBLIGE.
SAINT MUNGO'S CITY. | THE HUGUENOT FAMILY.

UNDERHILL.—WALTER BESANT: A Study. By John Underhill.
With Portraits. Crown 8vo, Irish linen, **6s.** [Shortly.

UPWARD.—THE QUEEN AGAINST OWEN. By Allen Upward.
With Frontispiece by J. S. Crompton. Crown 8vo, cloth extra, **3s. 6d.**

VASHTI AND ESTHER. By the Writer of "Belle's" Letters in *The
World.* Crown 8vo, cloth extra, **3s. 6d.**

VILLARI.—A DOUBLE BOND. By Linda Villari. Fcap. 8vo, **1s.**

**VIZETELLY (E. A.).—THE SCORPION: A Romance of Spain. With
a Frontispiece.** Crown 8vo, cloth extra, **3s. 6d.**

WALFORD (EDWARD, M.A.), WORKS BY.
WALFORD'S COUNTY FAMILIES OF THE UNITED KINGDOM (1895). Containing the Descent,
Birth, Marriage, Education, &c., of 12,000 Heads of Families, their Heirs, Offices, Addresses,
Clubs, &c. Royal 8vo, cloth gilt, **50s.**
WALFORD'S SHILLING PEERAGE (1895). Containing a List of the House of Lords, Scotch and
Irish Peers, &c. 32mo, cloth, **1s.**
WALFORD'S SHILLING BARONETAGE (1895). Containing a List of the Baronets of the United
Kingdom, Biographical Notices Addresses, &c. 32mo, cloth, **1s.**
WALFORD'S SHILLING KNIGHTAGE (1895). Containing a List of the Knights of the United
Kingdom, Biographical Notices. Addresses, &c. 32mo, cloth, **1s.**
WALFORD'S SHILLING HOUSE OF COMMONS (1895). Containing a List of all the Members of the
New Parliament, their Addresses Clubs, &c. 32mo, cloth, **1s.**
WALFORD'S COMPLETE PEERAGE, BARONETAGE, KNIGHTAGE, AND HOUSE OF COMMONS
(1895) Royal 32mo, cloth, gilt edges, **5s.** [Shortly.
TALES OF OUR GREAT FAMILIES. Crown 8vo, cloth extra, **3s. 6d.**

WALT WHITMAN, POEMS BY. Edited, with Introduction, by
William M. Rossetti. With Portrait. Cr. 8vo, hand-made paper and buckram, **6s.**

**WALTON AND COTTON'S COMPLETE ANGLER; or, The Con-
templative Man's Recreation,** by Izaak Walton; and Instructions how to Angle for a
Trout or Grayling in a clear Stream, by Charles Cotton. With Memoirs and Notes
by Sir Harris Nicolas, and 61 Illustrations. Crown 8vo, cloth antique, **7s. 6d.**

WARD (HERBERT), WORKS BY.
FIVE YEARS WITH THE CONGO CANNIBALS. With 92 Illustrations by the
Author, Victor Perard, and W. B. Davis. Third ed. Roy. 8vo, cloth ex., **14s.**
MY LIFE WITH STANLEY'S REAR GUARD. With a Map by F. S. Weller,
F.R.G.S. Post 8vo, **1s.**; cloth, **1s. 6d.**

WARNER.—A ROUNDABOUT JOURNEY. By CHARLES DUDLEY WARNER. Crown 8vo, cloth extra, 6s.

WARRANT TO EXECUTE CHARLES I. A Facsimile, with the 59 Signatures and Seals. Printed on paper 22 in. by 14 in. 2s.
WARRANT TO EXECUTE MARY QUEEN OF SCOTS. A Facsimile, including Queen Elizabeth's Signature and the Great Seal. 2s.

WASSERMANN (LILLIAS), NOVELS BY.
THE DAFFODILS. Crown 8vo, 1s.; cloth, 1s. 6d.
THE MARQUIS OF CARABAS. By AARON WATSON and LILLIAS WASSERMANN. Post 8vo, illustrated boards, 2s.

WEATHER, HOW TO FORETELL THE, WITH POCKET SPEC-TROSCOPE. By F. W. CORY. With 10 Illustrations. Cr. 8vo, 1s.; cloth, 1s. 6d.

WESTALL (William).—TRUST-MONEY. Post 8vo, illust. bds., 2s.

WHIST.—HOW TO PLAY SOLO WHIST. By ABRAHAM S. WILKS and CHARLES F. PARDON. New Edition. Post 8vo, cloth limp, 2s.

WHITE.—THE NATURAL HISTORY OF SELBORNE. By GILBERT WHITE, M.A. Post 8vo, printed on laid paper and half-bound, 2s.

WILLIAMS (W. MATTIEU, F.R.A.S.), WORKS BY.
SCIENCE IN SHORT CHAPTERS. Crown 8vo, cloth extra, 7s. 6d.
A SIMPLE TREATISE ON HEAT. With Illusts. Cr. 8vo, cloth limp, 2s. 6d.
THE CHEMISTRY OF COOKERY. Crown 8vo, cloth extra, 6s.
THE CHEMISTRY OF IRON AND STEEL MAKING. Crown 8vo, cloth extra, 9s.
A VINDICATION OF PHRENOLOGY. With Portrait and over 40 Illustrations. Demy 8vo, cloth extra, 12s. 6d.

WILLIAMSON (MRS. F. H.).—A CHILD WIDOW. Post 8vo, bds., 2s.

WILSON (DR. ANDREW, F.R.S.E.), WORKS BY.
CHAPTERS ON EVOLUTION. With 259 Illustrations. Cr. 8vo, cloth extra, 7s. 6d.
LEAVES FROM A NATURALIST'S NOTE-BOOK. Post 8vo, cloth limp, 2s. 6d.
LEISURE-TIME STUDIES. With Illustrations. Crown 8vo, cloth extra, 6s.
STUDIES IN LIFE AND SENSE. With numerous Illusts. Cr. 8vo, cl. ex., 6s.
COMMON ACCIDENTS: HOW TO TREAT THEM. Illusts. Cr. 8vo, 1s.; cl., 1s. 6d.
GLIMPSES OF NATURE. With 35 Illustrations. Crown 8vo, cloth extra, 3s. 6d.

WINTER (J. S.), STORIES BY. Post 8vo, illustrated boards, 2s. each; cloth limp, 2s. 6d. each.
CAVALRY LIFE. | REGIMENTAL LEGENDS.
A SOLDIER'S CHILDREN. With 34 Illustrations by E. G. THOMSON and E. STUART HARDY. Crown 8vo, cloth extra, 3s. 6d.

WISSMANN.—MY SECOND JOURNEY THROUGH EQUATORIAL AFRICA. By HERMANN VON WISSMANN. With 92 Illusts. Demy 8vo, 16s.

WOOD.—SABINA: A Novel. By Lady WOOD. Post 8vo, boards, 2s.

WOOD (H. F.), DETECTIVE STORIES BY. Post 8vo, boards, 2s. each.
PASSENGER FROM SCOTLAND YARD. | ENGLISHMAN OF THE RUE CAIN.

WOOLLEY.—RACHEL ARMSTRONG; or, Love and Theology. By CELIA PARKER WOOLLEY. Post 8vo, illustrated boards, 2s.; cloth, 2s. 6d.

WRIGHT (THOMAS), WORKS BY. Crown 8vo, cloth extra, 7s. 6d. each.
CARICATURE HISTORY OF THE GEORGES. With 400 Caricatures, Squibs, &c.
HISTORY OF CARICATURE AND OF THE GROTESQUE IN ART, LITERA-TURE, SCULPTURE, AND PAINTING. Illustrated by F. W. FAIRHOLT, F.S.A.

WYNMAN.—MY FLIRTATIONS. By MARGARET WYNMAN. With 13 Illustrations by J. BERNARD PARTRIDGE. Crown 8vo, cloth extra, 3s. 6d.

YATES (EDMUND), NOVELS BY. Post 8vo, illustrated boards, 2s. each.
LAND AT LAST. | THE FORLORN HOPE. | CASTAWAY.

ZOLA (EMILE), NOVELS BY. Crown 8vo, cloth extra, 3s. 6d. each.
THE DOWNFALL. Translated by E. A. VIZETELLY. Fourth Edition, Revised.
THE DREAM. Translated by ELIZA CHASE. With 8 Illustrations by JEANNIOT.
DOCTOR PASCAL. Translated by E. A. VIZETELLY. With Portrait of the Author.
MONEY. Translated by ERNEST A. VIZETELLY.
LOURDES. Translated by E. A. VIZETELLY.
EMILE ZOLA: A Biography. By R. H. SHERARD. With Portraits, Illustrations, and Facsimile Letter. Demy 8vo, cloth extra, 12s.

LISTS OF BOOKS CLASSIFIED IN SERIES.

. *For fuller cataloguing, see alphabetical arrangement, pp. 1–25.*

THE MAYFAIR LIBRARY. Post 8vo, cloth limp, 2s. 6d. per Volume.

A Journey Round My Room. By XAVIER DE MAISTRE.
Quips and Quiddities. By W. D. ADAMS.
The Agony Column of "The Times."
Melancholy Anatomised: Abridgment of " Burton's Anatomy of Melancholy."
Poetical Ingenuities. By W. T. DOBSON.
The Cupboard Papers. By FIN-BEC.
W. S. Gilbert's Plays. FIRST SERIES.
W. S. Gilbert's Plays. SECOND SERIES.
Songs of Irish Wit and Humour.
Animals and Masters. By Sir A. HELPS.
Social Pressure. By Sir A. HELPS.
Curiosities of Criticism. H. J. JENNINGS.
Holmes's Autocrat of the Breakfast-Table.
Pencil and Palette. By R. KEMPT.
Little Essays: from LAMB's Letters.

Forensic Anecdotes. By JACOB LARWOOD.
Theatrical Anecdotes. JACOB LARWOOD.
Jeux d'Esprit. Edited by HENRY S. LEIGH.
Witch Stories. By E. LYNN LINTON.
Ourselves. By E. LYNN LINTON.
Pastimes & Players. By R. MACGREGOR.
New Paul and Virginia. W.H.MALLOCK.
New Republic. By W. H. MALLOCK.
Puck on Pegasus. By H. C. PENNELL.
Pegasus Re-Saddled. By H. C. PENNELL.
Muses of Mayfair. Ed. H. C. PENNELL.
Thoreau: His Life & Aims. By H. A. PAGE.
Puniana. By Hon. HUGH ROWLEY.
More Puniana. By Hon. HUGH ROWLEY.
The Philosophy of Handwriting.
By Stream and Sea. By WM. SENIOR.
Leaves from a Naturalist's Note-Book. By Dr. ANDREW WILSON.

THE GOLDEN LIBRARY. Post 8vo, cloth limp, 2s. per Volume.

Bayard Taylor's Diversions of the Echo Club.
Bennett's Ballad History of England.
Bennett's Songs for Sailors.
Godwin's Lives of the Necromancers.
Pope's Poetical Works.
Holmes's Autocrat of Breakfast Table.

Jesse's Scenes of Country Life.
Leigh Hunt's Tale for a Chimney Corner.
Mallory's Mort d'Arthur: Selections.
Pascal's Provincial Letters.
Rochefoucauld's Maxims & Reflections.

THE WANDERER'S LIBRARY. Crown 8vo, cloth extra, 3s. 6d. each.

Wanderings in Patagonia. By JULIUS BEERBOHM. Illustrated.
Camp Notes. By FREDERICK BOYLE.
Savage Life. By FREDERICK BOYLE.
Merrie England in the Olden Time. By G. DANIEL. Illustrated by CRUIKSHANK.
Circus Life. By THOMAS FROST.
Lives of the Conjurers. THOMAS FROST.
The Old Showmen and the Old London Fairs. By THOMAS FROST.
Low-Life Deeps. By JAMES GREENWOOD.

Wilds of London. JAMES GREENWOOD.
Tunis. Chev. HESSE-WARTEGG. 22 Illusts.
Life and Adventures of a Cheap Jack.
World Behind the Scenes. P.FITZGERALD.
Tavern Anecdotes and Sayings.
The Genial Showman. By E.P. HINGSTON.
Story of London Parks. JACOB LARWOOD.
London Characters. By HENRY MAYHEW.
Seven Generations of Executioners.
Summer Cruising in the South Seas. By C. WARREN STODDARD. Illustrated.

POPULAR SHILLING BOOKS.

Harry Fludyer at Cambridge.
Jeff Briggs's Love Story. BRET HARTE.
Twins of Table Mountain. BRET HARTE.
Snow-bound at Eagle's. By BRET HARTE.
A Day's Tour. By PERCY FITZGERALD.
Esther's Glove. By R. E. FRANCILLON.
Sentenced! By SOMERVILLE GIBNEY.
The Professor's Wife. By L. GRAHAM.
Mrs. Gainsborough's Diamonds. By JULIAN HAWTHORNE.
Niagara Spray. By J. HOLLINGSHEAD.
A Romance of the Queen's Hounds. By CHARLES JAMES.
Garden that Paid Rent. TOM JERROLD.
Cut by the Mess. By ARTHUR KEYSER.
Teresa Itasca. By A. MACALPINE.
Our Sensation Novel. J. H. MCCARTHY.
Doom! By JUSTIN H. MCCARTHY.
Dolly. By JUSTIN H. MCCARTHY.

Lily Lass. JUSTIN H. MCCARTHY.
Was She Good or Bad? By W. MINTO.
Notes from the "News." By JAS. PAYN.
Beyond the Gates. By E. S. PHELPS.
Old Maid's Paradise. By E. S. PHELPS.
Burglars in Paradise. By E. S. PHELPS.
Jack the Fisherman. By E. S. PHELPS.
Trooping with Crows. By C. L. PIRKIS.
Bible Characters. By CHARLES READE.
Rogues. By R. H. SHERARD.
The Dagonet Reciter. By G. R. SIMS.
How the Poor Live. By G. R. SIMS.
Case of George Candlemas. G. R. SIMS
Sandycroft Mystery. T. W. SPEIGHT.
Hoodwinked. By T. W. SPEIGHT.
Father Damien. By R. L. STEVENSON.
A Double Bond. By LINDA VILLARI.
My Life with Stanley's Rear Guard. By HERBERT WARD.

HANDY NOVELS. Fcap. 8vo, cloth boards, 1s. 6d. each.

The Old Maid's Sweetheart. A. ST. AUBYN.
The Modest Little Sara. ALAN ST. AUBYN.
Seven Sleepers of Ephesus. M. E. COLERIDGE.

Taken from the Enemy. H. NEWBOLT.
A Lost Soul. By W. L. ALDEN.
Dr. Palliser's Patient. GRANT ALLEN.

THE PICCADILLY NOVELS.

LIBRARY EDITIONS OF NOVELS, many Illustrated, crown 8vo, cloth extra, **3s. 6d.** each.

THE PICCADILLY (3/6) NOVELS—*continued.*

By DICK DONOVAN.
Tracked to Doom. | Man from Manchester.

By A. CONAN DOYLE.
The Firm of Girdlestone.

By Mrs. ANNIE EDWARDES.
Archie Lovell.

By G. MANVILLE FENN.
The New Mistress. | Witness to the Deed.
The Tiger Lily. | The White Virgin.

By PERCY FITZGERALD.
Fatal Zero.

By R. E. FRANCILLON.
Queen Cophetua. | King or Knave ?
One by One. | Ropes of Sand.
A Dog and his Shadow. | Jack Doyle's Daughter.
A Real Queen.

Pref. by Sir BARTLE FRERE.
Pandurang Hari.

By EDWARD GARRETT.
The Capel Girls.

By PAUL GAULOT.
The Red Shirts.

By CHARLES GIBBON.
Robin Gray. | Of High Degree.
Loving a Dream. | The Flower of the
The Golden Shaft. | Forest.

By E. GLANVILLE.
The Lost Heiress. | The Fossicker.
A Fair Colonist.

By E. J. GOODMAN.
The Fate of Herbert Wayne.

By CECIL GRIFFITH.
Corinthia Marazion.

By SYDNEY GRUNDY.
The Days of his Vanity.

By THOMAS HARDY.
Under the Greenwood Tree.

By BRET HARTE.
A Waif of the Plains. | Colonel Starbottle's
Sally Dows. | Client.
A Ward of the Golden | Susy.
Gate. | A Protégée of Jack
A Sappho of Green | Hamlin's.
Springs. | Bell-Ringer of Angel's.

By JULIAN HAWTHORNE.
Garth. | Beatrix Randolph.
Ellice Quentin. | David Poindexter's Dis-
Sebastian Strome. | appearance.
Dust. | The Spectre of the
Fortune's Fool. | Camera

By Sir A. HELPS.
Ivan de Biron.

By I. HENDERSON.
Agatha Page.

By G. A. HENTY.
Rujub the Juggler. | Dorothy's Double.

By JOHN HILL.
The Common Ancestor.

By Mrs. HUNGERFORD.
Lady Verner's Flight. | The Red-House Mystery.

By Mrs. ALFRED HUNT.
The Leaden Casket. | Self-Condemned.
That Other Person. | Mrs. Juliet.

By R. ASHE KING.
A Drawn Game.
"The Wearing of the Green."

THE PICCADILLY (3/6) NOVELS—*continued.*

By E. LYNN LINTON.
Patricia Kemball. | Sowing the Wind.
Under which Lord ? | The Atonement of Leam
"My Love !" | Dundas.
Ione. | The World Well Lost
Paston Carew. | The One Too Many.

By H. W. LUCY.
Gideon Fleyce.

By JUSTIN McCARTHY.
A Fair Saxon. | Waterdale Neighbours.
Linley Rochford. | My Enemy's Daughter.
Miss Misanthrope. | Red Diamonds.
Donna Quixote. | Dear Lady Disdain.
Maid of Athens. | The Dictator.
Camiola. | The Comet of a Season

By GEORGE MACDONALD.
Heather and Snow.

By AGNES MACDONELL.
Quaker Cousins.

By L. T. MEADE.
A Soldier of Fortune.

By BERTRAM MITFORD.
The Gun-Runner. | The King's Assegai.
The Luck of Gerard | Renshaw Fanning's
Ridgeley. | Quest.

By J. E. MUDDOCK.
Maid Marian and Robin Hood.

By D. CHRISTIE MURRAY.
A Life's Atonement. | By the Gate of the Sea.
Joseph's Coat. | A Bit of Human Nature.
Coals of Fire. | First Person Singular.
Old Blazer's Hero. | Cynic Fortune.
Val Strange. | The Way of the World.
Hearts. | BobMartin's Little Girl.
A Model Father. | A Wasted Crime.
Time's Revenges. | In Direst Peril.

By MURRAY & HERMAN.
The Bishops' Bible. | Paul Jones's Alias.
One Traveller Returns. |

By HUME NISBET.
"Bail Up !"

By W. E. NORRIS.
Saint Ann's.

By G. OHNET.
A Weird Gift.

By OUIDA.
Held in Bondage. | Two Little Wooden
Strathmore. | Shoes.
Chandos. | In a Winter City.
Under Two Flags. | Friendship.
Idalia. | Moths.
Cecil Castlemaine's | Ruffino.
Gage. | Pipistrello.
Tricotrin. | A Village Commune.
Puck. | Bimbi.
Folle Farine. | Wanda.
A Dog of Flanders | Frescoes.
Pascarel. | Othmar.
Signa. | In Maremma.
Princess Napraxine. | Syrlin. | Guilderoy
Ariadne. | Santa Barbara.

By MARGARET A. PAUL.
Gentle and Simple.

By JAMES PAYN.
Lost Sir Massingberd. | High Spirits.
Less Black than We're | Under One Roof
Painted. | From Exile.
A Confidential Agent | Glow-worm Tales.
A Gr pe from a Thorn. | The Talk of the Town.
In Peril and Privation. | Holiday Tasks.
The Mystery of Mir- | For Cash Only.
bridge. | The Burnt Million.
The Canon's Ward. | The Word and the Will.
Walter's Word. | Sunny Stories.
By Proxy. | A Trying Patient.

THE PICCADILLY (3/6) NOVELS—*continued.*

By Mrs. CAMPBELL PRAED.
Outlaw and Lawmaker. | Christina Chard.

By E. C. PRICE.
Valentina. | Mrs. Lancaster's Riva..
The Foreigners. |

By RICHARD PRYCE.
Miss Maxwell's Affections.

By CHARLES READE.

It is Never Too Late to | Singleheart and Double-
Mend. | face.
The Double Marriage. | Good Stories of Men
Love Me Little, Love | and other Animals.
Me Long. | Hard Cash.
The Cloister and the | Peg Woffington.
Hearth. | Christie Johnstone.
The Course of True | Griffith Gaunt.
Love. | Foul Play.
The Autobiography of | The Wandering Heir.
a Thief. | A Woman-Hater.
Put Yourself in His | A Simpleton.
Place. | A Perilous Secret.
A Terrible Temptation. | Readiana.
The Jilt. |

By Mrs. J. H. RIDDELL.
The Prince of Wales's | Weird Stories.
Garden Party. |

By AMELIE RIVES.
Barbara Dering.

By F. W. ROBINSON.
The Hands of Justice.

By W. CLARK RUSSELL.
Ocean Tragedy. | Alone on a Wide Wide
My Shipmate Louise. | Sea.

By JOHN SAUNDERS.
Guy Waterman. | The Two Dreamers.
Bound to the Wheel. | The Lion in the Path.

By KATHARINE SAUNDERS.
Margaret and Elizabeth | Heart Salvage.
Gideon's Rock. | Sebastian.
The High Mills. |

THE PICCADILLY (3/6) NOVELS—*continued.*

By HAWLEY SMART.
Without Love or Licence.

By T. W. SPEIGHT.
A Secret of the Sea.

By R. A. STERNDALE.
The Afghan Knife.

By BERTHA THOMAS.
Proud Maisie. | The Violin-Player.

By ANTHONY TROLLOPE.
Frau Frohmann. | The Way we Live Now.
The Land-Leaguers. | Mr. Scarborough's Fa-
Marion Fay. | mily.

By FRANCES E. TROLLOPE.
Like Ships upon the | Anne Furness.
Sea. | Mabel's Progress.

By IVAN TURGENIEFF, &c.
Stories from Foreign Novelists.

By MARK TWAIN.
The American Claimant. | Tom Sawyer Abroad.
The £1,000,000 Bank-note. | Pudd'nhead Wilson.

By C. C. FRASER-TYTLER.
Mistress Judith.

By SARAH TYTLER.
The Bride's Pass. | Lady Bell.
Buried Diamonds. | Blackhall Ghosts.

By ALLEN UPWARD.
The Queen against Owen.

By E. A. VIZETELLY.
The Scorpion.

By J. S. WINTER.
A Soldier's Children.

By MARGARET WYNMAN.
My Flirtations.

By E. ZOLA.
The Downfall. | Dr. Pascal.
The Dream. | Money. | Lourdes.

CHEAP EDITIONS OF POPULAR NOVELS.

Post 8vo, illustrated boards, 2s. each.

By ARTEMUS WARD.
Artemus Ward Complete.

By EDMOND ABOUT.
The Fellah.

By HAMILTON AIDE.
Carr of Carrlyon. | Confidences.

By MARY ALBERT.
Brooke Finchley's Daughter.

By Mrs. ALEXANDER.
Maid, Wife or Widow? | Valerie's Fate.

By GRANT ALLEN.
Strange Stories. | Blood Royal.
Philistia. | For Maimie's Sake.
Babylon. | The Tents of Shem.
The Devil's Die. | The Great Taboo.
This Mortal Coil. | Dumaresq's Daughter.
In all Shades. | The Duchess of Powys-
The Beckoning Hand. | land.

By E. LESTER ARNOLD.
Phra the Phœnician.

By ALAN ST. AUBYN.
A Fellow of Trinity. | The Master of St. Bene-
The Junior Dean. | dict's.

By Rev. S. BARING GOULD.
Red Spider. | Eve.

By FRANK BARRETT.
Fettered for Life. | Honest Davie.
Little Lady Linton. | A Prodigal's Progress.
Between Life & Death. | Found Guilty.
The Sin of Olga Zassou- | A Recoiling Vengeance.
lich. | For Love and Honour.
Folly Morrison. | John Ford; and His
Lieut. Barnabas | Helpmate.

SHELSLEY BEAUCHAMP.
Grantley Grange.

By WALTER BESANT.
Dorothy Forster. | For Faith and Freedom.
Children of Gibeon. | To Call Her Mine.
Uncle Jack. | The Bell of St. Paul's.
Herr Paulus. | Armorel of Lyonesse.
All Sorts and Condi- | The Holy Rose.
tions of Men. | The Ivory Gate.
The Captains' Room. | St. Katherine's by the
All in a Garden Fair. | Tower.
The World Went Very | Verbena Camellia Sta-
Well Then. | phanotis.

By W. BESANT & J. RICE.
This Son of Vulcan. | The Ten Years' Tenant.
My Little Girl. | Ready Money Mortiboy
The Case of Mr. Lucraft. | With Harp and Crown.
The Golden Butterfly. | 'Twas in Trafalgar's
By Celia's Arbour. | Bay.
The Monks of Thelema. | The Chaplain of the
The Seamy Side. | Fleet.

Two-Shilling Novels—*continued.*

By AMBROSE BIERCE.
In the Midst of Life.

By FREDERICK BOYLE.
Camp Notes. | Chronicles of No man's
Savage Life. | Land.

By BRET HARTE.
Californian Stories. | An Heiress of Red Dog.
Gabriel Conroy. | Flip.
The Luck of Roaring | Maruja.
Camp. | A Phyllis of the Sierras.

By HAROLD BRYDGES.
Uncle Sam at Home.

By ROBERT BUCHANAN.
Shadow of the Sword. | The Martyrdom of Ma-
A Child of Nature. | deline.
God and the Man. | Annan Water.
Love Me for Ever. | The New Abelard.
Foxglove Manor. | Matt.
The Master of the Mine | The Heir of Linne.

By HALL CAINE.
The Shadow of a Crime. | The Deemster.
A Son of Hagar.

By Commander CAMERON.
The Cruise of the "Black Prince."

By Mrs. LOVETT CAMERON.
Deceivers Ever. | Juliet's Guardian.

By AUSTIN CLARE.
For the Love of a Lass.

By Mrs. ARCHER CLIVE.
Paul Ferroll.
Why Paul Ferroll Killed his Wife.

By MACLAREN COBBAN.
The Cure of Souls.

By C. ALLSTON COLLINS.
The Bar Sinister.

MORT. & FRANCES COLLINS.
Sweet Anne Page. | Sweet and Twenty.
Transmigration. | The Village Comedy.
From Midnight to Mid- | You Play me False.
night. | Blacksmith and Scholar
A Fight with Fortune. | Frances.

By WILKIE COLLINS.
Armadale. | My Miscellanies.
After Dark. | The Woman in White.
No Name. | The Moonstone.
Antonina. | Man and Wife.
Basil. | Poor Miss Finch.
Hide and Seek. | The Fallen Leaves.
The Dead Secret. | Jezebel's Daughter.
Queen of Hearts. | The Black Robe.
Miss or Mrs.? | Heart and Science.
The New Magdalen. | "I Say No!"
The Frozen Deep. | The Evil Genius.
The Law and the Lady. | Little Novels.
The Two Destinies. | Legacy of Cain.
The Haunted Hotel. | Blind Love.
A Rogue's Life.

By M. J. COLQUHOUN.
Every Inch a Soldier.

By DUTTON COOK.
Leo. | Paul Foster's Daughter.

By C. EGBERT CRADDOCK.
The Prophet of the Great Smoky Mountains.

By MATT CRIM.
Adventures of a Fair Rebel.

By B. M. CROKER.
Pretty Miss Nevill. | Bird of Passage.
Diana Barrington. | Proper Pride.
"To Let." | A Family Likeness.

By W. CYPLES.
Hearts of Gold.

By ALPHONSE DAUDET.
The Evangelist; or, Port Salvation.

By ERASMUS DAWSON.
The Fountain of Youth.

Two-Shilling Novels—*continued.*

By JAMES DE MILLE.
A Castle in Spain.

By J. LEITH DERWENT.
Our Lady of Tears. | Circe's Lovers.

By CHARLES DICKENS.
Sketches by Boz. | Oliver Twist.
Pickwick Papers. | Nicholas Nickleby.

By DICK DONOVAN.
The Man-Hunter. | A Detective's Triumphs
Tracked and Taken. | In the Grip of the Law.
Caught at Last! | From Information Re-
Wanted! | ceived.
Who Poisoned Hetty | Tracked to Doom.
Duncan? | Link by Link
Man from Manchester. | Suspicion Aroused.

By Mrs. ANNIE EDWARDES.
A Point of Honour. | Archie Lovell.

By M. BETHAM-EDWARDS.
Felicia. | Kitty.

By EDW. EGGLESTON.
Roxy.

By G. MANVILLE FENN.
The New Mistress.

By PERCY FITZGERALD.
Bella Donna. | Second Mrs. Tillotson.
Never Forgotten. | Seventy-five Brooke
Polly. | Street.
Fatal Zero. | The Lady of Brantome.

By P. FITZGERALD and others.
Strange Secrets.

ALBANY DE FONBLANQUE.
Filthy Lucre.

By R. E. FRANCILLON.
Olympia. | Queen Cophetua.
One by One. | King or Knave?
A Real Queen. | Romances of the Law.

By HAROLD FREDERIC.
Seth's Brother's Wife. | The Lawton Girl.

Pref. by Sir BARTLE FRERE.
Pandurang Hari.

By HAIN FRISWELL.
One of Two.

By EDWARD GARRETT.
The Capel Girls.

By GILBERT GAUL.
A Strange Manuscript.

By CHARLES GIBBON.
Robin Gray. | In Honour Bound.
Fancy Free. | Flower of the Forest.
For Lack of Gold. | The Braes of Yarrow.
What will the World | The Golden Shaft.
Say? | Of High Degree.
In Love and War. | By Mead and Stream.
For the King. | Loving a Dream.
In Pastures Green. | A Hard Knot.
Queen of the Meadow. | Heart's Delight.
A Heart's Problem. | Blood-Money.
The Dead Heart.

By WILLIAM GILBERT.
Dr. Austin's Guests. | The Wizard of the
James Duke. | Mountain.

By ERNEST GLANVILLE.
The Lost Heiress. | The Fossicker.

By HENRY GREVILLE.
A Noble Woman. | Nikanor.

By CECIL GRIFFITH.
Corinthia Marazion.

By JOHN HABBERTON.
Brueton's Bayou. | Country Luck

By ANDREW HALLIDAY.
Every-day Papers.

By Lady DUFFUS HARDY.
Paul Wynter's Sacrifice.

TWO-SHILLING NOVELS—*continued.*

By THOMAS HARDY.
Under the Greenwood Tree.

By J. BERWICK HARWOOD.
The Tenth Earl.

By JULIAN HAWTHORNE.

Garth.	Beatrix Randolph.
Ellice Quentin.	Love—or a Name.
Fortune's Fool.	David Poindexter's Dis-
Miss Cadogna.	appearance.
Sebastian Strome.	The Spectre of the
Dust.	Camera.

By Sir ARTHUR HELPS.
Ivan de Biron.

By HENRY HERMAN.
A Leading Lady.

By HEADON HILL.
Zambra the Detective.

By JOHN HILL.
Treason Felony.

By Mrs. CASHEL HOEY.
The Lover's Creed.

By Mrs. GEORGE HOOPER.
The House of Raby.

By TIGHE HOPKINS.
Twixt Love and Duty.

By Mrs. HUNGERFORD.

A Maiden all Forlorn.	A Mental Struggle.
In Durance Vile.	A Modern Circe.
Marvel.	

By Mrs. ALFRED HUNT.

Thornicroft's Model.	Self-Condemned.
That Other Person.	The Leaden Casket.

By JEAN INGELOW.
Fated to be Free.

By WM. JAMESON.
My Dead Self.

By HARRIETT JAY.

The Dark Colleen.	Queen of Connaught.

By MARK KERSHAW.
Colonial Facts and Fictions.

By R. ASHE KING.

A Drawn Game.	Passion's Slave.
"The Wearing of the	Bell Barry.
Green."	

By JOHN LEYS.
The Lindsays.

By E. LYNN LINTON.

Patricia Kemball.	The Atonement of Leam
The World Well Lost.	Dundas.
Under which Lord?	With a Silken Thread.
Paston Carew.	The Rebel of the
"My Love!"	Family.
Ione.	Sowing the Wind.

By HENRY W. LUCY.
Gideon Fleyce.

By JUSTIN McCARTHY.

A Fair Saxon.	Camiola.
Linley Rochford.	Dear Lady Disdain.
Miss Misanthrope.	Waterdale Neighbours.
Donna Quixote.	My Enemy's Daughter.
Maid of Athens.	The Comet of a Season.

By HUGH MACCOLL.
Mr. Stranger's Sealed Packet.

By AGNES MACDONELL.
Quaker Cousins.

KATHARINE S. MACQUOID.

The Evil Eye.	Lost Rose.

By W. H. MALLOCK.

A Romance of the Nine-	The New Republic.
teenth Century.	

TWO-SHILLING NOVELS—*continued.*

By FLORENCE MARRYAT.

Open! Sesame!	A Harvest of Wild Oats.
Fighting the Air.	Written in Fire.

By J. MASTERMAN.
Half-a-dozen Daughters.

By BRANDER MATTHEWS.
A Secret of the Sea.

By LEONARD MERRICK.
The Man who was Good.

By JEAN MIDDLEMASS.

Touch and Go.	Mr. Dorillion.

By Mrs. MOLESWORTH.
Hathercourt Rectory.

By J. E. MUDDOCK.

Stories Weird and Won-	From the Bosom of the
derful.	Deep.
The Dead Man's Secret.	

By MURRAY and HERMAN.

One Traveller Returns.	The Bishops' Bible.
Paul Jones's Alias.	

By D. CHRISTIE MURRAY.

A Model Father.	Cynic Fortune.
Joseph's Coat.	A Life's Atonement.
Coals of Fire.	By the Gate of the Sea.
Val Strange.	A Bit of Human Nature.
Old Blazer's Hero.	First Person Singular.
Hearts.	Bob Martin's Little
The Way of the World.	Girl.

By HENRY MURRAY.

A Game of Bluff.	A Song of Sixpence.

By HUME NISBET.

"Bail Up!"	Dr. Bernard St. Vincent.

By ALICE O'HANLON.

The Unforeseen.	Chance? or Fate?

By GEORGES OHNET.

Dr. Rameau.	A Weird Gift.
A Last Love.	

By Mrs. OLIPHANT.

Whiteladies.	The Greatest Heiress in
The Primrose Path.	England.

By Mrs. ROBERT O'REILLY.
Phœbe's Fortunes.

By OUIDA.

Held in Bondage.	Two Little Wooden
Strathmore.	Shoes.
Chandos.	Moths.
Idalia.	Bimbi.
Under Two Flags.	Pipistrello.
Cecil Castlemaine's Gage	A Village Commune.
Tricotrin.	Wanda.
Puck.	Othmar.
Folle Farine.	Frescoes.
A Dog of Flanders.	In Maremma.
Pascarel.	Guilderoy.
Signa.	Ruffino.
Princess Napraxine.	Syrlin.
In a Winter City.	Santa Barbara.
Ariadne.	Ouida's Wisdom, Wit,
Friendship.	and Pathos.

MARGARET AGNES PAUL.
Gentle and Simple.

By C. L. PIRKIS.
Lady Lovelace.

By EDGAR A. POE.
The Mystery of Marie Roget.

By Mrs. CAMPBELL PRAED.
The Romance of a Station.
The Soul of Countess Adrian.

By E. C. PRICE.

Valentina.	Mrs. Lancaster's Rival.
The Foreigners.	Gerald.

By RICHARD PRYCE.
Miss Maxwell's Affections.

Two-Shilling Novels—*continued.*

By JAMES PAYN.

Bentinck's Tutor.
Murphy's Master.
A County Family.
At Her Mercy.
Cecil's Tryst.
The Clyffards of Clyffe.
The Foster Brothers.
Found Dead.
The Best of Husbands.
Walter's Word.
Halves.
Fallen Fortunes.
Humorous Stories.
£200 Reward.
A Marine Residence.
Mirk Abbey.
By Proxy.
Under One Roof.
High Spirits.
Carlyon's Year.
From Exile.
For Cash Only.
Kit.
The Canon's Ward.

Talk of the Town.
Holiday Tasks.
A Perfect Treasure.
What He Cost Her.
A Confidential Agent.
Glow-worm Tales.
The Burnt Million.
Sunny Stories.
Lost Sir Massingberd.
A Woman's Vengeance.
The Family Scapegrace.
Gwendoline's Harvest.
Like Father, Like Son.
Married Beneath Him.
Not Wooed, but Won.
Less Black than We're Painted.
Some Private Views.
A Grape from a Thorn.
The Mystery of Mirbridge.
The Word and the Will.
A Prince of the Blood.

By CHARLES READE.

It is Never Too Late to Mend.
Christie Johnstone.
The Double Marriage.
Put Yourself in His Place.
Love Me Little, Love Me Long.
The Cloister and the Hearth.
The Course of True Love.
The Jilt.
The Autobiography of a Thief.

A Terrible Temptation.
Foul Play.
The Wandering Heir.
Hard Cash.
Singleheart and Double-face.
Good Stories of Men and other Animals.
Peg Woffington.
Griffith Gaunt.
A Perilous Secret.
A Simpleton.
Readiana.
A Woman-Hater.

By Mrs. J. H. RIDDELL.

Weird Stories.
Fairy Water.
Her Mother's Darling.
The Prince of Wales's Garden Party.

The Uninhabited House
The Mystery in Palace Gardens.
The Nun's Curse.
Idle Tales.

By AMELIE RIVES.

Barbara Dering.

By F. W. ROBINSON.

Women are Strange. | The Hands of Justice.

By JAMES RUNCIMAN.

Skippers and Shellbacks.
Grace Balmaign's Sweetheart.
Schools and Scholars.

By W. CLARK RUSSELL.

Round the Galley Fire.
On the Fo'k'sle Head.
In the Middle Watch.
A Voyage to the Cape.
A Book for the Hammock.
The Mystery of the "Ocean Star."

The Romance of Jenny Harlowe.
An Ocean Tragedy.
My Shipmate Louise.
Alone on a Wide Wide Sea.

GEORGE AUGUSTUS SALA.

Gaslight and Daylight.

By JOHN SAUNDERS.

Guy Waterman.
The Two Dreamers.

The Lion in the Path.

By KATHARINE SAUNDERS.

Joan Merryweather.
The High Mills.
Heart Salvage.

Sebastian.
Margaret and Elizabeth.

By GEORGE R. SIMS.

Rogues and Vagabonds.
The Ring o' Bells.
Mary Jane's Memoirs.
Mary Jane Married.
Tales of To-day.
Dramas of Life.

Tinkletop's Crime.
Zeph.
My Two Wives.
Memoirs of a Landlady.
Scenes from the Show.

Two-Shilling Novels—*continued.*

By ARTHUR SKETCHLEY.

A Match in the Dark.

By HAWLEY SMART.

Without Love or Licence.

By T. W. SPEIGHT.

The Mysteries of Heron Dyke.
The Golden Hoop.
Hoodwinked.

By Devious Ways.
Back to Life.
The Loudwater Tragedy.
Burgo's Romance.

By R. A. STERNDALE.

The Afghan Knife.

By R. LOUIS STEVENSON.

New Arabian Nights. | Prince Otto.

By BERTHA THOMAS.

Cressida.
Proud Maisie.

The Violin-Player.

By WALTER THORNBURY.

Tales for the Marines. | Old Stories Retold.

T. ADOLPHUS TROLLOPE.

Diamond Cut Diamond.

By F. ELEANOR TROLLOPE.

Like Ships upon the Sea.

Anne Furness.
Mabel's Progress.

By ANTHONY TROLLOPE.

Frau Frohmann.
Marion Fay.
Kept in the Dark.
John Caldigate.
The Way We Live Now.
The Land-Leaguers.

The American Senator
Mr. Scarborough's Family.
The Golden Lion of Granpere.

By J. T. TROWBRIDGE.

Farnell's Folly.

By IVAN TURGENIEFF, &c.

Stories from Foreign Novelists.

By MARK TWAIN.

A Pleasure Trip on the Continent.
The Gilded Age.
Huckleberry Finn.
Mark Twain's Sketches.
Tom Sawyer.
A Tramp Abroad.

Stolen White Elephant.
Life on the Mississippi.
The Prince and the Pauper.
A Yankee at the Court of King Arthur.

By C. C. FRASER-TYTLER.

Mistress Judith.

By SARAH TYTLER.

The Bride's Pass.
Buried Diamonds.
St. Mungo's City.
Lady Bell.
Noblesse Oblige.
Disappeared.

The Huguenot Family.
The Blackhall Ghosts.
What She Came Through
Beauty and the Beast.
Citoyenne Jaqueline.

By AARON WATSON and LILLIAS WASSERMANN.

The Marquis of Carabas.

By WILLIAM WESTALL.

Trust-Money.

By Mrs. F. H. WILLIAMSON.

A Child Widow.

By J. S. WINTER.

Cavalry Life. | Regimental Legends.

By H. F. WOOD.

The Passenger from Scotland Yard.
The Englishman of the Rue Cain.

By Lady WOOD.

Sabina.

CELIA PARKER WOOLLEY

Rachel Armstrong; or, Love and Theology

By EDMUND YATES.

The Forlorn Hope.
Land at Last.

Castaway.

OGDEN, SMALE AND CO. LIMITED, PRINTERS, GREAT SAFFRON HILL, E.C.